T0106529

For a Knight of the Swan, any mission might lead to fortune—but the chance for love comes once in a lifetime . . .

Margaret Grace is the lady of Fletchers Landing, earning what she can as a beekeeper and mead maker, and playing a nerve-wracking game with the mercenaries who demand payment to ensure her village's safety. When an unknown man appears on horseback one day, Meg knows she can't trust him—especially when the dashing knight claims to be looking for fabled lost riches. But her desires are harder to control . . .

Tormented by the memories of his imprisonment at the hands of a vicious mercenary, Sir Nathan Staves is glad to be abroad on a quest for His Majesty. His task promises the chance to recover a legendary lost bounty, but also throws him into the path of the beguiling Meg. Their breathtaking passion awakens just as a familiar danger does, forcing Nathan to decide which is the greater prize—an elusive treasure, or the love of a woman he will die to protect . . .

Visit us at www.kensingtonbooks.com

Books by C.C. Wiley

Knights of the Swan
Knight Secrets
Knight Quests
Knight Treasures
Knight Furies

Published by Kensington Publishing Corporation

Knight Furies

Knights of the Swan

C.C. Wiley

LYRICAL PRESS
Kensington Publishing Corp.
www.kensingtonbooks.com

Lyrical Press books are published by
Kensington Publishing Corp. 119 West 40th Street New York, NY 10018

First Electronic Edition: July 2018
eISBN-13: 978-1-5161-0753-7
eISBN-10: 1-5161-0753-5

First Print Edition: July 2018
ISBN-13: 978-1-5161-0754-4
ISBN-10: 1-5161-0754-3

Printed in the United States of America

For my family and the magnificent men in my life.

Acknowledgments

I am eternally grateful for my readers and the opportunity to share my stories.

I cannot begin to express my appreciation for my critique and plot partner, Kimberley Troutte, for letting me ramble on as we look for the possibilities together. I miss our long walks where we would peel apart a story and then create something better than it was before. Thank goodness for email and cells phones.

A huge thank you also goes to my dear friend, Susie Fourt. Your careful reading brings insight and clarity to the tale.

To my lifetime friend and warrior, Cindy Jackson, you embrace courage, compassion, discipline, and training. Thanks so much for cheering me on. I learn from you every time we're together.

And as always, please accept my deepest gratitude to my loved ones for their love and patience. I wouldn't want to stay on this ride without you.

Chapter 1

The impact of blade against blade shuddered up Sir Nathan Staves's arm. The mercenaries continued to come at him. They were like ants marching out of an anthill. He raised his broadsword and advanced his assault, pressing his enemies across Balforth's dungeon. Never again would he allow them to take him prisoner.

He found their leader, Sir Vincent DePierce, Lord of Balforth. Their blades met and swung again. One more strike and that damn man would no longer keep his head.

"I shall cut out your heart and feed it to the crows," Nathan swore. He drew back to land the deathblow.

"Sir Nathan," the voice worked its way into the battle. "Pax! Cease your advancement."

"Mercy!" someone shouted.

"For God's sake, Nathan. Stop!"

Darrick?

Nathan's arm hovered overhead. The sword wavered. He clawed his way through the nightmare's many veils. A shuddering breath racked his body, searing him as if it came from a fiery furnace.

Daylight seeped into his blood-red delusional state. He blinked at the bright sun. Clearmorrow Castle's tiltyard came into focus. The men he had trained with that afternoon now stared at him as if he were their enemy.

He wiped the blood and sweat from his brow. Why was Darrick lying on the ground?

"Darrick?" Nathan croaked as he struggled to find his way to reality.

"How could you," Lady Sabine cried as she ran to her husband. "Darrick is your dearest friend," she scolded as she elbowed her way past the soldiers working to staunch the bleeding.

"No." Nathan spun on his heel. Where was DePierce? His men?

"Is Darrick alive?" Elizabeth, the Lady of Clearmorrow cried. "Does my brother live?"

Her husband, Taron, Lord of Clearmorrow, shouted out orders to the men hovering around their wounded friend. "Fetch the surgeon."

"Bring me my sewing kit," Sabine said, kneeling on the ground.

"What have I done?" Nathan dropped his head in defeat. "Forgive me." He stumbled from the bailey yard like the monster that he had become.

* * * *

Nathan stood on Clearmorrow's parapet and could not tear his gaze away from the stain spreading down his sword. 'Twas his friend, Sir Darrick, Lord of Lockwood's blood.

There was a time when he would have never noticed the sounds of clashing swords, the visceral grunts as power pushed through his limbs and his weapons made contact with his enemy. But that time was lost at the hands of Vincent De Pierce. The time in the torturous oubliette had seen to that.

It had taken months for his muscles to stop their cramping, seizing him as he slept, determined to remind him of every hour he was kept in darkness. The screams inside his head silenced everything and everyone until the swirl of pain brought him back to reality.

Nathan's callused hands trembled against the stone crenulation as he gripped the ledge. Sweat trickled under his gambeson. This time, the bout of agony had led him down a path that had nearly removed Darrick's life. He rubbed the stain of blood. His heart clutched. The sting of watery pain made him blink against the sun. How was he to live with the fear that he could no longer escape the terror of that damp, dark hole?

The oubliette had allowed for him to stand, his feet taking all his weight, his arms stretched overhead. His tormentors left him to rot for days, bringing him out when they felt the need to "play" with him. If not for Lady Sabine, he would still be in that place of death.

He glanced down at the Lockwood family huddled beside Darrick. Why did they not come for him and place him in Clearmorrow Castle's dungeon? The newly wedded Lady Sabine looked up as if searching for the madman who nearly killed her husband.

His breath caught. Instead of outrage, he saw sorrow and pity gleaming from her countenance. She offered him an unsteady smile before ducking her head to speak to Darrick.

Guilt hacked through Nathan like a broadsword. Although they had yet to make the announcement, Nathan knew that Darrick and Sabine were expecting their first child. He'd seen her run to the privy more times than he cared to count. She placed her hand over the life growing in her belly as if reading his thoughts.

The swelling of new life had begun to show and change everything. Gone were the days when he and Darrick fought side by side, against those who chose to take what was not theirs. His stomach twisted and he felt as green as the color usually associated with Sabine's pallor when they all broke their fast in the great hall. They could ill afford to have him around. What if the next time he cleaved Darrick's head from his neck? The ladies of Clearmorrow or Lockwood would never forgive him. And he would never be able to live with himself.

He no longer belonged. It was getting harder to be around Darrick and Sabine and that love-drenched couple, Taron and Elizabeth.

Their boy, Chance, was growing strong, toddling into trouble wherever the child could find it. It gave him shivers to think of the mischief waiting for his discovery. What if something were to happen to the babe while under his watch? Bile rose in this throat.

Nathan shoveled his hands through his hair, tugging as if it would release him from the growing pinch in his belly. His lungs burned and grappled for air. The world began its vicious spin off its axis.

Henry was still in France. Drem and Brigitte were in Wales along with Drem's sister Terrwyn and her husband, James Frost, and they too were in a family way. Tate, Taron, and Sabine's half-brother were sent off to be fostered. Once they had bided their time and done their duty to the king, they too might join the rank of knight. Their lives would fill with adventure and the challenges that brought some men to their knees. And one day, they too would find someone to lean on when they were feeling weak and afraid. Hell, even Thunder had found a mate.

Change had taken hold, and Nathan didn't know how to stop it. Family. Or rather, the lack of family had never mattered as long as he had a quest to have victory over. He'd had a year to wrestle the task of rebuilding and fortifying Clearmorrow. Now that the majority of the stronghold would stand against any attack mounted against it, he felt the itch between his shoulder blades.

Perhaps he was too broken to save. Destined to be alone. He saw the looks between his friends and knew they had all shared private conversations. Apparently, judging by the swiftness in which the subjects changed when he joined them, it had been about him.

Had they noted the nights that he prowled the halls, unable to escape the dreams that haunted every hour that he drew breath? He glanced down. His knuckles seemed to protrude through his skin. When had they begun to look like chicken bones? His wrists, too, had become thin.

The invisible weight he carried on his back threatened to bend him over. The memories of battles and lives taken were piling up like cords of wood. Others might not see it, but he could whenever he caught his reflection in a pool or his shadow trailed after him.

The ladies still had their appeal, but they could not hold his attention for long. Perhaps it was the lack of sleep and no appetite for life that kept him lost.

When sleep did come, the nightmares rose up from the hole that had burrowed into his mind. And when he did break free, the exhaustion left him weak in mind and body. He had tried the lists, beating the memories into submission with his sword. But this afternoon's time at the turns showed him that he was indeed a broken knight. Instead of Darrick and Taron in the tiltyard, he had seen DePierce and his mercenaries. They'd come at him, weapons drawn. And all he had wanted to do was end the torment and take their lives.

A shuddering breath broke through the wall forming in his chest. He needed to leave. Needed to go…from this place so those he cared for were kept safe. To clear his mind. To fight the demons that had latched on to his soul. But where? Mayhap 'twas time to return to France. Perhaps King Henry would send him on another mission. He had no land to support him. All he had was his sword arm and even that was unpredictable.

"He knows you did not mean to harm him," Elizabeth said.

Nathan looked down at the slender fingers resting on his leather gauntlet. It took all the courage he could muster to raise his head. He did not want to see pity shadowing her gaze. "He is my friend and I could have killed him."

"But you didn't. Nathan, you are more than any friend." Her grip tightened around his wrist. "You are part of our family. We'll help you through this. Taron and I are still haunted by DePierce's ill treatment. We know the dark memories that take on a life of their own. Give yourself more time to heal."

He covered her hand with his. "I cannot take that chance. What if I became lost again in my mind and turned on someone else?"

"'Tis only a scratch," Darrick said from the stairway. He limped over, the old wound from their siege of Harfleur more pronounced today. "You'll stay here until you are well."

Nathan eyed his friend. They had shared so many years, fostering together with the same lord, serving their king, sharing the secrets of the brotherhood. They were Knights of the Swan and they were nearing their end. How many more years did they have on this earth?

A fresh linen bandage wrapped around Darrick's shoulder and held his injured appendage still. What made Lady Sabine give her approval to leave her care so soon? There was an air of apprehension in Darrick's stare.

"What truly brings you up on the parapet so soon after...?" Nathan's attention drifted to the tiltyard.

"So soon after I let my guard down and let you almost defeat me?" Darrick finished for him. He gripped Nathan's forearm, as if to prove that he was hale and hearty. "'Twas an error on my part. Not yours."

Nathan itched under their scrutiny. Did he dare confront what they discussed behind closed doors? Hell, why not? "Both of you know this isn't true. I've known of the talk amongst you. Felt the shame that my hands tremble. My muscles still tire from a bit of swordplay." He swiped his palm over his overheated face. How did one feel hot and clammy at the same time? "I cannot sleep. The haunting dreams of that hole are so real that I fear I have been captured and returned to Balforth Castle." Taron and Sabine stepped out on to the parapet, united as brother and sister. Nathan began to wonder if perhaps they were about to lay siege to his sanity.

"And when you are awake, you have the look of a man being tortured. And you were," Taron said.

Nathan swallowed, hating the building panic. "Do you fear that I will turn on you? As I did today?"

Taron clasped Nathan's arm. "We all were harmed in some way by that bastard."

A growl threatened to prowl up his spine. "I know this," Nathan said through clenched teeth. "I am grateful that we survived. But when I see you all together, I cannot stop the thoughts. I am reminded all over again."

Nathan turned away from the only people he called family. "Working to rebuild Clearmorrow has allowed my body to regain some of its strength. But the wounds of the mind have refused to heal. I need to leave before anyone else is damaged."

"Then 'tis good that we've received word while you were working with the men in the bailey," Taron said. The smile he sported never seemed to warm his dark obsidian eyes.

"A messenger?" Darrick asked. He turned an accusing glare on his brother-in-law and was met with a shrug.

"I would have told you sooner," Sabine said as she unconsciously ran a soothing hand over her belly. The action proved worthy as it drew Darrick's ire away from her brother and made him, instead, think of their babe. "However, I thought staunching your blood loss was more important."

Worry creased Darrick's brows and shadowed his gaze as he placed his hand over hers. "I am safe and I thank you for your care." He lifted Sabine's hand to his lips.

Taron cleared his throat, saving Nathan from pitching himself over the battlement. 'Twould be a kinder fate than to continue seeing love all around you and knowing that it would never be yours. No land to lord over or name to pass on to your children. For what purpose would you sire a child if you had nothing to give them?

"The king's messenger waits in the great hall," Taron motioned for them to follow. "He bears a disc with a swan etched into its surface."

"Then we best be at it and hear what news he carries," Darrick said. He spun on his heel and made the descent down the narrow stairway.

Sabine and Elizabeth shared a look between them. Their rosy cheeks had paled as they clutched each other's hand. Did they fear for their men and the lives they had started to rebuild?

Nathan waited for them before taking his leave of the parapet. King Henry desired their service. The Knights of the Swan were needed once again.

He drew back his shoulders, stretching the tense muscles until they burned. Relief, the thrill of the hunt, the challenge, the quest, they burbled up like a spring coming to life. Did a peregrine feel the same way when released from the darkness under its hood? He imagined it soaring over the countryside, searching out its prey. And in its hunt, did it have a renewed sense of purpose? Aye, it had to. For in this simple possibility of change... his change, he might find peace.

He clattered down the steps, nearly running to catch up with the only people foolish enough to include him in their family circle. They gathered in the solar that stood off from Clearmorrow's great hall. As lord, the missive was delivered first to Taron. He read it in silence, his face paling against two red splotches blooming on his cheeks. The vellum rustled as he passed it over to Darrick.

Nathan squinted, trying to see over his friend's sleeve. "By all the saints," he said. "I trust that it will be to return to France and continue Henry's good fight."

"I fear not," Darrick said. His mouth barely moved as he spoke. "Someone must ride north. Toward the debatable land."

"But is not Carlisle's keep nearby?" Sabine asked. "Surely they are closer."

He slid his thumb over her lip. "'Tis not what the king desires. He wishes for information."

The gray in Darrick's eyes turned the color of ice chips as his jaw worked to release the rest of the message. "We are to ride to Fletchers Landing."

Nathan grunted. "'Twas one of Vincent DePierce's holdings."

"No." Elizabeth and Sabine's gasp wove its way through their little group.

The messenger gripped his hat and pulled a leather packet from his cape. "If you please, my Lady Sabine, our king wishes to return this. He believes there may be clues in the land to the north and he asks that its meaning is discovered."

He slapped his woolen cap back on his head and waited for their reply.

Taron stepped forward. "Go to the kitchens. Ask Cook to find something to tide you over until this eve. If you wish, you may bed in the stables. On the morrow, we'll have a message for you to deliver."

"Aye, my lord, I thank you for your hospitality. 'Tis a fair long ride." Making a bow, he hurried off, a hungry look widening his eyes as he searched for the cook.

Sabine held out her hand. "Father's journal." They stared as she unfolded the leather wrapping. "'Tis the one that speaks of treasure that Rhys and DePierce were willing to kill for."

Nathan suppressed a shiver and lifted his chin in defiance. "I'll go. Alone."

"You can't," Taron said.

Nathan felt the boil of rage begin to hurl its way through his limbs. He tamped down the beast that he feared he may become. If he did not do something he knew it was only a matter of time before his friends' worries were confirmed. "And why not?"

"The memories," Elizabeth said. She caught her lip with her teeth. "Will you be able to manage them?"

Her concern warmed his soul. There had been a time in his boyhood, when he thought that his heart would break should Elizabeth never notice him. He knew that it was no longer possible for her love to be his. She had given her love to Sir Taron, Lord of Clearmorrow. But in those moments that he wandered the halls of late, he did dream of someone to care whether he lived or died. And he had come to decide that someone could only be found in another place other than Clearmorrow or Lockwood Castles.

"I am stronger than I look." He bent low, lifting her fingers to his lips. A bit of mischief made him linger over long until Taron shifted his feet into position so that his fist might make contact with Nathan's jaw.

Appreciating an uninjured face over the torment that he caused Elizabeth's new husband, he released her hand and ducked. The thought of being on the lands connected to the villain DePierce was nearly obliterated from his mind. At least until he closed his eyes. Time would reveal whether he could keep his sanity a while longer.

He pressed down the whispered questions that normally only tormented him in the dark hours of the night. He had to place his attention elsewhere, and swiftly.

"Darrick. Taron. 'Tis too soon to leave Castles Clearmorrow and Lockwood untended. The lands need your care. They are still recovering from that bastard DePierce and his nephew Hugh."

"Did our king state who should go?" Taron asked.

Though the movement was slight, Nathan noted Elizabeth's hand slide over her abdomen. Ah, so yet another child to fill her arms was on its way, too. Did the others notice?

"No," Darrick growled as he searched the king's words. He fisted the missive in a stranglehold. "In fact, it mentions to forgo troops on this mission."

"Your families need you here." Nathan itched as all four pairs of eyes stared, pouring out their concern. "I'm the best knight for this quest. And I vow, as a Knight of the Swan, to hold my sanity together." Despite the trail of panic streaming down his back, he released a slow wink. "Mayhap I will even find the king's treasure."

* * * *

Meg stomped through the meadow. She, Margaret Grace, may technically be the lady of Fletchers Landing, but she certainly did not receive deference for that station. A heavy sigh whose source seemed to come from deep inside, and she felt clear to the soles of her shoes, whispered past her lips.

The milk cow ambled along the path, mindless of the trouble it was for someone to chase after her. Meg danced out of the way of the bovine's lumbering hooves. 'Twas not the first time Maisie had taken off through the open gate, but not before knocking over bee skeps. It took three days for the bees to find their queen and return to the hive. Not to mention the villagers' complaints of stings and swelling. Her sister, Anna, was kept busy creating poultices and calming the disfiguring knots left by the angry hive. If it weren't for their need of milk, Meg would be tempted to let the beast wander off to some other poor soul. She feared that one day the contrary thing would next knock over a lantern and start a fire. But their little sister, Phillipa, swore Maisie produced the sweetest milk. And Anna needed the cream for her unguents, and her potions brought coin to Fletchers Landing. So who was Meg to argue? Her ire shifted. Actually it was their brother's carelessness that took her from her chores. If there was blame to be placed it should be on Baldric's head. Again.

"How many times must I remind him to ensure the gate is closed properly?" she muttered to the blasted cow. Her brother was old enough to complete the task of tending the beasts in the barn. Had they the funds and connections he should have been sent off for fostering three years ago. But thanks to that damn Vincent DePierce and having to pay the others for protection, their coffers were as empty as last year's bird's nest.

"'Tis for certain Baldric has had plenty of warnings." She jerked off her veil and swatted at the annoying gnats attacking her head. If only someone would take him in hand and teach him the ways of being a lord.

Maisie paused to snag a mouthful of grass and released a plaintive grass-scented moo.

"Come along, now," Meg urged. The stick she used to tap along the cow's backside no longer had any effect. She dodged Maisie's tail as it swished the flies sticking to her roan coat. The cow refused to take another step.

"Poor beastie," Meg crooned. "Have you worn yourself down to skin and bones?"

She swiped at the hair escaping her braid. Tendrils stuck to her cheek like vines climbing a castle tower. The summer heat had begun to sweep over the countryside. Usually the breeze blowing off the firth was enough to cool the air. But the infernal Maisie had strayed farther than usual and now they faced a long walk home.

Meg folded her arms and searched the shaded path while she waited for the stubborn cow to fill her many stomachs. It appeared both of them were hungry and exhausted. She dared not shut her eyes. Could she?

The space between her shoulder blades twitched and burned. The payments for protection may help their village and keep the reivers from crossing the land between England and Scotland, but it did little to protect anyone outside Fletchers Landing's walls. If only she had someone to help shoulder the weight of all that fell on her. It felt like ages since she sat down and took her ease.

A butterfly flitted by, its gossamer wings brushing her cheek before settling on a bush. The lapis and black wings opened and closed as if finding a cooler spot to rest. Meg tilted her head to listen. The sound of water rolling and crashing, polishing rough stones until they were smooth, came from the grove of trees. The promise of a refreshing dip.

Spring had come early this year, and with it came the melt of ice and snow. She had forgotten the small stream that meandered through the meadow and down to the firth. The melt had filled the banks and now left behind an oasis that called to her.

The butterfly lifted from its perch and led the way.

Who was she to ignore a sign to follow? She tapped on Maisie to gain her attention and cut a path between the bushes to reach the stream.

Meg tied the cow to a nearby tree and left her to graze. Unwilling to lose another minute, she stripped off her hose and shoes, then dipped her toes into the water. The chill tore her breath from her lungs and left her giddy. She could not let this opportunity pass her.

After scanning the banks to make certain only she and the cow were by the stream, she tucked the hem of her skirt under her wide belt and pulled it through. Hot air caressed her calves. A groan of pleasure escaped her lips before she tamed it back where it belonged: to the cage where she chained it and kept it under control.

She stepped into the water. It lapped and licked her legs and she went in deeper. A finger of ecstasy slid down her back, reminding her that she was not always its master. She nodded, and let the carefree sensation roll over her. "Just this once," she whispered. Then she would climb that hill and return to her responsibilities.

She dipped lower to splash her face and dampened a corner of her skirt, using the soft wool to drip cool water over her neck. It lapped at her collarbone, trickling down her bodice.

A song she heard one of the boys singing the other evening popped into her head. First it was just a hum, then a whisper. Before she knew it she was belting the song out at the top of her lungs.

And suddenly, a baritone joined in the chorus. Meg stumbled and nearly fell on her bottom. She splashed about like an unhappy duck until she could solidly plant her feet on the streambed.

"Who's there?" she cried. DePierce's marauders? Smugglers? Reivers? How did she manage to forget all the possibilities of danger she could encounter out on her own? She slowed down the rapid heartbeat that shook her body. It would never do to let anyone see her fear. No matter whom they might be. The distance to the keep yawned farther away than she would like.

The singing had stopped. Only the babbling stream answered her query. Its contents continued to slide over the rocks and occasional tree limb. She sucked in a breath to slow down the pounding in her head. Eyes narrowed, she searched the trees on the opposite bank.

What was that behind the old birch tree? Feet? Male bare feet. Strong. Striking. And manly.

"I see you," she croaked. Heat rose until she thought her ears might catch fire. Dear God, she actually found them to be attractive. "Come out from behind that tree."

There was movement and then silence. Did he travel alone? Biting her lip, she prayed that DePierce had not returned.

Fear kept her rooted to the streambed despite the relentless attack of icy needles against her feet and legs. They were becoming too much to endure.

There were no signs of other traveling companions. Nor did she see a horse nearby. If she moved swiftly, she could be out of reach before he came close.

She scrambled up the bank and pulled the little knife she carried in her belt. In her other fist, she clutched the stick she used to direct the cow. It would probably do little to scare the man off, but she had to do something. She was the protector of Fletchers Landing. Who did he think he was to scare her half to death?

"Show yourself, damn you."

Long legs encased in leather chausses stretched out as languorous as a cat awakened from a nap. Bare toes curled, his feet arched. Then his legs folded out of sight. Meg waited, her arm outstretched as if she thought to stab him from across the stream. Realizing how ridiculous it might look, she brought her arm in and reared her shoulders back.

The stranger who emerged from the tree nearly stole her breath. A mane of auburn curled about his head like a halo. Even from their distance apart his height made her tip her chin. He was tall and broad shouldered. The muscles in his arms and across his chest stretched the jerkin's material. Yet it hung neatly over his belly and hips. Metal studs gleamed from leather gauntlets wrapped around his forearms. Her attention caught on his leather chausses encasing his thighs. And sweet lord, his bare feet. His toes curled into the moss, like a cat playing in meadow flowers. Dear God, when did she give a fig about a cat's habits?

She tore her gaze away, forcing it back to his face. A square jaw framed his mouth. It appeared to be twisted in something resembling a smile. She couldn't be sure because it kept shifting behind the scruff of his copper-colored beard. His brows arched then furrowed into a frown.

She shivered. Probably nothing more than going from snow-chilled water to late spring sun. Something caught in her belly, swirling around like that lapis-painted butterfly. She pushed the pleasure back in its cage. Dear God, she nearly growled.

Chapter 2

Nathan blinked into the sun. The maiden. Nay, the woman, stood in defiance of the fear he knew was coursing through her veins. A grin tugged at his mouth. Ah, what a sight to behold. A servant, with obsidian hair, stood before him, threatening him with a stick and a blade so small that most would think it unworthy of its name. But he had seen firsthand that the weapon need not be great in size. Sometimes small and unwavering caused more damage.

Shite. Waves of memories returned in a flash. Lightning in a storm. Except this was in his mind. It took all that he could draw from the depths of his soul to stand strong. Thank God his legs did not give out under his weight. Sweat beaded and slid down his neck. The betrayal of his body made him want to weep. He fought back the demons that scoured his soul. When would it cease?

Freeing his thoughts from the stranglehold, he focused on the warrior woman. The hem of her skirt still tucked under the belt wrapped around her narrow waist, exposed her flesh, rosy from the stream. She stood, shapely legs braced. Protecting…a bovine of dubious descent. He'd never seen so bony a cow present so swollen a bag. He almost pitied the beast.

The maiden's raven tresses had escaped the braid that kissed the swell of her back. A tender spot he had always found enthralling. Her eyes, the color of the most entrancing obsidian, glittered back at him, promising a most challenging fight. Memories of her pale, perfect skin flashed behind his eyelids. And when he tried to remove the vision, it returned to him, her nipples exposed through the thin material covering her breasts.

He hated that he had fallen prey to her seductive voice. She had carried him to a place of peace he'd had little experience with after the oubliette.

Her voice drew him from one of those dark places that seemed to cling to his spirit. She freed him. And when she poured out her heart in song, he could not stop himself from joining in.

He should have kept quiet. Enjoyed the scenery. Then search for her later. The maiden wore a serviceable dress of wool. No lady here. Only a servant. In truth, no threat to him. He should have found her in the village. Persuaded her to spend some time with him as he searched out the information that his king commanded.

Ah, but the flesh is weak and the spirit is willing. Or was it the other way around? Either way, he had made a mess of things. Was there a husband to whom she would run? Demand payment for his rude behavior? By God, he hoped not. He wanted to get acquainted with the maiden from Fletchers Landing and that did not include anyone with claims on her person.

He blinked as his nether region tightened. It had been nearly a year since he'd last lain with a woman. And that did not end on the best of notes when she wrapped her arms around him. The fear of suffocating had caused him to withdraw, retreating for fear of harming her.

And yet, here he stood, his…need, standing full, erect, and very proud.

Nathan shook his head, feeling like a piece of his soul, something as small as a dust mote, had returned to him. He blinked as he tried to gather his thoughts that were like goose down in a storm. Aye, there was a duty to perform, but Henry's edict did not say that he could not partake of the Fletchers Landing delectable fare.

He moved forward and swiftly questioned his plans when she jabbed her blade in his direction.

"Who are you?" she shouted from the opposite bank. Her voice carried over the rushing water. "What do you want?"

As soon as she opened her mouth, he was relieved that at least a portion of his upper brain still worked.

What did he want? His thoughts would terrify her. Even though the one in his lower region wanted to take control. Why didn't the bastard stay as quiet as it had the last several months? He needed to prove to himself and to his friends and those in higher places that he was still a Knight of the Swan. Nay, he was better than he ever was. His hands flexed as if searching for the protection of his sword. Still, he had to work to form words that would not make him sound like a madman.

"I'm in search of Fletchers Landing."

A wary tip of her head reminded him of a wren as it prepared to take flight.

"Village is that way," she said, pointing in the direction he recalled he had already come. And nay, there were no villages to receive him.

How interesting. She had pointed him in the opposite direction. "You're from here?" he asked.

She gathered her cow and clambered up the bank. In that simple space that stretched farther away, he felt like he was losing grasp of something he might never regain.

Eager to not lose her, he grabbed his meager possessions from behind the birch tree. His horse, Madrigal, nickered as Nathan unloosed the reins from the tree. The horse and he loped across the rushing stream.

In her haste, the maiden left behind her hose and shoes. He scooped them up, imagining her reception and the gratitude that was guaranteed to follow.

"Wait," he called. Relief filled him as she paused, a question arching her eyebrows. He came closer to her and presented her shoes. The thin woolen hose wrapped around his arm like tentacles on a sea monster he'd seen on one of his missions for the king. It had taken both hands to pry the things from his skin. Did her cheeks just flush the color of pomegranates?

A small gasp was enough to make it clear that she realized he had received a plentiful view of her shapely legs. A wave of disappointment washed over him as she yanked the skirt down.

"You forgot these," he croaked. When had his throat become parched? The hose and shoes hung from his fingertips.

"Thank you," she murmured. Her silken voice slid over his skin like a lover's caress.

Now that he was closer, he could see that he had been incorrect. Her eyes might be as dark as obsidian, but for a moment they were warm and almost friendly.

She hugged the shoes to her chest. Nathan stifled a groan when she caught her lower lip between her teeth. Her eyes settled somewhere in the vicinity of his mouth.

A breeze ruffled the tendrils clinging to her slender neck. Should he claim a reward for his gallantry? Nathan's thoughts raced to keep his nether region from making an appearance. Nay, 'twould be best if she offered it to him. He waited, wanting to discover the sweetness of her lush lips.

The tree limbs arching overhead rustled as they created a canopy of privacy and seclusion. The shushing of their leaves called to him, whispering to lift the curl nestled on the curve of her breast.

The cow chewed on her cud, waiting for them to break the silence. Nathan began to despair the woman's offer would never come. The warmth in her eyes dissipated. Her gaze glittered back at him, brittle as a stone chipped from the caves of Clearmorrow.

Nathan blinked, caught by surprise when she tugged on the cow's rope and moved away instead of sitting down to repair her clothing. She cast a cool glance over him as if he were in dire need of a bath.

"Why are you following me?" The silk of her voice still had the ability to make his stomach coil in anticipation.

Nathan supposed he probably could use a bath. The ride from Clearmorrow Castle had taken him several days. Bathing had been his intention when he paused beside that stream. The need to rest both man and steed had taken him by surprise. He had almost fallen asleep. But all that changed when she arrived and disturbed his peace.

He refrained from the instinct to sniff his person. He supposed now he would have to wait until he took up residence in the keep. Wasn't it the custom for the lady of the castle to offer to bathe their guests? Not that he'd request it. Well, maybe in the past, but not now. He'd seen the demands of those in power put upon women like Elizabeth and Sabine. He could have, had he chosen the plan to blend in, become a part of the little village. Feeling her curious gaze, he figured he best respond to her questions before she used that little knife still clutched in her fist.

"I'm called Nathan Staves."

"We're not used to strangers. You should know that there's nothing in Fletchers Landing for you." She took her attention off the cow and the path ahead to direct it over his horse. "'Tis a fine steed. A destrier, isn't it?"

"Aye. He's called Madrigal."

"My sister would be enthralled with him," she whispered. Nathan watched her draw up, right before she stumbled and caught her breath. He winced, feeling her pain ripple through his body. Empathy? He supposed that was another new experience he never expected. He reached out to steady her elbow.

The delicate skin around her eyes tightened. She quickened her pace. "I must make haste. I bid you farewell."

He supposed he could have used the king's power and stated his reason for being there. It would impress some. He had a feeling that this one would trust him even less. Truth be told, it rather hurt his pride that she did not fall so willingly under his charms. "Why did you send me in the wrong direction?" he called out.

Her footsteps slowed as she turned. "I thought perhaps you were mistaken in your destination." Her full lips pouted. They were made for making love. He wanted to bury himself in their lush unspoken promises. One reason among many held him back from pursuing his desires.

Having spent time at the royal court and in back alleys, Nathan knew when someone was lying to him. And this was one of those times that did not catch him by surprise.

He stepped cautiously, as though he was creeping up on a dove, and closed the gap between them. "I can't imagine not finding something endearing in your little village. 'Tis by the sea, is it not?"

"But you'll not find anything of worth near the Solway Firth." She kept her head turned from him. The little stick tapped at the lumbering cow's backside as they set off again. "'Tis possible that you wished to travel to Carlisle," she continued. "I suggest you take the path back at the crossroad. I vow it would be more to your liking. I bid you Godspeed."

To Nathan's utter amazement and speechlessness, she jacked her shoulders back to show him who was master and led her beast away. He wondered, did she realize that in doing so, her breast stood proud and almost as erect as his cock?

That woman had awakened something in his soul that he thought had died in that treacherous hole. To his surprise, another piece of him returned so hard, its impact made his rib cage hurt. He watched her hips sway as she strode away.

Nathan picked up Madrigal's reins and continued down the path that infuriating and extremely intriguing wench took. The one thing he did know right then, he was definitely not traveling to Carlisle.

But first he needed to relocate the stream. It would take a great deal of time to regain his balance. And then he would make his way to Fletchers Landing.

The challenge was on.

* * * *

Meg could not believe she had treated the stranger so poorly. Her parents would have been horrified. Of course, that was not the only thing she had been forced to do that would have made her mother go into one of her rants. Hospitality had been one of Lady Beatrice of Fletchers Landing's mantras.

But Meg had had more than enough overbearing men to suit her. First, her betrothed, who not only took advantage of her dreams of love, but also proceeded to destroy her family. Then the Lord of Balforth had arrived to claim his lordship, demanding heavy taxes, only to leave after pieces of gold were placed in his hands. He was no better than Duncan Graham, who only offered protection for a price. Fletchers Landing was crowded with men who brought nothing but torment to her life.

Now, God forbid, here was a new stranger in their midst. A certain male who called himself Nathan Staves. One who she feared would threaten the tower of stones that she had carefully erected under the name of those who counted on her for protection and provision; her family and the people of Fletchers Landing.

His very presence made her tremble. Why was he truly here? He was not simply a wanderer looking for work. The steel of his sword was finely wrought, the hilt gilded with gold. The horse's saddle and bridle were not that of a poor man. However, both of his hands were callused, proving that he did indeed know the meaning of labor.

But what labor did he do? She had witnessed DePierce's soft hands. The very thought made her shiver with revulsion. Nor were they rough hands of the fishermen and the farmers. The protectors and marauders had similar calluses on one hand. His were on both.

She had seen them when he nearly touched her arm. In that moment, one breath between parted lips, she had nearly disgraced herself, her family, and broken her vow. The cage where desire resided rattled with need, begging for release. She looked over her shoulder. Did he persist in following her?

The path was empty. And inexplicably, Meg had to fight the need to release a tear. Letting go of Maisie's rope, she sat down on a boulder and tugged on her hose and shoes. No need for anyone to take notice of her state of undress. Not that anyone probably would.

Her clothing in place, she rose, resolute in returning to the keep and forgetting the stranger that made her heart quicken. That task might be harder than she first thought. Whatever his reason for riding nearby, she had the feeling that life in her little village was about to change.

Her feet dragging, she led Maisie into the outbuilding and settled her in. Phillipa rushed over before she secured the gate.

"Where have you been? Oh my lord. The poor thing is nearly ready to burst."

Meg sighed. "Then milk her and be done with it. And see that she doesn't cause anymore mischief." She glanced up at the sun. If she hurried, she would be able to attend the meeting in the cavern by the sea.

Mayhap, she would find out what the smugglers knew about the man called Nathan Staves.

Chapter 3

Nathan stepped out of the stream. His thoughts cleared with each shivering tremble of his muscles. A shrug of his stiff shoulders brought pain, reminding him once again that he was still healing. His feet bore the wounds where DePierce's men had honed their techniques of torture. Not all wounds were visible, but all wounds would carry scars in some shape or form. He limped over to Madrigal and rummaged through the satchel tied behind the saddle.

After drying off with his used jerkin, he pulled out a clean linen shirt and donned his leather jerkin. The chausses would serve until he could find someone to clean them.

He had tarried long enough. The day was slipping away. It was time for him to make his mission official and find a place to lay his head for the night. He would prefer sleeping as the raven-haired maiden's guest, but he still needed to discover whether she already had a man to protect her.

He toweled the remaining droplets from his face and swept back his damp hair. Madrigal nickered. Nathan swung around, his sword already in hand before he realized it.

He'd seen enough people in trouble to recognize it. A boy with thick black hair stumbled from the brush. His blue eyes widened and seemed to take up most of the room on his pale face. "My pardon. I...I don't mean you harm," the boy squeaked. He opened his hands, proving they were empty of weapons.

"What's your name?" Nathan asked. He glanced over the trees, searching for others. "Why are you alone?"

His eyes shined with intelligence. "Are you a knight?" he whispered in awe.

"Mayhap. Why do you ask?"

"I've only seen swords and horse leather nearly as fine as yours once before. But they were soldiers and weren't to be trusted."

Surprised that the boy noticed so many details in such a short time, brought respect and wariness racing through his veins. "They're gone now?"

"Yes, they came and went. But they'll return. I'm certain of it." He leaned to peer closer. "My father once had a mighty sword. But I do not know where it went."

Nathan smoothed his hand over the hilt and slid the sword into its sheath. "To lose one's weapon is a sad thing indeed."

"I wish that I might learn the art of swordplay. To protect our village."

"'Tis an honorable reason to learn."

He chewed on the edge of his thumb and studied Nathan as if he would poisonous vermin. Apparently, he came to a decision and abandoned the safety of the bushes. He held out his hand. "I'm called B-baldric, my lord," he said.

"My pleasure," Nathan said. The gravity of the boy's countenance made him look even closer and see the streaks marring his cheeks. "And what are you doing out here by yourself?"

"I'm searching for something that I lost," he admitted. "I fear I shall have to bear her wrath again." He made a face that reminded Nathan of Darrick's dog, Thunder. "Older sisters are not to be crossed and they can become impossible to please."

"Aye," Nathan nodded. "I hate to expose one of their secrets, but most women are impossible to please."

Baldric considered this news and nodded with a sigh. "'Tis as I feared. Though I don't remember my mother being so difficult." He shook his head. "'Twas so very long ago. It's hard to fully recall."

The thought of dealing with that bag of emotions sent Nathan scrambling for other topics. "I'm headed for Fletchers Landing. Do you know it? Have I far to travel?"

"Know it? 'Tis my home." A grin stretched, lighting Baldric's whole face. "You have but to climb up yonder hill and then down to the valley below."

"Are there establishments to tend for my horse? Mayhap an alehouse?"

"Course. Wayland our blacksmith will be able to direct you. And if it's food and ale that you seek, you must ask for Harrigan. But honey mead is what Fletchers Landing is known for."

Nathan bowed low. "Many thanks, young Baldric. Would you care to join me on my final trek to your home?"

"I still must search for a while longer. If I don't return home before nightfall, my sisters will be sorely angry."

"As you wish." He gathered Madrigal's reins and decided to walk for a while. His mission was about to begin. He pondered Baldric's comment about the soldiers. Had they been there to serve DePierce and his foul plan?

Feeling as though he had developed a new ally in the village, he turned to wave at the lad. Mayhap he would teach him to wield a sword. The weight of his tongue held back his offer. Baldric leaned heavily against a wooden staff as he limped down the road. Nathan's mind busied with details of how he might alter the training to fit the boy's needs. Of course, judging from his own experience, in doing so, the villagers would be more willing to accept him as one of their own. 'Twas the way of things.

Nathan rounded the hill that led to Fletchers Landing. The scent of salt and sea that coated the air met him as he took a breath. Midday sun cut through the clouds, illuminating the pale stone that stood over the village like a guardian angel.

He paused to see the lay of the land. The outer curtain wall stretched around the village, keeping its inhabitants safe from strangers like him. Straight ahead, the cliff reached out, a sentinel against the enemy. Steep paths led to where fishermen's boats bobbed on the waves. The tide would roll through the Solway Firth below the cliff and into the sea. A grove of trees filed past the southern wall. The rest of the land held neat rows of cottages and lush green fields. To the north stood the large keep. Behind it were more fields teeming with people working the rows.

A wave of gratitude swept through him. The great building was made of stone more than of timber. He'd witnessed the damage caused by fire and hoped to never have to rebuild another fortification again. Though as a Knight of the Swan, he supposed that was probably inevitable once he returned to the king's side.

Though smaller than Clearmorrow, the keep looked to be made of sturdy craftsmanship. Outbuildings surrounded the keep. A steady billow of smoke and the clang of iron against iron announced the blacksmith's workhouse.

A frown tugged his brow. The barns and sheds were jammed together far too close to the main hall. Their thatched roofs were a fire hazard. Now that DePierce was no longer in control, the land had transferred into King Henry's hands. Nathan would have to speak to whoever now stood as manager of the land and see that changes were made.

He swung his leg over the saddle and settled into the well. His destrier pranced, drawing the villagers' attention. A few stopped what they were doing and stared after them.

Nathan drew up on Madrigal's reins while he searched for the blacksmith. Nestled in the shadow of the keep stood the building he'd seen from the hill. Heat billowed from the doorway, stroking his face before he dismounted.

He led the horse to the trough and let him drink deeply before tugging him away. Much like his master, his mighty steed had a penchant for overindulging. They were on a mission for the king and this was the first time Nathan had been away from those who would protect and forgive him if he lost his grip on sanity. The last thing both of them needed was to let go of that thin thread of control.

The ringing of hammer and anvil stilled. The silence was nearly unbearable. Nathan winced. It might as well have been a horn trumpeting his arrival.

He approached the man, wary of the weapons still in his beefy hands. "Good day," he said.

"G'day," the blacksmith said around the iron nails caught between his lips. "What'd you want?"

Their lack of hospitality toward strangers almost took Nathan back a step. Instead, he recalled that he was the king's man and expected to be treated thus. Long were the years when he hadn't earned that respect, nor did his name carry any weight. But today, he arrived on the king's command and he intended to find out why Fletchers Landing held more than the attention of the king.

He stepped forward, entering the giant's lair. "I've traveled far and I wish a place to rest my horse."

Glacial gray eyes glittered back at him over the fire. He pumped the bellows, raising the flames. Heat threatened to scorch their eyebrows.

"Be you Wayland?" Nathan refused to give him space. Instead, he moved deeper into the hut, toward the fiery pit. "I have king's coin and I intend to stay here for a few days. Maybe more."

"That so? Without Lady Margaret's permission, I won't be tending to anything for you." His glance cut to Madrigal. "'Tis a magnificent beast. Him, I'll serve for your coin. But you... You'll need to speak to the woman at the keep before you think to rest your head in Fletchers Landing."

"Aye? And who might be managing the king's land?"

The blacksmith laid down his hammer, folding his tree-trunk arms across his chest; the ice in his glare a stark contrast against the stoked fire in the pit. "As I told ye, speak to Lady Margaret. She'll set you straight."

Nathan scrubbed the bristles coating his jaw. Lord Godwin and Lady Beatrice were the only ones reported to have held the land before DePierce. And they were all dead. Who was this Lady Margaret?

* * * *

"Meg, I cannot believe you mean to take this chance again," Anna rolled a ball of beeswax between her palms. "The people of Fletchers Landing do not expect you, Lady Margaret Grace of Fletchers Landing, to make this sacrifice."

Lord, when Anna said her name it sounded as heavy as the responsibilities felt. She rolled her shoulders as if to free herself from all the worries that continued to plague her. It was useless. They stuck to her like a bur.

She hated feeling unsettled by the gnawing demands of change. She hadn't been able to shed it ever since she met the stranger by the stream. She should have sent men off to deliver a warning. His presence was not encouraged. But she had been unable to make the command. When she opened her mouth, all she could think of was what his lips might taste like. She was certain he meant to steal a kiss. She'd been prepared to inform him of the cur that he was. Heat infused her cheeks. And yet, she did neither. In truth, she had hoped he would step closer, infuse the air with his strength. Ah, to sip from the powerful nectar of confidence. To lean on someone who gave her strength instead of taking it; to ease her needs.

The flesh between her legs throbbed with heat, swelling until she had to press her thighs together. The innermost core of her being ached, searching like a ship lost at sea, as if her life depended on his return. She snorted at the ridiculous way her mind tried to explain away her reaction to this Nathan Staves.

"Meg," Anna persisted. "You're not even listening to me."

Meg set the hive smoker aside and stared at her sister. The scent of smoking wood and sweet honey lost its ability to soothe her nerves. She ignored the tug of wistful thinking. Besides, 'twas certain he had already forgotten their encounter.

Anna was correct. There was more to concern herself with than the handsome stranger she had sent away and directed to Carlisle.

She had been lucky that it was not one of DePierce's mercenaries. The last time they came ashore they made it clear that they intended to return and wanted payment for peace. She expected to see them around every corner. Their message rang in her ears until she could not distinguish it from the sound of her pounding heart. Without payment, their patience would disappear. She needed time to figure out what to do, how to free them all from this tangled mess.

The meeting with the others would have to take place. Tonight.

She shook out her skirts, mindful not to agitate the bees buzzing nearby. The number of hives had increased once she started having more skeps built. If only it was enough to pay for everything they needed. She stretched the low arch in her back and licked a drop of honey from her finger. "And what would you have me do instead?" she asked, to appease her middle sister.

"You could marry."

"Marry? To whom?"

Anna ducked her head. "There are some in the village who would give you their hand in marriage. I suppose, Mother and Father would have wanted you to marry first, you being older than the rest of us." She raised her head, her eyes bright, nearly outshining her honey-colored hair. "It would solve our problem. 'Tis all I'm pointing out to you."

Meg folded her arms across her middle. Would the pain of loss never cease? "And what good would it do me? One more mouth to feed and nothing in return. That's what it'd be. You know as well as I that no man in this village has the coin to send those vermin packing. Nor the muscle, strength, or weapons. Even if they were sent off, I fear they'd return again. No, my opportunities for making a fine match are long gone."

"Then we should look elsewhere." Anna paced the small space where Meg kept the apiary. "We could spend a season at the royal court. Someone is bound to remember our parents and help to make an arrangement. I am of age and Phillipa has but a few years. Mayhap you would catch someone's eye. A merchant or..." She twirled her finger in the air, aggravating not only Meg but also the swarm of bees. "Someone not too old. He should at least have most of his teeth."

"How kind of you," Meg muttered. She could not believe she was having this conversation, let alone actually giving it a second's thought. "And how would I pay for fitting you and Phillipa out in the proper attire? And what of Baldric? He needs fostering more than you need dresses for dancing and finding your leisure on someone's arm."

"Opportunity." Anna ducked her head. "Education. More benefit would come for us if we were to make our situation known.

Meg felt the blood drain from her face, her head woozy at the thought of anyone finding out the trouble that they were in. The king would see them ripped from their home.

"If you would at least consider it," Anna snapped.

Meg tugged off her leather gloves. She shoved the wisps of hair frolicking against her dampened cheek from her face. What did her sister really desire? "We cannot just leave for London. Arrangements must be made.

Introductions. Of which we have no one to speak for us now that Mother and Father are no longer with us."

"Unlike you, there are those of us who have thoughts of marriage and... and a life elsewhere." Her lip caught between her teeth as if in concentration. She bent her neck and managed to avoid meeting Meg's gaze. "Phillipa, for instance. 'Tis certain."

Meg folded her arms. She narrowed her eyes, divining her sister's motivation for concern for their little sister. "And what would you know of it?"

"If you were to marry, then I would be next in line. Then Phillipa." Anna swatted at the bees flying near her head. "'Tis all I'm saying."

Ah, so there was a motive. Meg suspected as much and searched Anna's face. There was a flush to her cheeks. Meg had never noticed that before. Anna was now ten and eight years old. When had her middle sister grown into the bloom of a woman? She would have to watch her more closely. But to marry? To whom? To a stranger? Impossible. They would marry for love or not at all. Was that what her sisters wanted? Anna had her medicines and her garden. Phillipa had the animals to mend. The horses to breed. Did they choose to let all that go for a life of marital servitude?

And Baldric. Did he wish to abandon her too? He had yet to realize his strengths lay hidden in the courage to ignore the frailty of his young body. He was born to one day be lord of Fletchers Landing. But that was stripped from him when the reptilian lord of Balforth, Sir Vincent, appeared and threatened them with King Henry's edict that the land needed a lord's hand at the helm, not a young woman such as herself.

As for Meg, that one kiss shared with the man she had been betrothed to had been a disaster. It sent their family on a course never imagined. No, she would never desire to find love again. And love, was the only reason to tie yourself to another person. If anything came from the death of their parents it was the lesson she learned five years ago. No one should ever be forced into a marriage. No matter how badly one needed financial gain.

She shook free of the darkening thoughts. "Anna, you have your gardens and potions. Surely, you have no desire to tend a man."

Once again, her thoughts betrayed her. No desire for strangers with broad shoulders and tall as an oak. Lush lips. Or strong masculine feet.

"I know 'tis better than working harder than most of the villagers. Look at you. You are Lady Margaret Grace of Fletchers Landing. Not some..." She paused, searching as she waved her hand. "You are dealing with smugglers," Anna hissed as she took another angle. "They bring nothing but trouble. And put you in harm's way."

"Hush." Apprehension made Meg glance over the field. "They bring us money to pay our taxes and the tithing fees that the ones from the north are charging for protection."

Why was her sister so insistent? Their safety depended on secrecy and payment. In that order. As for marriage, Meg was not about to take another chance and cater to her own happiness. She was kept busy watching over her family and Fletchers Landing. It's what her parents would have expected of her.

Anna swished her skirt as if she had practiced it a hundred times. Meg knew better. It was not in her sister's nature to act the wanton wench. Hers was a heart that sought out those in need of healing.

"'Tis time for me to find a man. He'll be strong and virile. Passionate, and…" Anna added in a rush, "he'll kiss me until I swoon."

Meg's neck heated. There was a time when she too had those same desires; to be kissed until her legs gave out. But then that was before one kiss brought disease and death to their family.

And what of the man at the stream? her conscience asked. Since he would never return and she would never have to speak to him, he did not count, she argued.

What did demand her attention was Anna's open desire for a mate. She feared her sister would find herself in deeper trouble than anyone could imagine.

"You'll do well to keep those thoughts to yourself, Anna. There are men aplenty who will be happy to do your bidding, but a marriage vow won't be part of the bargain."

"Nonsense. Just because you failed at love doesn't mean that I will do the same. Perhaps you aren't created for love." She spun around, finally able to look at her. "I know already in my heart that I am ready for love."

Meg gasped, whether it was Anna's sharp tongue or that her sister came dangerously close to bumping one of the hives, she did not examine it. The skep, made of wicker and straw, was a fragile thing compared to a person's foot striking it in anger.

Mayhap she wasn't made for love. There was never another who took her breath or made her willing to take a chance on a new life.

What of the stranger?

No. The cost was too high and she had too many responsibilities to keep everyone safe. Even now, she faced a heavier price than she had anticipated. It was one thing to put her person in peril of the demands the smugglers continued to make. She had thought that she could bargain with the devil's demons and then send them on their way.

Now she feared she might lose everything that she'd fought so hard to keep safe.

Her knees folded, forcing her to sit on the low wall. Breathing became more difficult under the weight of so much responsibility. How she missed her parents, wanted them back.

Tears burned as she forced her eyes open. Fletchers Landing was surviving, indeed, she was certain that if not for the ridiculous price set for protection, they would be thriving.

The grove of trees grew tall and straight. The gardens were ripe with fruit and vegetables. The hives produced honey and from that she made the mead and candles. Anna saw to it that sickness did not visit them. Thanks to Phillipa, the beasts of the field were strong and healthy.

She barely noticed as Anna sat beside her and stroked her back.

"I'm sorry I hurt you," Anna whispered. "I fear for you. Being lady of this village, of the keep, managing all that you do. 'Tis too much to ask of you."

The sound of the surf crashing into the shore cast a soothing rhythm. It broke apart the fears that threatened to take over.

Perhaps she should make inquiries and send her sisters to safety. But which was worse? A season filled with stolen kisses or coerced bargains made with smugglers and those who promised to protect but took what they wanted instead?

"Meg, make haste!" Brother John raced into the field. His halo of gray curls bounced as he trotted toward them. "A stranger rode through our gates on a destrier. They say he is as big as a mountain and carries a sword so fine, the like of which none have ever seen."

* * * *

Wisdom called for Nathan to ignore the cries coming from outside the smithy's building. He set down his mug of ale. He missed the heady taste of wine served at Lockwood and Clearmorrow. The fruitful drink they brought back from Calais held the ability to carry him far from the lingering dark thoughts.

Leaning back, he managed to see what drew his attention. Of all things, Nathan never expected to see Baldric grappling with the blacksmith. His dust-covered tunic showed signs of having rolled on the ground. He pushed himself up on all fours and stood toe-to-toe against the large man. A squirming bag lay on the ground between them.

"You can't do this," Baldric wailed.

Red-faced, Wayland held the boy off with one hand and dodged the swinging arms aimed at his body. His whitened knuckles were like dried bones against the raven hair. He grunted as one of the lad's fists made contact with his nether regions.

Nathan winced as the giant of a man took offense at the blows to his body.

"I'll be returning, Harrigan," Nathan said. He flipped a coin toward the alehouse keeper's direction. "We still need to discuss my night's stay."

The stout little man caught the exchange outside. His brows rose. "Best get out there and put a halt to it before his sister gets word of it."

Who was this sister who put the fear in men and boys?

Nathan downed the watery ale and raced out, feeling like he was about to take a stand between David and Goliath. He came to a skidding halt. What did he have to offer as a stranger?

Baldric turned, his eyes swollen with tears. "You can't let him do it," he cried. "You can't."

"It's a runt of the litter," Wayland growled. "Probably won't live past the night."

Nathan surveyed the scene. "What's in the bag, master blacksmith?"

"Nothing," he grunted. "Not important for someone as yourself."

"Well, I wouldn't rule me out. You never know what I might be interested in."

"Please," Baldric pleaded, clinging on his sleeve. "Make him let it out."

Nathan skirted around them until he backed Baldric. "Suppose we talk about this as men." The boy gave a grunt and Nathan added, "The three of us as men."

The bag began to wriggle on the ground. A muffled yip worked its way through the canvas.

Nathan stepped closer, putting Baldric behind him. His sword unsheathed, his arm was stopped by the small hand wrapped around his wrist.

"Don't hurt him," Baldric cried.

"Baldric, where have you been?"

Nathan jerked his sword arm aside as the wench ran toward them. She reminded him of a smaller, younger version of the maiden at the stream. Her hair flew behind her in a wave of ebony. The expression on her face was even darker.

"You were told to watch the cow."

"He's going to kill it, Phillipa," the boy cried.

"He saw what I aimed to do and wouldn't listen when I told him to get," the smithy said. An air of satisfaction brought a gleam to his already rosy cheeks. "'Spect you'll want to take him on to the keep."

Although she could not be more than fifteen years of age, she stood with her hands to her hips and continued with her lecture. "Smithy, you will do well to remember yourself." She turned on Nathan, removing the odd hope that she intended to ignore him. "You will stay that sword," she ordered.

Seeing that he was the only one holding an unsheathed weapon, Nathan turned his attention away from the fiery maiden. The sack writhed at his feet. Something fought to be free. "Aye, in a moment."

Panic, fear, heart pounding in his head, Nathan sucked in a breath. He was as hungry for air as that poorly treated beast. With a flick of his wrist, the blade whipped through the sack. Wide-eyed and panting, a pup of questionable lineage stuck its head out. Mottled shades of brown and black collapsed on its belly at Nathan's feet.

Flashes of torture in dark, dank holds, empty of fresh air, collided in his body. Could something as simple as an unwanted puppy actually take him to his knees?

He braced his legs, refusing to fall over on his face. Sweat streamed down his jaw, trailing a path down his chest.

A small hand pressed his sword arm down until the tip of the blade touched the earth.

Grateful for the distraction, Nathan clung to the contact. It reminded him of the present and allowed him to break free from the past.

The admiration glowing from the maiden's face made Nathan itch under her watchful gaze. "My sister will thank you."

Baldric knelt on the ground beside the little puppy. It climbed into his lap on three legs and licked his neck. Its fourth leg was missing a paw.

The tranquil village was a façade. At some point the villagers had come to surround them. There was apprehension in their untrusting eyes. So much for slipping in and gathering information. His plan to send a missive at first chance became a little more difficult. Someone was bound to note if a stranger hired a messenger.

"Told you the cripple needs to be put out of its misery." The smithy glowered, his tree trunk forearms pumping with anger. "Put it back in the sack, my Lady Phillipa. I'll finish what I started."

Phillipa bent down to take the small animal from Baldric's arms. Nathan's chest clutched. Did she intend to hand it over?

"You will never lay another hand on my brother or this pup again," she snapped. "Where is its mother? We'll take them both to the keep."

"Bitch is dead." The man's eyes bulged with rage.

Nathan admired the way the girl did not blink. She reminded him of the raven-haired maiden at the stream. Instead, the warrior princess stood taller, drawing the boy and puppy in tow. "All the more reason for us to take the little mite."

"I expect payment," he growled.

"Take it up with Lady Margaret," she snapped.

"Bitch'n wenches," Wayland muttered as he turned on his heel and stomped away. "You'll get yours. 'Tis for certain."

Warning flares heated the back of Nathan's eyelids. It took discipline to keep from running the fool through with his sword. The blacksmith would be someone to watch.

Nathan found his way back to the alehouse and finished the mug of ale in one long drawn-out swallow. The bitter liquid, slid down his parched throat. He had thought a change of scenery would keep the darkness at bay. Mayhap the memories would prove too strong to silence. But he had to try.

"My lord," whispered Harrigan. "'Tis certain, you've made yourself an enemy."

"I wager I will have to find another building to house Madrigal."

It would never do to stable your horse with a new enemy. And he had a feeling the blacksmith Wayland would get his pound of retribution.

"My thanks." He clasped the man's hand. Mayhap he could still gain an ally outside the keep. The two extra coins slid on the table were covered and palmed. "If someone should come for me, they'll be looking for Sir Nathan Staves."

Harrigan's one good eye roved over Nathan's face. "Staves of nowhere, is it?"

"For now," he said.

"Looks like his lordship has taken a liking to you. Yonder he comes."

Nathan's brows rose. Lordship?

Baldric ran back. His one good leg leading the shorter one with a skip and a hop. "Come with us." He tugged on Nathan's sleeve and pointed to the keep on the hill.

Phillipa turned. Impatience spilled from her steps. She juggled the squirming spotted puppy in her arms. "Baldric. Bring your stranger."

"You must join us for the evening meal," Baldric said. "'Tis certain my sister will want to reward you for your good deed."

"Best heed my Lady Phillipa and Lord Baldric," Harrigan said. He swiped the moisture beading over his upper lip. "But mind, if you don't make it past Lady Margaret's gate, I'll find a place for both you and your charger."

Chapter 4

Nathan looped the reins over Madrigal's neck and swung into the saddle. The little lord and lady had determined that they would wait for him to gather his destrier from the blacksmith's stable. Did they, too, feel more than animosity boiling from the fire pit? Thankfully, Wayland had hid himself away from the shop and they had only to deal with his assistant. Though Nathan relished a meeting, it would prove more fruitful if he left it for another day.

He smoothed his palm over the great horse's thick neck. "What has our king gotten us into?"

Brother and sister led the way up the road to the keep. Another set of gates were closed and fortified well enough that it would withstand a siege. Pale stone glistened in the setting sun, turning crimson as the day began to end.

But where were the soldiers? They would need more men at arms to defend the keep against disgruntled people like the blacksmith. He squinted into the sun's glare. A gleaming path of white stone led to the water below. A young servant ran up to Phillipa and Baldric. The serving girl bobbed her head as the commander of their little troupe issued out orders.

"Don't let her know," he overheard her say as he rode up beside them.

Ah, so there was someone else who held the village in order and under stern rule?

"Halt," the voice came from behind the gate. Phillipa, Baldric and the servant froze. Judging by the apprehension etched on their faces, Nathan itched to feel the comforting cool metal of his sword gripped in his fist. Madrigal stomped his great hooves and snorted.

The gate swung out on oiled hinges.

Two more women stood in the entrance. The taller of the two kept to the shadows, her arched hand protecting her eyes from the sun. She stepped out, her attention on the children. A pristine white cloak swung from her shoulders and covered her from head to toe. A gauzy veil of lace hung over her face, hiding her features. Slim hands, fisted a pair of leather gloves the color of mourning doves.

"What have you to say for yourselves?" asked the tall woman. Her throaty voice wove its way through the veil.

Nathan lifted his head to peer under the silk wall. There was a familiarity about it that made the beat of his heart pick up speed. Those same fingers that itched to hold a sword now ached to reveal her face. What did she hide? Was her countenance disfigured from plague or fire?

If not for the boy, he would have bent down from the saddle and stripped the mask away. Who was this woman? Mother? Mistress of the keep? The dreaded Lady Margaret?

Baldric's shoulders drooped. "I'm sorry I left the gate open, Meg."

Meg?

"I saw the blacksmith," Baldric continued, pleading his case. "I knew he meant the mother dog harm." He lifted his head. "And I was right."

"Your responsibility was to our livestock. What you did was allow one of our cows to wander off. Someone else could have found and claimed her. Then who would answer to her calf waiting for his mother's milk?"

The boy paled under her scrutiny. "Me," he whispered.

"But it didn't," his sister said.

"You'll do best if you stay out of his mess," Meg warned.

"I saw to them," Phillipa insisted. "Maisie and her calf are fine. Besides, 'tis time to ween him from her teat." She shifted her hold on the sleeping puppy, her fingers stroking its ears with relentless compassion.

"You spend too much time in the barns as it is."

Phillipa's head reared back in defiance. Her jaw clenched. "What do you intend to do to the blacksmith?"

The woman swathed in white, stiffened. "What do you mean?"

The woman beside her gasped. Her hair the color of golden chestnuts, was pulled back, braided and pinned to perfection. "What happened?" Her eyes were doe soft. An air of gentleness seemed to surround the children. "Is someone hurt? Should I get my things?"

"No," the children said; a united front. They shared a look between them.

The woman they called Meg unwrapped the many layers. The veil fluttered to the ground like the reveal of an exotic dancer. Layers of material piled at their feet. "Thank you, God." She embraced them, her head bowed under a mighty weight.

"If not for this stranger, Master Wayland would have injured Baldric just so that he could murder this puppy," Phillipa pointed out.

A collective turn of heads pulled their full attention to Nathan. His breath stuttered.

He tipped his head. His lady at the stream. Disguising his discomfort with a bow, he shifted in the saddle, allowing room for his cock to fill at the most inopportune time. If not for the tremble of fingers against her unbound hair, he would never have guessed that she recognized him.

"Anna, take the children inside. We've given a performance for all to gossip about already. And that," she said, pointing at the puppy, "will stay outside."

"But Meg," Baldric wailed. "We need to take care of Pod. He needs me."

Gone was Nathan's smiling young wench from the stream. In her place was a stern, tight-lipped, bitter woman. "You've named that little beast already?"

The boy rubbed his nose as he hobbled toward her and tugged her sleeve. "His full name is Tripod."

"What an odd name."

His eyes brightened. "'Tis because he's a bit like me."

Her head tipped to one side, noticing the way Phillipa stroked the pup's deformed appendage. Meg took in a sharp breath. "I don't see anything that compares to you."

Nathan wished he could ride away at that moment. He did not need or want to witness another private moment among family members. Apparently they had forgotten he still sat astride Madrigal. An escape should be easy enough.

"Meg, 'tis certes, that you see his foot isn't quite right."

Her complexion paled. "Yes. I see that now, little brother." She gave his shoulder a gentle nudge. "He has a white spot on his paw. Why not call him Whitefoot, instead?"

Baldric's smile warmed and Nathan had the feeling they had all been taken into his plan. He lifted the smaller spotted paw. "Of course. I should have noticed that. Aren't you brilliant? It'll be good to have him nearby. For protection. Once he's grown, that is."

"And who shall clean up after it?" Her voice quavered.

"I shall do it all. I promise. You won't even notice that he is here."

Her dark eyebrow, the color of a raven's wing, arched in doubt.

"You won't send him away because he's different, will you?" Baldric rubbed Whitefoot's ears. "'Twould be as mean and cruel as that blacksmith."

A collective gasp passed through them. Meg stiffened, yanking her hands behind her back.

"Baldric," Anna ordered. "Take the puppy to the barn."

"For now," Phillipa added before he could object. She tucked the puppy into his arms but not before yanking his ear. Contrite, he turned smartly on his heel and made a hasty retreat.

Nathan would have liked to have been the one to console Meg, but her sisters beat him to it. They huddled around Meg, rubbing her arms as they whispered in her ear. He felt a bit like an insect when they stopped chattering to stare over their shoulders in his direction.

He rested his elbow on the saddle's horn. The royal court held nothing to compare to the interaction between the ladies and their little lord. It was the like of which he had never experienced.

"No, I'll do it," Meg assured them. Waving them on, she stood rooted until they slipped through the small postern gate in the wall. She spun around and marched toward him, her back as stiff and straight as any well-trained soldier.

"You," she said, keeping her voice low enough that Nathan had to lean forward. "What are you doing here?"

Her breath blew across his skin, prickling it like a goose missing its feathers. He suppressed a shiver. Must be the breeze blowing in from the tide. He had hoped for a better reception. But that was before it appeared Meg was someone of importance at the keep. He still had yet to ascertain if there was a man in her life other than Baldric.

"Apparently, I missed the turn for Carlisle." A twitch of her lips drew him to her mouth. He slowly dismounted and was relieved when she did not retreat. The top of her head came to the middle of his chest so that she had to tip her head back, exposing her slender neck. Her lush lips pouted up at him. A droplet of liquid glistened at the corner of her mouth. It attracted him as a flower attracts a bee to its pollen. "I'm told I have a penchant for saving those in need of help."

She made a face, rolling her eyes at his attempt at humor. The shawl came up to her chin. "Come inside the keep, before we add more fodder for the people to gossip about."

"A moment, my lady." Unable to resist, he ran his thumb over the sticky substance near her succulent mouth. His brow arched as he licked the honey from his skin. Ah, that was the source of her sweetened breath. Aroused, a groan slipped from his lips as his groin clenched. He closed his eyes and leaned in to taste if the rest of her was as sweet and nearly tumbled through the empty chasm where she once stood.

A scratchy throat cleared beside him. Nathan craned his neck and suppressed his surprise at the height of its owner. The man of the cloth, complete with wooden cross hanging from his neck, a halo of bushy gray hair, and woolen gown that reached his ankles, was not a small man by any means.

"I'm called Brother John," the man said. His face, wrinkled by time and the sun, beamed down at him. Piercing blue eyes stared back, divining between deception and truth.

Nathan narrowed his gaze. Enough meddling clergymen had filled his past to last a lifetime. He drew back his shoulders, defying the sudden urge to ask for forgiveness for so many sins, too numerous to count and that would probably send the old man to an early grave.

He tipped his head. "Sir Nathan Staves."

"Ah, a knight of the realm." The friar ran his palm over Madrigal's shiny black coat. His bony fingers traced the medallions marking the saddle. "A favored one, at that."

From somewhere hidden under the many folds of his mud brown long tunic, he produced a red apple. The destrier, trained to obey only one master, that being Nathan, took the treat from the old man's hand. Juice ran from his lips. The horse nickered, blowing against the monk's cowl.

Traitor. Since when had his charger been accepting of strangers?

"Our friend here appears to have an appetite." The monk waved to the shadows and a servant trotted up. The young man paused, hesitant to take command of the powerful beast.

"Show me the way, lad," Nathan said. "My boy, Madrigal, is inclined to be a bit testy. 'Tis best that I tend to him myself."

"No matter," Brother John said. "Follow me." He set off, his hands hidden inside the voluminous sleeves, and chatted on. "Lady Phillipa is probably pacing the stables so that she might get her hands on him. She works miracles with all the animals."

Nathan scowled. What manner of man from the church came without judgment? He almost liked him. At least the man didn't don himself with velvets and silks. He would have had to run him through just on principle alone.

"The young girl. Lady Phillipa. She's the one who came to the boy's rescue?"

"I heard the tale that you had a hand in helping Lord Baldric." His smile stretched. "'Tis good to aid someone in need. Is it not?"

Nathan rubbed the back of his neck. The only true person he ever vowed to help and protect was his king. Albeit, those few he knew who were connected to the Knights of the Swan would gain his help if needed. But in truth, even then, it still was done in the name of the king.

"Young Baldric may have a challenge here and there, but it has given him a charitable heart. He'll make a wonderful lord of Fletchers Landing when he comes of age," Brother John said.

The path took a circuitous route inside the keep wall. Outbuildings crammed against each other until there seemed hardly any room to breathe. Why place everything inside the wall when you had villagers who obviously worked the fields? Did they worry their people would steal the stores?

Nathan turned back his thoughts. "Sir Vincent DePierce was given lordship by King Henry, was he not?"

A change washed over Brother John. A tightness of the lips and jaw. "Here are the stables."

The building, three times the size of the others, housed several horses, some of which Sir Ranulf, Lord of Sedgewic would be envious. The spacious tack room resided at the end of the building. The thatched roof concerned him. He'd need to see that changed while he uncovered Fletchers Landing's secrets. The barn and stalls were immaculate, giving testament to the care the old friar professed.

After they settled Madrigal in a stall that would make Darrick weep with envy, Brother John motioned for one of his minions. They seemed to appear out of the mist and shadows. But he saw no sign of Baldric and his sister tending to the puppy as they were ordered.

Madrigal pushed at his shoulder, lipping his sleeve. Nathan cut his eyes to the shadows. Who listened and watched? The space between his shoulders crawled with suspicion and if he should ever admit it, anticipation.

"He'll be well cared for. Much more than if still under the blacksmith's roof. Someone will see to his brushing."

"Aye. No reason not to put tack away." Nathan carried bridle and saddle to the tack room, leaving it on the bench for cleaning. He swung his satchel over his shoulder. "What's going on here, Brother John? Tension leaks through the stones and washes through the village."

"It's nothing for a stranger to concern himself with." He puffed a breath. "As for Blacksmith Wayland, he has yet to learn our ways. 'Tis certain we will pray for his soul."

Nathan would rather take a stronger means other than prayer. It was his observation that it did little good to pray.

Bells rang out.

"'Tis time for us to make ready for our evening meal," the old monk explained. "We eat after vespers and when all the tasks are completed. I believe Lady Margaret intends for you to join us. I imagine you would prefer a wash up before attending the ladies in the solar."

The man's voice scratched over Nathan's nerves. He imagined the parishioners fell under the neutral tones until they were cast under religion's spell. "Aye, a good wash would do. Have you a trough or well?"

Nodding in understanding, the old man motioned for him to follow on. The path kept winding and Nathan began to wonder if he was expected to take a plunge in the firth.

"Fletchers Landing is more civilized than asking our guests to splash around in the beasts' drinking water. Besides, my lady Phillipa considers it unhealthy for the animals."

"She has a passion for them, does she?"

Brother John grunted. "Aye."

Silence stretched. Had the man of the cloth reached the stage of forgetfulness? Even a cup of water would be a welcome sight so that he could remove the road grit clinging to his neck.

The sound of water crashing against the shore kept them company as they climbed the stairs to the overlarge doors. Impressed with their size, Nathan measured their arch would reach twice as high as any other that he'd seen in all of his travels. Only the doorways at King Henry's court would rival their workmanship.

Expecting it to take two servants to open the great wooden panels, he was surprised when they swung easily on oiled hinges.

They entered the great hall. The room opened out, bringing its inhabitants and attention to the center. Fresh rushes softened the sound of their footsteps. The scent of crushed herbs followed behind them.

"The bell will ring once more. I suggest you make haste. My lady does not appreciate tardiness." Brother John pointed to an alcove. "You'll find accommodations to your liking." And with that assumption, he left Nathan standing at the door.

Nathan eased into the room. It held a washbowl and a pitcher. He sniffed at the perfumed water. Then tested it. It had been heated in anticipation of his use. Perhaps he did indeed feel someone's eyes upon him.

Taking the old monk's advice he made quick use of the water scented with rosemary and lavender. Then went in search of the solar.

* * * *

Meg paced the solar. She could not believe that her own flesh and blood had turned against her. "I thought I made it perfectly clear that the stranger should stay in the stable with his horse."

"But he's already been invited to sup with us. We can't go back on our word. What would Mother and Father have said?" Phillipa argued.

Baldric and Phillipa shared a look before he chimed in. "Yes, Mother and Father."

"They would have asked: 'Who is this man? Can he be trusted?'"

Visions of him standing on the banks of the stream, barefoot and pleasing to the eye, claimed her attention. He wore his charm like a fine tunic. And then he dared to touch her in front of everyone. Her hand slipped up, wavering over the place where he had caressed her with his thumb. The warmth had stuck to her like honey. And her serviceable dress, work-worn and faded, made her feel like a mud wren. She tugged on the bodice neckline that gaped since weight loss. The plans to repair its fit had never been deemed important enough to give it time.

"Meg," Anna said quietly. "It is but a meal. Surely we are not so mean spirited to send him away after he took it upon himself to help our brother."

"And we will make certain to eat quickly. Won't we, Baldric?"

"Our duty fulfilled," Anna added.

Meg touched the ache between her brows. Was even the ever-biddable Anna against her? They did not know of the meeting she had been forced to attend. Nor would they ever as long as she slipped into the night once darkness had set.

"I suppose, if we kept the stranger occupied, offered him a seat at our table…"

"He's called Sir Nathan Staves," Anna said. Their stunned looks made her lips quirk to the side. She shrugged. "Brother John does have his merits in ferreting out information."

Meg's insides jumped. "A knight?"

"And he is frightfully handsome."

"And strong," Baldric added.

"Did he say where he is from?" Meg asked. *Dear Lord, please do not let him be one of DePierce's mercenaries.*

"Meg, he is the king's man. Brother John advises that we offer him a room while he is here."

"But we don't know why he's here." Meg lowered her voice, saying through gritted teeth, "What if he discovers…things?"

"Greetings." His moss-green eyes lit with amusement.

The man they spoke of now stood inside the solar. He had changed into a tunic that matched the color of his eyes. His dampened hair, combed away from his face, exposed the column of his neck. Golden threads wove through the whiskers on his jaw. Leads of muscle bulged from his shoulders. A wavy lock of hair fell in front of his eyes.

She fisted her hands, hiding them in the folds of her drab brown skirt and resisted the urge to smooth back her hair. Fire raced up her neck. Even her scalp tingled at having been caught in the act of gossiping about the man.

He bowed deeply. A curl teased his jerkin, drawing attention to his neck and broad shoulders. Upon rising, mischief lifted his lips. "I believe I can satisfy your questions once your Lady Margaret makes her appearance." He winked conspiratorially.

Her middle sister glided toward him and curtsied, the rounded décolletage exposing more breast than Meg believed proper. When did Anna sew that new neckline?

"I'm Anna," she said, her voice, ever soothing, as she rose with the help of his hand. "The middle sister."

"A beauty to behold. In truth, I have never seen such beautiful sisters. Not even in King Henry's court."

Anna giggled. Meg stared at her sister and had to snap her mouth shut. Anna hadn't giggled since their parents passed away. A blush stole over Anna's skin, brightening her cheeks. "'Tis very kind of you to say."

His gaze stroked over them, touching each with his attention. "Lady Phillipa and Master Baldric. 'Tis good to see that you are none the worse from the altercation in the village."

"The smithy is a good man." Phillipa smiled as she cut a look in Meg's direction. "I'm certain he will think twice before setting his hands where they don't belong."

"Our sister has already handled it," Baldric said. "He's to spend time with the lambing."

Sir Nathan's eyes widened. "And how is that punishment?"

Baldric grinned as he rubbed his hands together with treacherous glee. "He hates the sight of blood."

"'Tis good for him to witness life coming into the world," Phillipa added. "Though I would have had him serve longer, our sister feels too much time away from his anvil will cause our village to suffer."

"And when might I meet Lady Margaret? I'm told she is a veritable dragon. A paragon of impatience. Should I be afraid? Must I unsheathe my weapon to win her over?"

Meg's brows rose. She stepped forward, refusing to retreat from him again. "I can assure you that should she be here, she would wonder why someone would speak of her in that way."

"Meg," Anna hissed.

"'Tis unfair to play with her, Sir Nathan," Phillipa said. White faced, she strode to Meg's side, looping their arms together. "Of course you recall meeting our sweet Margaret."

His lips twisted and that mischievous gleam had returned as he met Meg's gaze. Would he reveal that they spoke beside the stream?

"Aye, we met at your keep's gate."

Baldric's elbow poked him in the side. "She's Lady Margaret Grace," he whispered out the corner of his mouth.

If it weren't so mortifying to learn you were spoken of without regard, she would have found it amusing. Her brother and sisters were doing everything they could to free the knight from his misstep.

"She's..." He turned his head, searching her from head to toe. Somehow, her fingers had found their way into his hands. Warmth seeped through her limbs. "'Tis true you are formidable, my lady, but certainly not a dragon."

Christ's blood. Fire had replaced the warm glow. If only she could extract her fingers from his grasp.

"'Cept we call her Meg," Baldric yelled from across the solar.

Bless him. Meg needed to speak with Brother John regarding her brother's training, immediately.

To his credit, Sir Nathan blushed. Good. Her skin had yet to lose its heat ever since she met him at the stream. They could endure the stew together. Meg nearly found it in her heart to let him off without an apology. Almost.

She tipped her head in acknowledgement. Until she knew his true purpose it would serve her well to be forgiving. "'Tis good of you to join us."

"Nor are you of an age to manage this holding for the king."

What a pity. He spoke. Meg frowned as she extracted her person from his hold and put a decent space between strangers. "Thank you for your concern. We are doing well enough. As you will see when you partake of our food."

The bell tolled, announcing time for their evening meal.

"Ah, even time must do your bidding." The mischievous gleam reclaimed his countenance. He bowed so deeply, she feared he might topple over his fine, calfskin boots. "If you will allow me..."

She looked down at his outstretched hand. Long tapered fingers wiggled for her acceptance. At least, no one but the children would witness his display.

"Lady Meg, I'd count it a privilege to escort you to the table."

Hesitant, she touched his sleeve and ignored the thrill of something like summer lightning, skipping over her skin. "No doubt," she said dryly. "Otherwise, you would be lost."

Shadows slid over his eyes before he shielded them with ridiculously lush lashes. He turned his head. Did he murmur something to the effect that he already was?

"Come, children," she said, hoping to regain the playfulness they had known so little of for the past five years.

Chapter 5

Meg sat in her mother's chair at the long high table. Lady Beatrice had been no small person, and her mother's great chair was a reminder of her own small stature. Her father, Lord Godwin's, chair still remained empty over all those years. One day, the new lord of Fletchers Landing would take command. The only time someone had attempted to claim it, Meg had feared she would surely die from heartache. Vincent DePierce, Lord of Balforth and presumably the king's newly appointed Lord of Fletchers Landing, had foolishly thought he could take up her father's seat. They had not seen that man for nearly a year. The next time would be too soon.

Her fingers dug into the dark polished wood. A bloodthirsty vision came to mind. She would never be the person her father or her mother had been, but she would see Father's chair burned before that bastard sat in it again.

Brother John walked in behind them. His bushy gray brows rose as he took in the dinner scene. How long had it been since they'd had a guest at their tables? Did he question Sir Nathan's presence? Meg sorted through appropriate responses should he question her decision to invite a stranger to their evening repast.

To her surprise, he nodded at the knight. "I bid you good eve. I see that you found your way to the table."

The monk who had passed down so much knowledge to Meg's family deserved a higher seat. Instead, he purposefully sat near Baldric. Meg watched the knight through the edges of her lashes. Sir Nathan kept the banter going over the next course of poached flounder.

"Tell me," he said, carefully placing his eating knife beside his trencher. "What news have you regarding the pup? Has it settled into its new home?"

Phillipa shoved an overlarge bite of meat into her mouth. She tore off a huge chunk of bread and gave it to Baldric. If not for him ducking at the last minute, the whole thing would have been shoved in his gaping mouth. Mortified, Meg realized they had a lot to work on if they were to even think about being presented for a marital match.

They all waited while the youngest of the group continued to chew.

Anna, ever the peacemaker, shifted in her seat. "I'm certain Phillipa has the poor little thing tucked in a bed in the stables. They would never disobey you, Meg. Isn't that right, Brother John?"

Brother John cleared his throat. "I, uh, forgot to check on the beast. Mayhap I will say a prayer before bedtime." He plucked a bit of fish from the trencher and chewed as if it had been dried in the smokehouse over winter. His wide sleeves swung out, threatening to dip into the remains of the sauce. Draining their best honey mead wine from the cup made of horn, he rose from the table. "I must leave you now." He paused, bowing first to Meg and then Sir Nathan. "My lady, I've done as you bid for our king's guest." Silence stretched. The chatter between Baldric and his sisters stopped as they waited for her response.

"Yes?" Dear Lord, what did he think she bade him do? She took a long drink of cool mead to drench her parched throat. "What…news have you?"

"Accommodations are set, my Lady Meg."

"I see." She turned on the man who'd tormented her thoughts all evening. "I hope it not too much to assume you might wish to stay in our keep."

"Much better than sleeping under the trees beside a stream," Sir Nathan said. The corners of his mouth twitched. "I'm honored."

"Yes, well then," she said. Him sleeping under the same roof brought visions of bare limbs. God help her; his bare feet. She would have to do penance for her straying thoughts. "Brother John…"

"As you requested." The tunic and cowl nestled around the old monk's shoulders drooped as he dipped his head. "The bedchamber that sees the morning sun is prepared for our king's man."

"Oh, yes, 'tis a lovely thought," Meg whispered to no one in particular. "The morning sun is glorious there. And much cooler at night." And far away from the shores and the coves across the firth.

Arms folded, he added, "May your evening be blessed."

Phillipa nudged Baldric, tipping her head toward the doorway. "I think we should check on Whitefoot, don't you?"

A flash of rebellion hardened his jaw. "But I haven't eaten my custard."

"Cook will save you some. I'll see to it." She rose from her chair so fast that it threatened to tip over. Her pocket bulged where she must have slipped an extra morsel for the puppy.

Warning bells pealed. How did no one else hear the deafening sound? Phillipa and Baldric were up to something. But when Anna rose to join them, Meg nearly fell out of the great chair.

"Welcome to our home," Anna said. She took a breath before continuing. "'Tis certain you will enjoy our hospitality."

"I beg your pardon," Meg said, peering after brother and sisters. They nearly collided in their efforts to escape the room. "I've never seen them act this way before. Perhaps we should have more guests join us for a meal."

The corner of his mouth tilted up and for once that evening he did not have a quick reply.

Her plan to feed the stranger and be done with him was foiled. So, they talked of farming and the many good things grown on the land.

The meal stretched into the evening. She glanced toward the window. Darkness was falling. She would have to send a message to her business partners that she had been detained. Partners. 'Twas a far stretch to define smugglers as her partners.

Her stomach churned. Please God. Keep them patient.

Nathan cut a pear in half and handed her a slice. Fire raced through her fingertips as they connected with his. She started to pull her hand away and stopped when he trapped them in his. His thumb grazed over her wrist. A shared breath hung between them before he released her.

"Thank you," she whispered. "For…protecting my brother, and…seeing that he was unharmed. He is still young, you see. His limp is not so easy to notice at times. 'Tis believed that one day it will be gone."

His focus returned to the fruit and began slicing it into thin strips. "How do you manage it?"

Meg didn't know whether to be grateful or disappointed that he avoided contact by holding out a plate for her to select a piece of fruit. She made a show of selecting the best one.

"When my parents died it was left to me to keep our village thriving. At first the villagers did not care for my orders. But soon they understood I did this to keep them safe and fed."

"Vincent DePierce. He was appointed lord by King Henry."

Her jaw clenched. How dare he bring that man's name to her table? She fought down the desire to fling the fruit across the room. "'Tis of no concern. Soon the question of ownership will be cleared and Fletchers Landing back in the rightful heir's control. No matter what is said, that man will not be lord here." She slapped her hand over her mouth. Dear God, she'd said that to the king's man?

He reached out, peeling her hand away. His finger brushed over her lips.

Meg tasted his callused flesh with the tip of her tongue. She ached to lean into him and trust that he would catch her if she fell. "Why are you here?" she croaked.

He withdrew his hand, leaving an empty cavern between them. "Vincent DePierce can no longer harm you. He died nearly a year ago."

A sob leaked through Meg's chest. If only that were true. His mercenaries no longer cared whose coin they took. They were there. Watching and waiting for their prey to make a mistake.

"Our king has yet to decide who shall be deemed the new lord." He caught a tear from her cheek.

The kindness in his eyes made her feel weak and lost. She had to maintain her strength if she was to hold on to Fletchers Landing for her family. Their future.

"Then I shall offer additional prayers for our king's improved wisdom." Palms pressed into the trestle table, she rose from her mother's chair. She was not abandoning her position. Only retreating until she had figured out another plan. "If you will excuse me."

"My lady." Nathan caught her hand. "Lady Meg. Thank you for your hospitality."

Ignoring the warmth, the tenderness in his touch, she steeled her control. "You are here on King Henry's orders, are you not?"

He ducked his head. "I do not mean to cause you distress."

She shivered as his breath whispered over her skin. "And yet, here you are."

"True. But had I not been sent, we would not have met. My tender heart would have been shattered."

"I sincerely doubt that, Sir Nathan. One's heart cannot miss what it does not know."

"On that I must disagree."

Shadows swept in, furrowing his brow. If not for him still holding her hand overly long, she feared she would have smoothed away the heavy thoughts. Her gaze dropped to their joined fingers. His; callused and strong. Hers; work worn and in sore need of Anna's unguents. She snatched back her hand. What was she thinking?

"Please, I pray," his voice rumbled. "If you will allow it, I shall escort you to your bedchamber and then you may direct me to my own."

How was it that his voice had the simple power to make her legs go weak? "We shall call the servants. To help you."

"Must they be called? I am but a simple knight. I'm certain we can manage on our own. Don't you?"

Meg lifted her shoulders, tipping her chin to grant permission. "Yes."

How else was she to rid herself of his shadow? The smugglers had called for a meeting and she dared not be any later. They were sure to take umbrage at her tardiness and demand to renegotiate the terms of their agreement.

"My Lady Meg, lead the way."

* * * *

Nathan walked beside Lady Meg. He'd nearly lost his control when the whisper of a groan slipped between those luscious full lips. A simple shrug of her slender shoulder tore him from his concentration of the mission of discovery. And when she rose, her curves hidden under the bodice of her serviceable gown had threatened to reveal her rosy buds...he feared he would have tumbled into the remainder of his trencher. He suppressed the need pumping through his veins. He must silence his little head, for that would only lead to trouble.

She strode purposefully beside him. Though her posture would please the staunchest of instructors for lady of the keep, he could not bring himself to think of her as the dreaded dragon, Lady Margaret. Smaller in stature she may be, but she was stronger than she looked. In mind and spirit. And that, he admired. It was a gift he once believed could never be taken from him. And he was so very wrong.

A few of her tresses had loosened from the braid and curled around her shoulder. It glistened under the torchlight. Like a siren, it called to him. His breath came quicker and 'twas not based solely on his rising desire for the woman. A frown tugged at his brow.

Her steps had certainly picked up pace. If he did not know any better, he would guess that she had a rendezvous with a lover. His mood darkened. Determined to stall whatever plans for the remainder of the night that did not include him, he planted his feet in front of what must be the family gallery.

He pointed up at the narrow-faced man and tall plump woman sitting astride black muscular beasts. "My God, they are magnificent!"

Meg puffed a breath. Her hands on her hips, she stared at him as if he were a contrary child. She swept back her hair and returned to his side. "They are?"

"Just look at the mass of muscle, the strength and power."

"Ah, yes, I suppose I've never thought of them in that light." She bit her lip, drawing his attention away from the tapestry.

"Are they Percherons?" he asked. "Are they still alive? Have they bred others?" Could this be the reason for DePierce's attraction?

Confusion clouded her eyes. "I beg your pardon?"

Nathan blinked and pointed to the dark warhorses that any good knight would kill for and protect. They were the stuff of which legends were written. "The horses. I must know who their sires are."

Her eyes widened, their depths glittered back at him. "Oh!" Her chest rose and fell as if she ran a race.

Entranced by the movement, Nathan leaned in closer. All thought of DePierce and the king's mysteries surrounding the land fell away. His breath hitched as she reached out. To touch him? Stroke his jaw? Did she feel the growing need too? Would she ever admit it? His muscles, preparing for the onslaught of sensations that he was certain would come at her lightest touch.

"I thought you were interested in my parents." She traced the tapestry's threads. "Lady Beatrice and Lord Godwin."

Heat rose up Nathan's neck until he swore it could catch the damn painting on fire. "My apologies. I—"

She waved him off. "Just don't speak of it to my sister."

"I meant your family no harm." He scrubbed his jaw. "I seem to be making a mess of things ever since we met over the stream."

"On the contrary. I've enjoyed the distraction." Her sad smile tugged at some small corner of what used to be someone who cared deeply. A blush bloomed over her cheeks. "'Tis but these are not Percherons. Our family began dabbling in breeding Friesian horses when my father returned from his many..." She waved the air. "Trips. He found the breed much to his liking."

She arched her back to examine the subject of great interest. A chuckle reverberated from her slender throat. "Brother John and my sister Phillipa are quite protective of them."

Enthralled by the sight, Nathan whispered. "Beautiful."

Her dark eyes, deep pools of glittering passion, turned to him. Ebony lashes fluttered against her high cheekbones.

Nathan's hand hung in the space between them. He needed only to stretch out his finger, trail it over her collar and up her neck.

As if aware of his thoughts, she stepped out of reach. "I will be sure to share your enthusiasm with my sister. She's already hard to live with, but now that the king's knight has an interest, she will be impossible." Meg's shoulder lifted. "She is certain to keep you entertained with all manner of breeding theories."

Though he had no plans on being tied to a little girl who thought she knew a thing or two about horses, he nodded in agreement. "I shall be indebted to her at gaining some of her knowledge."

Meg motioned for them to return to the path through the halls. They climbed the stairs to the second floor. Unsure of where they were going, he allowed her to lead the way. Besides, he rather enjoyed the position. It gave him a view of her backside, swaying under layers of soft wool. He stumbled on the next step and frowned. Never one to be a lumbering ox he frowned at the possibility that something new was becoming unhinged.

Meg paused at the top of the stairs. The wide hallway stretched to both sides. "Brother John has seen that your bedchamber has been prepared. I hope you're an early riser. The sun shines through the window at morningtide."

Nathan clutched his chest. "My fair lady, do not make me go back on my word."

Her brows arched, a twist of the corners of her mouth, proved she had a bit of humor in that very controlled person that she portrayed. "Another broken heart? Say it is not so."

"Only a small crack." He shook his head. "I fear that should I not see you safely to your chambers, 'tis certain it shall shatter."

The suffering sigh warned that he had pushed her to her limits. "As you wish, Sir Knight."

Triumphant in stalling her, he cupped her elbow and lifted the candles high. "Lead on my lady."

They came to the end of the hall. Sconces littered the wall, their tapers lighting the way. A window opened out over a narrow courtyard and the shore below. Her arms folded across her middle, she blocked the door to her bedchamber.

"And this is as far as you will go," she said.

Her palm pressed gently against his chest. Did she feel his heart thundering toward her, reaching out for some bit of comfort?

"I bid you but one more request before we say goodnight."

Suspicion widened her eyes. "Your room is down that way," she said as she turned to unlatch the door. "Until tomorrow."

"Wait." Refusing to think anymore, he cupped her arm, sliding his palm up her soft woolen sleeve. How did they make it so soft? He filed that question away for tomorrow. At that very moment all he wanted to concentrate on was her lush lips. The feel of her in his arms. "I ask but one kiss. To help me sleep of sweet dreams. With you on my lips."

He allowed himself to stroke her lower lip with his thumb. Ah, to sip, to cover her mouth with his lips. Eyes closed, he leaned forward inhaling her sweet honeyed perfume that seemed to linger on her clothes, in her hair.

Bracing his hands on the doorframe, he leaned in and pressed his lips to hers. Their bodies so close, the air between them heated with their breath.

He dove into a kiss that made him feel like he had finally come home, returning from a long and weary battle. She tasted better than he had imagined. He wanted to pleasure her until dawn.

They stood on a precipice, desire and passion waiting for Fate's winds to push them in either direction. His fingers dug into the wooden frame to keep from touching her as he desired. He waited, willing her to plead with him to take the leap together.

Her silence gave him pause. Did she tremble from desire or out of fear? He could not bear it was out of fear of him.

He did the most torturous thing that he could ever imagine and dragged his mouth from hers. His limbs quaked with need. He touched his forehead to hers. Shuddering breaths shook their bodies. "I must... We must..." Groaning, he gave into his little head's whispers. One more taste of her sweetness.

Her fingers forked through his hair, tugging, drawing him closer, deeper.

"Damn," he growled against her resistant mouth. Torn from the fantasy he snapped open his eyes. Fire scraped across his scalp. He reared back, her fingers tangled in his hair, yanked his head away.

Her chest rose and fell as she gasped for deep breaths. Tears glistened from her darkened gaze. Her desirable lips, rosy from his lust. "You will take your person to your bedchamber, Sir Nathan," she ordered. "And we will never speak of this again."

Nathan shook his head to clear it from passion's haze. Dear God, what had he done? Never had he taken advantage of a woman. They had always come willing to him. Is this another slip of the mind?

Realizing he still gripped the doorframe he released it and backed away. His knuckles ached from the stranglehold he'd had on his restraint.

"My Lady Margaret," he croaked. "Forgive me. It was a mistake."

"A mistake," she whispered under her breath. The latch gave under her hand and she slipped inside.

"Lady Meg," he called through the wooden planks.

The lock clicked in place, ensuring he could never persuade her to change her mind.

He pressed his forehead to the door and imagined he could feel her, just out of reach. "I never intended to hurt you," he whispered.

Nathan dragged himself away from her door and searched out his own room. He found it as she had directed. Despite his weariness, he paced the floor. He could not shake free of the fear that should he sleep, the dreams would return. And then once again he would awaken, empty and lonely as the large empty bed filling the bedchamber.

He grabbed a flagon someone had kindly left on the side table. An oversized chair waited beside the hearth. He sat down, eager to find solace in the cup, and poured himself a hefty drink.

He took a tentative sip. A fruity explosion coated his tongue. The sweetness of the mead surprised him. 'Twas not that weak ale served in the village.

It reminded him of Lady Margaret. Sweet, complex, and a little dangerous. "Meg."

He sifted through the events of the day and poured another drink. The coil, wound so tight that it threatened to break him, began to release its hold.

Chapter 6

Meg rested her head against the door and listened for his footsteps to announce his retreat. What had she done?

The door was the only thing that stood in their way. It would have taken just a simple nod, a tug on his sleeve, to take him to her bed. She had trembled, wanting and fearing that he would kiss her again. Not that she feared the man. No, she feared her wantonness. How could she desire a complete stranger while there were others who threatened her family and village?

Loneliness, the like of which she had never known before, swept over her. There would be no more shared kisses. She had made a promise to her dead parents. It could never be broken.

She pressed her fingers to her lips. They were hot, swollen; raw with need. She slipped her palm down her bodice, scraping her nails over her breasts. The apex between her legs ached to be stroked. Her thigh muscles squeezed together.

He said their kiss was a mistake. It may have been wrong for them to share a moment of weakness. But a mistake? A broken sob escaped. Emptiness met her need, stripping her of a desire she thought buried with her youthful dreams.

A single kiss. Another shared in a moment so many years ago had brought them to destruction. No matter that her betrothed was not only ill; his brutal kiss had been cold and filled with anger. He had pinched and grasped, demanding what was soon to be his. She had wished him dead on that awful afternoon. And that curse was set in motion.

She shook her head. Sir Nathan's kiss stirred something deep within that she thought had died along with those who had taken ill. But it no longer mattered that her future promised only empty arms and lonely nights. She had made that bed when she brought sickness to her family. She would not make that mistake again.

Meg unbound her braid and dragged her fingers through her hair. She splashed her face from the water the servant had set beside her dressing table. Though it cooled and refreshed her skin, the feel of Sir Nathan's lips remained.

She paused to look at her reflection in the polished silver plate that hung on the wall. Once confident all visible signs of her wayward desires were erased, she set off for the clandestine meeting.

* * * *

Nathan jerked awake. Sweat dripped down his chest, trickling over his rib cage. He stripped off the damp linen shirt and scrubbed it across his skin. The rough material acted like a tonic, drawing him from the remnants of nightmares that continued to haunt him. They stuck to his thoughts like a spider's web.

What tore him from the same dream? A sound that didn't belong? He abandoned the chair to listen at the door. Nothing but silence. No movement outside his window. But he couldn't let it go. Very few things could bring him up from the depths of fitful sleep.

He paced the bedchamber until it could no longer contain him. Except for the deep shadows cast upon the walls, the hall was empty.

The candlelight wavered as he strode past Meg's door. He knew he should not walk in her direction. But she called to him like a siren of the sea. What would he do should she open her door and beckon him to enter? What wouldn't he do? He paused, listening for footsteps on the opposite side of the door. Once again, silence ruled.

At the end of the hall a high arching window opened out to catch the breeze. The air's salty tang coated the roof of his mouth. It slid over him, drying his dampened skin. Cooled his heated flesh.

He walked over to the window and leaned over the ledge. A sliver of the moon hung overhead. The globe cast miserly light on the pathway below.

A faerie's burst of light, small and bright, caught his attention. It blinked on, then off. The change in shape and shadow wavered with movement. Whatever or whomever was down there took a chance on keeping their footing safe. And usually, that meant that they were up to no good.

Nathan stared into the night until his eyes watered. The keep and village were quiet, peaceful. There were no calls for help. No one shouted of the danger. He waited. Did he imagine it?

The headache threatened to return. He rubbed his stinging eyes. The gnawing fear that his imagination had taken over again caused him to turn away from his watch.

A shuddering sigh rumbled in his chest as he set off for his bedchamber. What good was he if he could no longer trust his instincts?

* * * *

Meg braced her legs and pretended to be stronger and more confident than she felt. Instead, her knees shook as she fought to contain the fury racing through her limbs.

Sweat dripped down her back, tickling the base of her spine. Although it was now summer, she had chosen the dark cloak to keep her hidden as she traveled the path to the cave below the keep. The small fire lighting the back of the cave heated the air.

She kept her clenched hands hidden under the folds of her cloak and worked her jaw loose. "How can you demand more payment for protection?"

Duncan Graham, spokesman of the clan residing on the edge of the land that divided Fletchers Landing and Scotland, pumped his wide shoulders. "There's more to protect now."

"Your calculations make little sense. Nothing has changed since our last agreement."

"Aye. It has." He stroked the dark whiskers shadowing his chin. "You've two younger sisters, do you not?"

Meg narrowed her gaze. "Yes. And again, I say nothing has changed."

"Well now, that's where we must differ." He picked the end of his thumb with his dagger. His glance up made her stomach ache. "I've watched 'em grow up. Comely as ripe pears, dripping in your hand. Juicy and ripe."

A feral snarl escaped. She touched the dirk hidden in her skirts. "Stay away from them."

"Och, now did I say that I wanted to taste of their English skin?" He shook his head. "I'm ashamed for the both of us for thinking such a thing." Duncan rose from the boulder, to tower over her. The dagger slid into its sheath. "But here's the thing, my wee lass, you have a great deal of strangers traveling through this land."

"'Tis no more than travelers bartering for supplies," Meg snapped.

"I'm not a fool, my lady. If they're not mercenaries, I'll eat my sporran," He nodded, certain he'd won that argument. "And the question begs to be asked: What would they want with the cottage wares you are so proud of?"

Meg bit her lip. Was she foolish enough to think no one noticed them lurking about the woods? "Who doesn't need good candles to light their path?"

"You canna think we don't watch everyone that comes and goes. 'Tis our agreed-upon task, is it not?" He shook his head. The thick mane of curls grazing his jerkin trapped the firelight. "I see them come and go. They don't carry supplies from your village. They bring them in by boat and sit and wait for something.

"And I can't help wondering what they want with your little spit of land. The village is nice enough, but not that it brings so much attention to strangers and mercenaries."

Meg folded her arms, holding in the fear that began to grow out of control. Where was he leading with his questions?

"And then I think of those young maiden sisters of yours. Someone will soon demand a taste of their wares. And that," he said, thumbing his chest, "is where our protection comes in."

"Brother John will see to the children's protection."

"'Tis a pity. Though a worthy opponent, I grant you. He is getting up in years."

"He serves us all well."

"He won't be able to protect you much longer."

Her hackles began to rise. "Is that a threat? Do you intend to go against your word as a Scotsman?"

She fisted her hands on her hips. The hidden dagger begged to be brought out on display. What madness had befallen her to think that she could outbargain this man? "I am paying you to keep the border reivers off our lands. You might hold your *sgian-dubh* at my throat, but I will not let you bleed me dry. I'll grant you no more."

"Then control your own damn people, my lady. I canna keep mine from retaliating when their livelihood is stolen from their protected lands."

"We do not rove across the lands. This is our agreement. The villagers know this."

"Well, damn your arrogance. If I'm telling you that someone is breaking the agreement, then I'm telling you the damn truth." His voice began to rise. "And you won't insult me by calling me a liar."

Meg stepped closer, motioning for him to be quiet. "Settle your ire. I didn't intend to hurt your pride." Worry dug into her brow. "But I know my people."

He gave his sporran a jerk, clearly still affronted. "Then you best look to those who aren't your people."

Her evening meal threatened to free itself and cover the cavern floor. Mercenaries. Smugglers. The king's knight. Not to mention her paid protectors. And now she had to consider someone from the village would put them all in jeopardy by reiving across the border? Who could be trusted?

"I will do what I can." His large hand swung out. Meg fought the urge to flinch and was relieved when he rubbed the back of his neck instead. "At least consider binding your brother and sisters to our clan."

"So that you may lay claim to Fletchers Landing? I think not, Duncan Graham."

"And why not? We have strong lads and comely maidens."

"They are but children."

"Lady Anna. Is she already spoken for? And your sister, the one who breeds the fine horses. She is nearly of age. Are they already betrothed?"

"You'll keep your distance, you thieving cur."

Deep furrows dug into his brow. "And you'll watch your bitter tongue. Is that why you bring the young knight into your keep? To take them from the valley?"

"I don't know who you're speaking of."

His brow arched. His gaze scraped over her from head to toe. "Have you already bartered with the king for their lives?"

"Of course not. They do not marry unless 'tis for love."

His cheeks flushed. "You know that is not the way of things," he sputtered.

"I've had word that Lord Balforth is dead. We are safe for now." She couldn't bring herself to promise that his men did not mean to take what they could. Without proof, Duncan and his men would take them on and as God is her witness, she did not want their Scottish blood on her hands.

"All the more reason to handfast the maidens and the boy," Duncan continued to press.

Why was he relentless in this rabbit he was chasing? "No." That should be simple enough for even Duncan Graham to comprehend.

"One day, lass, King Henry will demand his land. There will be a price."

"There is always a price," she snapped.

"Good. Then we are agreed."

"I said no to additional payment for protection. I'll speak with my people and make it understood no one is to reive your land." She held up her hand. "And no one is to be promised, betrothed, or handfast to you or your clan."

If she truly threw caution to the wind, she would have pushed his chin up to close his gaping mouth. Instead he did it for her. The crack of teeth almost made her jump.

"You're making a sorry mistake," Duncan Graham said. Shards of anger glittered from his stare, cutting through her courage like a finely honed sword. "You'll be begging for my protection soon enough."

"I've made my decision." Despite the building heat, she drew the cloak close to her throat. "The rest will take care of itself."

He picked up a bucket of seawater and doused the fire. Water hissed as it struck the flames. The empty bucket sailed through the air, striking the wall. "And what if there are others who will say different?"

Meg gritted her teeth. She'd had enough threats for the evening. "Tell them to take it up with the dragon of Fletchers Landing."

* * * *

Nathan stared at the door outside his chamber. The thought of entering was like sand abrading his skin. Inside, it held little hope that he would sleep for longer than an hour or two at the most. He turned on his heel. What manner of man feared an empty room? One who had known firsthand of the evil that lurks inside mankind.

He knew battles, been the one wielding the ax and sword. Seen the damage committed by a well-placed heavy mace. He had applauded a well thought-out plan of attack. Taken charge of a month-long siege at Harfleur. Marched and rode through freezing rain and brutal weather. Known the beast within all when hunger became your master.

But the oubliette. Never had he experienced the torture of hanging in a simple cell, without food and water, the constant bedeviling of fists and various tools of the trade. Not until that day DePierce's men attacked him and took him to Balforth Castle. Even that was not the worst. He had known that his body would withstand the physical abuse.

It was his mind that began to crumble. The darkness. The fetid air that stank of those who had died before him. Thoughts that soon became voices in his head, urging him to let go. Other times, to murder anyone who dared speak to him, to fight until death. And they became louder, stronger, when his body commanded him to sleep.

Nathan prowled the keep as had become his habit at both Clearmorrow and Lockwood Castles. If he kept moving, he would escape the need for sleep. At least hold it off for a while longer. Still too alert, listening for an intruder's steps, wary of an attack at night, he knew that sleep would not be his for a while longer.

He followed the hallways that wound through the keep. Several rooms were occupied by Baldric and the women. He could hear the snuffling and soft sighs through the door. Abandoning his search for intruders he explored the other floors.

One stairway led to another floor. Large carved panels claimed one side of the hall. He tried the latch on the double-wide door. But despite his many attempts, it remained locked. What did they hide that needed such a heavy lock? A private chamber of some sort? Perhaps the lord and lady's chamber? A room where they kept their record of accounts?

He leaned out another large window. This one, too, arched overhead until it nearly reached the crenulation shooting from the parapet. It would give them an advantage to see the comings and goings of those who sailed into their harbor. Mayhap the light he saw earlier would be easily explained.

Where was the stairway that led outside? He looked behind tapestries for hidden openings, felt along the wall for an unusual line or ridge in the stone. Time after time, his search ended in front of the locked chamber door. He dared not destroy his host's keep, but come morning, he would know what lay behind that damn door.

Sweating despite his lack of tunic, he returned to the narrow stairs leading to the floor below. Weary enough to try to sleep, he braced himself and entered his bedchamber. The empty bed called to him. Woolen bed panels, soft as lamb's wool, rustled with the breeze.

He stripped off his boots and chausses, and flopped onto the bed. The mattress accepted his weight, wrapping its feather down around him. His body, naked as the day his mother bore him, pebbled as the air caressed his skin.

Eyes squeezed closed, he seized the mattress, and let himself drift into the abyss.

* * * *

Meg clutched the cloak to keep it from flapping in the wind. A heavy weariness sat on her shoulders, pressing her feet deeper into the path. Although her bed called to her she would never be able to sleep. What price would she have to pay if she were to curse Duncan Graham and wish for his death?

She had stood her ground with that arrogant Scotsman. She would pay only what had been agreed upon in the beginning. No more. But his subtle threats against the children terrified her beyond anything she had ever known. He would come again. That she was certain. And demand more protection payment. The only way they could afford to continue this agreement was for her to sell more smuggled goods to tradesmen.

How she would do that while Sir Nathan was underfoot was beyond her. There had to be a way around him. Thoughts of that man, his arms, his kisses, brought a battle of chills and fire whipping through her body.

Her sister may think she was too cold to want love, but deep down, Meg knew that was a lie she even told to herself. No one must know her true feelings. She dared not examine them for if she did, her word, her vow would be lost. But her bed would no longer be empty. Her heart would no longer ache with longing for something that she could not have.

Meg rounded the last bolder and gazed up at the keep. All looked quiet and peaceful. Completely opposite of the worries that bent her shoulders. She tucked her braid under the cloak. There would be time enough for thinking while she lay awake in her bed, watching the moon slide past her window.

Slipping inside the kitchen door, she found the cup of mead Cook had set on the table for her. The sweetened liquid wet her lips, tingled on her tongue. It slid down her throat and left a trail of fire and joy. She poured another splash of the liquid gold into her cup.

The day had started off difficult and had continued on that path on into the night. It was bound to take more than one drink of mead to help her rest. She sipped slowly and resisted the urge to carry the flagon up to her room.

After stripping off her gown, she stood in the middle of her bedchamber wearing only her chemise. The breeze caught the curtains surrounding her bed. She sat on the edge of the mattress. Somewhere outside a dull thump drew her attention. Was the Scotsman making good on his threats?

Meg careened out the door. Her bare feet smacked the floor as she ran. One after the other she checked on her sisters and then Baldric. They all slept, nestled in their beds. Tiptoeing out of their bedchambers, her heart still racing in her throat, she started to return to her bed.

A crash and then hoarse shouting came from the hallway leading to Nathan's bedchamber. Did the reivers get past Brother John's guard?

Meg picked up the lead candlestick holder someone had left on the side table. Her body quaking, she raised her weapon high overhead and entered Nathan's room.

Chapter 7

Meg moved cautiously, ready in case someone lunged for her. No one came. Harsh breaths could be heard. Somewhere in the room a trapped animal panted.

"Sir Nathan," she called.

The empty bed held only sheets and blankets, torn from the mattress, pooling on the floor. To her relief she could not see signs of blood.

The panting grew as she neared the dressing screen. She gasped as she took in the destroyed chair and shattered flagon. It had taken two men to carry the thing down from her parents' private chamber. How did one man destroy it as if it were kindling?

Mindful of her bare feet, she stepped around the wreckage. Where was he?

"Nathan," she called again, speaking as she would to a frightened child. "Please. Let me know where you are. I can help."

A guttural groan, raw and loud as a wounded bear, erupted from behind the screen.

She peeked around the corner. The knight lay curled on the floor. The pale muscular planes of his hip glistened in the firelight. Fresh scars, pink and wide, gleamed across his shoulders. His limbs shook as he drew in ragged breath after ragged breath.

"Don't come near me," he warned through gritted teeth.

"Nathan," she whispered as she inched near. "'Tis I, Meg."

"I don't want to…harm…you."

"You won't." Meg crawled back to gather one of the blankets. She returned before he could launch an argument. "Here. Let me help you."

Once his nakedness was covered his hands began to unclench. "My… thanks," he croaked.

Encouraged, she slid closer. "Are you in pain?" His dampened curls clung to his powerful neck. She pressed her wrist to his forehead. "Fever?" To her relief, his skin was cool to the touch.

"Head," he muttered. "Need my mind strong again."

Meg nodded. She'd heard Brother John speak of the atrocities to which the men of war fell victim. Judging by Nathan's visible scars, there were more stories to tell.

"Meg!" One after the other, Phillipa and Baldric skidded into the chamber.

"Where are the intruders?" Phillipa demanded. Her eyes widened. "Sir Nathan! Where are your clothes?"

Nathan jerked as if he were struck.

"Quiet is what we need," Meg hissed. She checked the blanket to ensure his modesty was covered. "Questions are for later. Go find Anna and Brother John."

"Please." His fingers wrapped around her wrist, drawing her to his side. "Stay."

Meg smoothed his dark auburn hair from his face. The dampened curls wrapped around her fingers. "Calm yourself. I'm not moving from this spot until you say you are ready."

She looked up as Anna swept in with her basket of unguents. "The children say our guest is ill?"

Brother John followed on her heels. His gray hair and brows seemed fuller than usual. If it weren't for the fact that their guest was incapacitated she would have had the nerve to laugh at his flustered countenance. He flashed his drawn sword. "What goes on, Lady Meg? If 'tis fever, you must leave him where he lies."

"Brother John, I will do no such thing," Meg announced. "Phillipa and Baldric, back to your beds." As an afterthought, she added. "And mind that you lock your windows and doors."

The old monk glowered over everyone as the room was righted and Nathan was returned to his bed. She ignored their questioning glances. And set about readying a place for her to sit.

Anna poured some liquid from her supplies. "Sip it slow," she warned. "It has some heat, but will soothe you in no time."

Nathan waited until Meg nodded. "You'll find rest tonight."

"For you, Meg," Brother John said, holding out a blanket. Meg blinked, and looked down at her state of undress. Heat rushed up her neck and set fire to her cheeks. Grateful for his silence, she snatched the offered blanket and wrapped it around her shoulders.

The mischievous gleam in Nathan's eyes was enough to warm her clear through to her bones. "'Tis good to know you are almost back to yourself."

"Getting my balance back."

She bit her lip. "The pain in your head?"

His mouth twitched to form a sardonic smile. "I fear it has grown."

"More like the pain be in his arse," Brother John muttered.

Despite her efforts to do otherwise, her gaze drifted to Nathan's groin. Now that the danger had dissipated she could enjoy the memory of his smooth backside, his limbs sprinkled with hair the color of amber honey.

"'Tis certain the tisane will take effect and you will feel relief," Anna said.

Brother John grunted. His arms folded over his brown tunic. "I shall stay with him until it does."

Meg watched Nathan's lashes flutter. His shoulders drooped. Anna was correct. The tisane was helping him to relax and send him to sleep. "No, I shall stay with him."

"Now, Lady Meg, 'tis not for a lady in your position to nurse him."

"Brother John, you're a man of God. You know we must serve those in need. Especially if he is one of King Henry's knights." She took hold of his hand. "I am the lady of Fletchers Landing. And my sister is too young for such a task."

Rising from her chair she ushered them to the door. "Go now. Morning comes soon enough. All will be well."

"I shall pray for you and our guest." Brother John marched off, his stiff back showing his displeasure in her decision. Come tomorrow, there would be long services to save her soul.

Anna wrinkled her delicate features. "You will call out if you are in need." She cut her glance to the man sleeping in the bed. "Or in danger."

"I promise," Meg said. "Not to worry. Remember, I'm the dragon of the keep. No one dare cross me or harm my family."

Worry marred Anna's smooth forehead. "Your meeting?"

"Hush." Meg glanced over her shoulder. "We will speak of it when we are alone."

Anna kissed her cheek. "Be safe."

Meg nodded and shut the door. She pulled the high-backed chair closer to the bed and settled in for some long-awaited rest. Her patient no longer panted in pain, haunted by the past. She smoothed his brows and watched his face relax under her caress. His mouth should be laughing and kissing instead of twisting in agony. She traced his lip with the tip of her finger. His soft beard tickled her wrist.

His hand swung up and he held her palm pressed to his cheek and sighed.

Tears burned the edges of her eyes. How would she ever manage to keep her vow while he remained at Fletchers Landing?

* * * *

Nathan stretched his arms overhead. He'd slept. A peaceful sleep. One without dark memories to tear apart his rest. Meg. The tisane had helped, but it was Meg, her presence beside him, which allowed him to sleep.

He rolled to his side. "My lady…"

The chair that she had sat in through the early morning hours was empty. He shut his eyes and saw all that the others would have seen. The raw, fearful beast that he became when the past grew too heavy to bear. What caused it this time?

Was it the lights in the distance? The danger that he felt? It was palpable. Fingernails scraping across the back of his neck. There were secrets waiting to be whispered from dark corners and alleyways.

Now that the household knew of his affliction would they look at him differently? With fear? Or worse…pity?

He took a deep breath and swung his legs out of the bed. Time to find out where he stood in their eyes. Knight of the Swan or not, if they did not think they could trust him, he would never be able to find the answers to Henry's questions. The longer it took meant a delay in his return to serve by his king's side.

Feeling more rested than he'd been in months, he dressed and set off to find the dragon lady of the keep. The great hall echoed his footsteps. The sideboard against the wall was empty of the morning repast.

"You there, good women of the keep." The handful of servants turned from their tasks. Wide-eyed, they bobbed their respect and sped off before he could inquire where their lady might be.

"Christ's blood," he muttered. "'Tis as if they thought I threatened to cleave their heads."

He would win them over one by one, if only to prove that wenches still found him agreeable. The itch between his shoulders began creeping up his neck. Nathan frowned.

"Good day," Brother John's voice broke through the silence. "You've finally risen from your bed."

Nathan swung his hand toward the empty spaces the women left behind. "Have the women promised silence? Or is it your pious presence that makes them hare off? If you would, carry the message that I mean them no harm."

The monk's brows arched, cutting a ridge in his forehead. "That so? I've heard tales otherwise." The keys at his waist swung, rattling against his side like skeleton bones. "They're God-fearing people."

"Then they have nothing to fear from me." Nathan cringed. He should have kept his silence.

His stomach growled, surprising him with the sound. The desire to eat had been a stranger for some time.

Brother John snorted, belying his thoughts. "The day has already begun. You'll want to follow me."

The monk took them down the paths that led toward the garden he could see outside his window. "Why bring me here?"

"'Tis the way that you'll need to take." His long strides carried them farther from the keep. The crash of the tide, kept pace. Its hypnotic rhythm mimicking their steps.

They came to an orchard alive with activity. Nathan's senses filled. The sweet scent of apples and pears coated his tongue. Tree limbs bent with the weight of their fruit. Bees swarmed around the orchard of fruit trees. They settled on flowers, tasting the pollen. Buzzing. Fluttering. He swayed on his feet.

Brother John plucked a few apples from the tree. After pocketing several in the folds of his tunic, he tossed one to Nathan.

Nathan caught it and bit into its crisp flesh. Juice ran down his chin as he devoured his first meal of the day. Heaven. The king had sent him to heaven.

"Come, sir knight, there is more to fill your belly."

They came upon a garden filled with plants at different stages of growth. Nathan filled his hands with plump sun-kissed berries, gobbling them as fast as he could pick them.

A maiden, swathed in a gauzy material, tended the neat rows of vegetables. She bent to examine a plant, pull a weed, and then tuck her harvest into the basket. Leafy green tops swung in her hand as she caught sight of them.

Nathan's pulse leaped in anticipation. And then it stuttered. This was not Lady Meg. "Lady Anna," he called out.

"She'll desire to know of your health this morn," Brother John warned. "Mayhap too many questions." His gaze cut over Nathan, sharp as any knight's sword. "She's a good soul. You'll remember to treat her as such."

"Sir Nathan," Anna called out. She appeared to float over the garden toward him, like a milkweed seed caught on a breeze. "I see you have improved."

"I cannot thank you enough," Nathan bowed over her hand. "Before I take my leave, I must know the recipe of your tisane."

Her cheeks bloomed with color. "So soon?" She looped her arm through his and left the monk to follow them. Her wary glance to the hills behind her gave away her true feelings. "But you have just arrived."

"'Tis true that I must make haste and return to our king's side." He shook his head. "But I fear that I shall be here for a while longer." He took in a long, deep breath, and let his gaze travel over the landscape, then included the young maiden who clearly hoped he would ride out on his fine steed never to return. "Mayhap I will find a way to extend my stay."

"Tell me, sir knight, of King Henry. Do you ride with him? Is he as brave and strong as they say? And his court. Are there many dances and romances to keep you occupied?"

"Lady Anna," Brother John huffed.

Nathan patted her hand. Though Anna might be skilled in the ways of healing, she would be eaten alive by the ladies of the court. "Aye, the king is as you say. I've ridden by his side since I was fostered as a young boy." Too many battles. Too many wounds. Too many lives. Too many years he had ridden by him. He shook free of the dark storm threatening to form. "I fear there are not so many dances, for our king is a warrior and no longer has time for frivolity."

"And romances?" she pressed, batting her lashes at him.

Although his throat became parched, he managed to answer without receiving the pointy end of the monk's sword. "There is always time for romance."

Her mouth drew into a pretty pout. "But not love."

Long fingers clamped his shoulder, pulling him away from Lady Anna. "Bees. Sir Nathan. Are you afraid of bees? If so, mind your step when we enter the apiary. 'Tis where we will find our Lady Meg."

"Ah, look, there she is." Lady Anna tugged on his hand. "Come! You must bid my sister good morn."

Relieved to be steered away from talk of love and romance, he happily followed into a veritable wall of beehives. Smoke swirled around a woman swathed in gauzy white linen. She squeezed on the bellows, puffing it around the skeps constructed of bent willow and mud.

"Lady Meg?" Nathan said as he swatted at a pollen-laden bee that came precariously close to his face.

"You'll want to keep your distance," the old monk warned.

Anna stepped back. "There are some who do not react well to their sting."

"Yes," Nathan said, "I remember well a soldier who swelled from the venom." It was a sight he wished never to witness again.

"She'll be here for hours if we do not force her to rest." Anna squeezed his arm. "Mayhap you can draw her from her tasks and entertain her with your harrowing tales of battle."

"Be grateful, child," Brother John admonished. "The bees are God's gift that makes your gardens produce greater crops than those who live to the north."

"There is no reason to keep it all to ourselves. We could teach them the ways, just like you did when you came to Fletchers Landing."

"'Tis not the time to discuss this, child," he snapped.

"Forgive me, Brother John." Anna dipped her head, her jaw firm as she fought the bit of censure. "I should not have spoken to you thusly in front of our guest." Her slender fingers balled into fists. "Excuse me."

Nathan followed Anna's retreat. There was anger in her steps. All families had their difficulties. But there was something they were hiding. A secret that might break them apart.

Lady Meg motioned for them to wait and set the smoker on a bench. She began unwinding the veils from her head. A smile curved her sensuous lips.

The revealing of her curves distracted him from the hum of the busy hives. There must have been a bolt of material wrapped around her body. He leaned in as if to bring her closer. Finally she stood before him and he could not bring himself to tear his gaze from her mouth as she tugged the last glove off her hand.

"Sir Nathan?" she said.

He shook his head, lost in the vision. Had she addressed him once already? She was as beautiful as she had been drawn in his memory.

"My lady." Like a foolish boy at his first attempt at flirtation, he dipped a rushed bow. "I must speak with you. Privately." He cleared his clogged throat. "To thank you."

"Brother John," Meg said. Her voice as smooth as the honey dripping into the hive pans. "I think 'tis time for the children's lessons for the day. Sir Nathan and I shall join you in the stables anon."

"Take caution," Brother John puffed. "Our land has many places that allow for someone to disappear."

"Why, Brother John, I do believe you think I have no manners with the sweeter sex. I assure you, I've plenty of practice within the king's court."

"That brings me precious little comfort."

Meg tucked a curl behind her ear. "Sirs, I believe we are wasting time. There's no need to posture like roosters on my account."

Nathan grinned. "See there. Nothing to worry your gray head about."

"You'll find that I have little patience for puffery." Her hand slid close to her hip. A flash of metal caught the bright sun overhead. The little dagger used to cut away the honeycomb swung at her belt.

"Do you intend for us to challenge the other to prove whose weapon is bigger?" Nathan grinned.

The old monk angled his sword out from the folds of his long tunic and had the temerity to smile in that man-of-God way that promised to infuriate.

"Brother John," Lady Meg snapped.

His nostrils flared, hardly representing a man of the cloth, particularly that of a repentant monk. "As you wish." Brother John whipped around, a full-blown badger dressed in monk's clothing.

Nathan had seen that imperious countenance before. The itch between his shoulder blades had returned.

Chapter 8

Heat flushed Meg's cheeks as she stared after Brother John. What set him off on an angry tear this time? Was it Anna or their visiting knight?

"My lady." Sir Nathan held out his arm for her to grasp. "If you grant me but a moment of your time, I vow to escort you safely to any destination of your choosing."

He smiled down at her. Even though Duncan Graham and the monk stood head and shoulders above Sir Nathan, she felt safe in his presence. An odd way to think about a stranger.

Laying her hand upon his sleeve, she nodded for him to proceed. They walked past the outbuilding and the meadery. A cache of barrels waited in the cave for delivery. It would be another long night for her. At least Brother John would be there to lend a hand in loading them onto the skiff and sailing them across the firth. The coin they would receive would buy them another month of protection.

The silence stretched as she searched for something interesting to say. It was easy enough to argue with the thieving Graham. Fighting over how much she could afford to pay for the village's safety from reivers. She couldn't very well speak of her concerns.

They slowed to weave their way past the rocky path that led to the caves. She did not intend to bring him that direction. Apparently her feet had followed that well-worn path too many times. They paused to rest beside the large boulder that blocked the light at night.

"How did you find your bedchamber? Did it suit to your liking?" Oh, God, his forearm tensed. He paused turning her into his arms. "I did not mean to offend."

"On the contrary." His breath caressed her skin, over the nape of her neck. "I could think of only one thing lacking."

Her breath stalled as she waited for him to ask her to join him. How would she respond without breaking her vow? Perhaps a simple kiss. If he should ask. One kiss might not break her promise. "Yes?"

He cupped her chin, tipping it to look into his moss-green gaze. So soft, caring, and penetrating. Her secrets began to feel like weights.

"I would have you tell me of the lights that whisper under cover of the night. Of whom you meet and why you take that chance."

"Why, Sir Nathan, what a mystery you ask. I'm unaware of any lights over the gardens outside your window."

"I saw them. Last night."

She bit her lip. "From…from your window," she stuttered. "There are no windows in that direction. Only the crop fields and the herb garden. Mayhap it was a trick of the moon."

"'Twas nothing of the sort." His arms tightened, and then released.

Cold seeped through her sleeves despite the summer sun. *Please don't tell me your attention is a mistake. Not again.*

"I've had plenty of time. To wonder. How did you happen to hear me call out, my lady? You are on the other end of the keep. Are you not? And yet, you came to me in only your chemise."

"I could not sleep. And I thought to check on the children's safety."

His hand slid up her arm, over her shoulder, to rest on her jaw. "Tell me, is there another that I must vanquish before I am allowed to taste the honey clinging to your lips?"

"Sir Nathan, I…" Meg trembled, fighting the need growing inside. She could not give him what he wanted. A name. A reason. "No. No one," she whispered.

Her voice sounded to her ears like someone else: Someone who had never vowed always to protect. One who never allowed her heart to love and dream and feel the thrill of passion.

Jealousy welled for those who had the choice to love or not. Hope shriveled like a rotted blossom on the vine.

She twitched her skirts away from a thorny shrub. The delicate yellow flowers had faded and fallen away, leaving behind rigid spines to bedevil a careless passerby. The gorse needed clearing from the path. She muttered a curse when one nasty spine caught under her surcoat, scraping skin and tearing the woolen threads.

"My lady. Wait before it does further damage." Sir Nathan bent down to release her from the offending plant.

"I can do this myself," she muttered. Fire raced through her limbs as he picked up her foot and placed it upon his thigh.

He smiled up at her. The sunlight reflected in the amber hues hidden in his hair. "I trust you are able. But then I would still be in your debt." His golden lashes brushed his high cheekbones. "And it would be a shame to lose such an opportunity to improve your opinion of me. Would it not?"

Did he just have the temerity to give her a lazy wink? Her skin heated where his fingers brushed against her stocking. She glanced around to ensure no one nearby was watching. Flames crept up her neck. Her bodice became too tight. She plucked at the material overheating her chest. "I assure you. I keep no ledger."

"A pity. I rather enjoy improving the balance where you are concerned." His gaze lingered where her hand hovered over her breasts.

She snapped it down and did her best to glower where his hand encircled her ankle. "I insist you release me, Sir Nathan. 'Tis improper."

"I fear the thorns have done harm to your flesh." He frowned at the stain of blood on his fingertips. "Does no one tend to the gardening outside Lady Anna's domain?"

She stiffened, lifting her foot out of his grasp and stepping out of reach. "We'll do so when 'tis time to harvest the gorse."

Sir Nathan dusted his chausses as he rose. "Fodder for the beasts of the field may be all well and good, but there is such a thing as human comfort." He lifted his arm for her to take.

Mayhap he was used to the ease of royal life and did not understand one's duty of providing for your people and the keep. "To trim it back just for comfort of the path is wasteful when there are so many uses."

They arrived at the stables. As far as Meg was concerned, it was none too soon. She stifled a sigh of relief. "I shall leave you here. 'Tis certain you'll wish to see to your horse. You'll find my sister Phillipa will have ensconced him in the finest of stalls."

"Please." He caught her fingers before she could rush past him. "'Tis customary for the lady of the keep to show her guests about, is it not?

"Oh, but I'm certain you know your way to a stable yard." She could feel him reeling her in. How was she to accomplish everything by nightfall if she must entertain this king's man? A shipment of wool was expected. Why could he not just leave? She bit the inside of her lip. "Mayhap you will wish to exercise him."

"Madrigal. 'Tis his name." He smiled at her raised brows. "Yes, I'm aware 'tis a different name for a charger. But," he shrugged, "how could I

change it? 'Twas his name before he was gifted to me and I did not desire
to offend my friend."

A twinge of jealousy pinched. "A gift from a female, I presume."

He shook his head with what should have been a chuckle, but it came
out in a huff. Indeed, a rusty chuckle. "No, had that been the case, I would
have changed it within the first hour. I've found that our king has a sense
of humor when he wills it."

They arrived in front of a stall and the steed in question nickered and
lifted his head over the gate. Nathan produced an apple and held it out
for Madrigal to partake. He ran his hands over the horse's powerful neck.

"A gift from the king," Meg whispered under her breath. He was more
than the king's knight. "You are his…friend?"

A corner of his mouth kicked up. Shadowy thoughts drew his attention,
shuttering them away where she could not examine anything closely. "Does
a king ever have friends among his subjects? There is always the blurred
line between friendship and duty." He cut his eyes to meet with hers. "As a
subject of the realm, I'm certain you are aware that a day will come when
our king will expect you to do your duty and serve his wishes."

Meg fisted her hands at her side. She swallowed past her dry throat.
"And what would those wishes be, Sir Nathan?"

He shrugged and poured out some grain for Madrigal. His muscles
rippled under the jerkin. "It remains to be revealed. Mayhap there are
secrets that would serve him?"

She turned from watching the graceful movement of his shoulders. He
was the king's friend. And his loyalty would always remain with the king.
Should he discover their means of financial support he would be honor
bound to report them in his next missive.

A chill skimmed up her neck. "I fear I am but a simple lady from
England's North Country. We have so little to offer the king in the way
of intrigue." She ran her hands over Madrigal's sleek coat. The animal's
muscles shivered under her caress.

"Everyone carries a secret that they wish to keep to themselves." He
returned the empty bucket to the bench. Then refilled the horse's water
trough. A brush in one hand, he braced his palm beside her hand. The
difference of size and strength was striking.

The stroke of his strong hands over Madrigal's coat brought another
nicker. "Even a country miss observes things that they might wish to share
among family and friends."

"Ah, but once it is shared, there is no turning back." Meg shook her head. "For then there is always the temptation to share it with another and then another."

"Sir Nathan," Baldric called from the doorway. "Wait until you see…" His limping gate slowed.

"What ho, young lord," Sir Nathan said as he saluted him with the brush. "How does your new ward, the puppy, fare today?"

Relief washed over Meg in waves. Baldric's admiration for the knight was palpable. It would be good to turn Nathan's attention in another direction.

"Whitefoot now enjoys a warm bed. But don't tell my sis—" Baldric's brow wrinkled. "Meg, I didn't think to find you in the stables."

"'Tis good to see you, too, little brother. And what great thing did you have to show Sir Nathan?"

"There you are." Brother John towered over her brother. "I feared our guest had managed to spirit you away from our time in the chapel."

"Oh." Meg blinked, grateful for the monk's imaginary excuse. His lie may cost her extra time on her knees, but she would do so gladly. "Of course." She dusted her hands over her skirt.

"Mayhap our young lord will continue the tour." Brother John folded his hands over his stomach.

"You'll want to see our tiltyard," Baldric announced. "They haven't been used since the Lord of Balforth had his soldiers practice."

"Perchance, if you take Sir Nathan to the tiltyard he will offer his wisdom regarding the lists," the monk added. "A lord of the land must know how to protect his land. Should he not?"

The brush Nathan had been stroking over the horse's chest felt to the floor. His eyes narrowed as he bent to retrieve it. A white line had formed around his firm mouth. Meg could not ignore the tension between the two men.

Ever the one sensitive to those in need, Baldric hobbled over to the knight. "I can show you our armory, instead," he said, tugging on the knight's sleeve.

Nathan regarded the small hand. A flush bloomed on his high cheekbones. He bent his knee. "Lady Meg, I look forward to resuming our time together this eve."

"Mayhap we shall meet again after vespers," Meg offered.

"Our lady is quite busy this time of year," Brother John warned. "My Lady Margaret, our Lord in heaven waits for no one." He lifted her elbow, escorting her from the stables.

Once they neared the chapel, she shook off his grasp. "Cease this at once."

"I thought to relieve you of his attention," her father's longtime friend and confidant said. "There is much to accomplish before darkness falls. How do you intend to deliver when you have a king's knight underfoot?"

"We will move the ale earlier than planned. Mayhap we start while Baldric leads him through the tiltyard and armory. Fetch Anna and Phillipa. I must speak with them as well."

"I thought you desired to keep them uninvolved."

"I fear there is no other way. Together we will fulfill our agreement with the traders."

Ignoring his chastising frown, she cast a look over her shoulder to search for Sir Nathan. He had had the look of a wounded animal right before they parted ways. She prayed they did not have a repeat from the night before. If only because her willpower to keep from trying to kiss the pain from his haunted expression was weakening.

* * * *

Nathan resisted the urge to follow Meg. Once she and that monk turned the corner he tore his attention from their direction and pointed it onto the boy. "What say you, young Baldric? Lead the way."

They made their way through the maze of outbuildings. Nathan continued to take note of the thatched roofs crammed close together.

"This," Baldric said as he unlocked the door with fanfare, "is where most of our weapons are stored."

Nathan grunted. They were too far away from the main keep. "Where are those who are expected to wield such fine specimens?"

Baldric's throat lurched as he swallowed. "Sir Vincent DePierce sent them away. He said only his men were loyal to the crown. Our men were not." He stared at the wall of pikes, poleaxes, and mauls. "Their families still wait for their return. I fear they're dead." He bit his lip and shifted the leg that was slightly shorter than the other.

Nathan waited. The silence stretched.

"The villagers. All of us. We fear they will return. And kill us all in our beds. I think that is why my sister Meg walks the paths during the night. To protect us." He settled his soft blue gaze on Nathan. "'Tis why I need you to train me to fight. Teach me to protect my land. My family."

"DePierce is dead."

"I would have liked to have seen that," he said, his voice bloodthirsty with vengeance.

Nathan squeezed Baldric's shoulder. "I vow it to be the truth."

His face wrinkled in doubt. "But there will be more. His next of kin to stake claim of Fletchers Landing. His men."

"I know that he has no family left." Nathan shut his eyes. Would the memories awaken and take their vengeance just by thinking of the events at Balforth? He gathered all the strength that he could and gripped his sanity. "His nephew Hugh died by my hand."

Baldric nodded as he absorbed this news. "Might you still grant me training? There is no one to foster me." His hand stole over his thigh. "I understand that I'm not fit or strong enough to become a great knight as you."

Nathan shook his head. "There is nothing wrong with your body that cannot be corrected with the proper training."

"In truth?" The boy's grin was a riot of joy and relief. "When can we begin?"

Nathan chuckled at Baldric's enthusiasm. He rubbed his jaw. He felt better than he had in the months before.

Could he use Baldric's desire to train in combat to his advantage? Mayhap with the lad's help he would discover the tunnels, find the king's lost treasure, and be on his way. Besides, he feared he would indeed go mad without anything to keep his mind busy. And a physically tired body would ease the desire that appeared every time his thoughts drifted to Lady Meg.

"'Tis a man's game. Are you willing to work?" Nathan asked. "Your muscles will scream for you to stop. To rest. But you cannot." He stared into Baldric's determined face. "Not for one breath or someday it might be your last."

"I understand."

"Must you gain permission from your sisters? Brother John?"

"One day, when the king returns the land to us, I am to be Lord of Fletchers Landing. I need no permission."

Nathan knew he should wait to begin their training, but the weapons called to him. His body ached with the need to move his body. "Show me the training fields."

"'Tis only the ally between the wall and the keep. Near the bailey yard."

"Then that is where we will begin." He knelt down before Baldric. "We will return here to fit you with needed sword and shield."

Crestfallen, Baldric muttered, "'Tis certain nothing will fit me properly. My one leg is too short. At times, it folds under me. I should have never asked it of you."

"I will not let you give up before we even start. We shall determine what we need. Then see the blacksmith. It will be good to order him to create a sword to suit you."

"Mayhap I will order him to make one for you too."

Chuckling at the image of the red-faced blacksmith once he received the commission to make his lord a sword, they strolled toward the tiltyard.

The rusted locked gate was no match for Nathan when he pried it open. They would need to add that to the blacksmith's growing list. Outrage began to build at the laziness and lack of respect the villagers showed their lord and his lady sisters.

The entrance opened into a courtyard. It might have been used for training in the past but now it held a garden of flowers.

Nathan scratched his head. "Well, lad, it appears we've been uprooted from our yard."

"We won't be able to train?" Baldric kicked at a tuft of white chamomile flowers. "My sisters are forever befouling my plans."

"Not so fast to anger, my friend. If we are to carry weapons, we must always keep our temper in balance."

"I suppose so. But this will mean we'll need to speak to Meg about it. She's bound to refuse to let me train to fight with you."

Brother John's sour face came into Nathan's view. The monk had a quick mind like a fox. He had to have already suspected Nathan would agree with Baldric's request. "We will come at her on all flanks with our argument. Think on it as your first lesson in warfare."

He sighed dramatically. "At least this gives me time to let poor Whitefoot out to the bailey yard."

"Where are you keeping the poor little beast so that it cannot run freely to use the privy?"

"Nowhere special," Baldric scraped the toe of his boot across the earth. "Truly."

"Do you think the pup prefers your bedchamber over the stables?"

"Meg didn't quite refuse him entrance in the keep. Not really." The boy puffed his cheeks and wandered the garden, whacking off the heads of defenseless flowers. "Sometimes he needs extra help getting up. I cannot be there if he's made to stay in the barns. And Cook promised to check on him during the day."

"You don't think anyone will hear him cry out? I didn't see any other hounds in the keep. Inside or out. Why is that do you suppose?"

"Our sister says they cause too much work. But Whitefoot will be different. You'll see. He's quite smart. When he is older he'll offer protection in case we are attacked. You'll see."

"I doubt that I will be here when that happens. But I do believe in your conviction."

"You can't leave so soon." Baldric gripped his wrist. "We need you."

Nathan's chest ached. His jaws clenched as he worked to clear his throat. "Our king needs me."

"We all do."

Nathan rested his back against the stone wall and pulled the journal out of his tunic. He raised it to the sky, trying to locate the matching horizons.

"What have you there?" Baldric asked. He leaned over Nathan's arm to peer at the drawing on the parchment.

"A puzzle of sorts."

"Oh, I enjoy puzzles. Shall I help you?"

"I would appreciate it. 'Tis a mystery that has me baffled." Nathan passed him the journal. The pages fluttered in the breeze causing them to create another drawing hidden within the multiple pages.

"Laid flat it looks a bit like the way bees dance, when they report a field of flowers to their hive," Baldric observed. He squinted as he held it up to catch the wind again. "But turn the pages quickly and it looks like a map of some sorts. It looks familiar." He handed it back to Nathan. "Where do you suppose it leads?"

"That is part of the puzzle. We don't know really where to start. Nor where it ends."

"I wish my father were still alive. I don't recall much of him, but I do recall spending time in his private chamber. He had a spyglass that we used to look through. We could see to the other side of the firth." He sighed. "But that was a long time ago. Perhaps 'tis only my imagination."

Nathan's heart thundered in his chest. Was that the chamber he had found the first night he arrived? "Why would your father have a navigator's glass?"

"He and Brother John traveled the seas when they were younger. 'Tis how they met."

"Does it still exist?"

"The glass?" He shrugged again. "I wouldn't know. The room is locked and Meg keeps all the keys on her castellan's ring."

Chapter 9

Meg dragged her weary body up the path. It was already dark and past vespers. The smugglers had not received her note for an earlier delivery. They came later than she had hoped. They were becoming unruly and demanded more than what she could provide. If not for Brother John to help move the casks, she would still be down in the cavern arguing over the price that had been set weeks before.

Her stomach growled. She could not recall the last meal she ate. Perhaps she could make her excuses and ask Cook to send something up to her bedchamber.

Closing her eyes, she listened at the door of the solar. Nathan was in the midst of regaling them with an adventurous story when her brother and sisters laughed at something he said.

Her palm rested on the panels. It would be so easy to turn away and hide from his searching looks.

The latch turned. The door swung open. Candlelight swathed the room in golden light. It wrapped a halo around Nathan's auburn head of curls.

"You're here! Sir Nathan thought he heard someone scratching at the door," Anna said as she grabbed her hand and drew her into the solar. "I thought you sent word that your head ached too much to join us this evening." Anna tipped her head in her direction. "I see that the powder I sent you earlier did the trick."

"Yes." Meg touched her palm to her temple. "It did wonders."

"A miraculous recovery." Nathan lifted his mug, saluting Anna and Meg.

"I won't stay long. I wanted to ensure your evening went well. Everyone was well cared for."

"You must eat sometime," Nathan said as he led her to a chair.

How did he take command so easily? She started to rise on weakened legs. "I've asked Cook to send something up."

"But Meg," Baldric draped his arm over the back of her chair. "We've so much to discuss."

"We do?" Meg asked weakly. His cheery face gleamed with anticipation. She could not resist. "And what has you so elated?"

"Sir Nathan and I measured the weapons in the armory. None would fit my hand."

Meg nodded and rubbed her temple. The fictitious aching head swiftly became a reality. "That is because they were created for a man. Not a boy."

Baldric jumped up and bounced on his heels. "That is why we made a trip to the blacksmiths. I commissioned Wayland to create a sword that will fit my hand. And it will be the correct size for my height."

"You ordered him to make you a weapon? Why?"

"Sir Nathan has promised to teach me to fight like a knight."

"But darling, that will take a great deal of time." She rose and cupped his small chin. "He will not be staying with us forever."

How could he? She could not keep up the deception. She had already placed them in jeopardy. Now with him endlessly underfoot, someone would make an error and reveal all their secrets. Her ears began to ring.

"Who's to say how long my stay will keep me," Nathan's voice broke in. "I've warned Baldric that I will know when 'tis time to leave. And then I must be gone. But while I'm here, I shall share what I can and train you, brother."

Scratching came from the other side of the door. "Hurry, my lady Phillipa," the steward called.

Phillipa ran to open the door. "What is it, Matthew?"

"'Tis the sheep." He bunched his flannel cap between his hands. "Someone unlocked the pen and set the whole flock loose."

Phillipa cursed. "Who would do such a thing?"

"Will they not return come morning when feeding time comes?" Meg asked. She leaned upon Nathan's arm as she joined her sister.

"'Tis the wolves that've been prowling the woods of late. I fear there will be casualties come dawn."

"I vow, if it's the border reivers I'll have their ballocks," Phillipa's heels clicked on the stone as she raced out of the solar.

"Come now, Phillipa," Meg called after her. She swallowed the dread slithering up her spine. There had been payment. She smoothed her hair and prayed no one noticed the tremble in her hand. "I fear she spends too much time with the animals and too little time on her manners."

Anna sidled up next to her. "Do you suppose it's them?" she whispered.

"I think that someone forgot to lock the gate again." Meg squeezed her fingers and prayed her sister would keep silent about reivers. She put on a brave face and turned to the servant. "Matthew, fetch the others. See that our mounts are saddled and gather the torches."

"Stay here," Nathan said, guiding her to the stairway that led to her chamber floor. "Lady Margaret, I will help with the gathering of the flock."

"No, I must be there."

"You do no one any good if you make yourself ill." He kissed her fingers, then opened her palm and placed another kiss in its center. "I will come to your chamber when we have returned and give you my report."

Meg nodded, too weary to argue. She cupped her hands as if to hold the kiss for a while longer.

Anna joined her by the stairs. "We shall wait together."

Once they reached Meg's room, she stood at the window. Watching and waiting for news; for Nathan and Phillipa's return.

"Sir Nathan will keep her safe," Anna offered.

Meg stiffened. A light that did not belong winked over the firth. Her nostrils flared. She twisted her hands, wringing out the tension through her fingers. "What if the reivers are caught? Sir Nathan will make demands. Bring forces against them. Peace will be lost."

"Purchased peace that holds no true promise," Anna said. "Fragile as the next payment. Ye know this to be true. I've told you time and time again."

"Yes," Meg ground out. She hated being reminded of what she feared every day. "But it need not be this night." She spun on her heels and grabbed the cloak off the peg.

"Where do you think to go?" Anna asked. "Sir Nathan said to stay here. That he would send a messenger if there was news."

"Sir Nathan is not our lord, Anna. And I intend to ensure that he does not discover the caverns. Have you given any thought as to his opinion if he were to discover the smugglers' cave and the wares that wait for transport?"

She paused at the door. "Wait at the window. I will signal with the lantern if there is concern."

* * * *

Madrigal sidestepped over a log and around a felled tree. Nathan shifted in the saddle, the torch held high overhead. Stars winked in the pitch-black cloudless sky.

The man they called Matthew rode toward him. "There are all but ten that are still unaccounted for."

Nathan nodded. "'Tis good news, then." The villagers had joined in the search and helped round up the stragglers. All but a handful had made an appearance. Lady Meg, that stubborn woman whom he had ordered to stay put in the keep, remained out of sight. It pleased him that she had obeyed his wishes. He imagined her fiery reception would be filled with indignation. He would receive all that she had to say, and then perhaps silence her with a kiss. A smile caught his lips by surprise.

Her passion for the people of Fletchers Landing should be commended. When he made his report to the king he would ensure there will be recommendations for her family. Baldric and her sisters were in need of a desirable future that far outreached the North Country.

Phillipa remained at the pen, ensuring that none of the sheep were harmed. Meg's youngest sister gestured for him to ride closer. "Have you seen Brother John?"

Nathan narrowed his gaze, probing the crowd for the tall elderly monk. Brother John's absence was commented upon by several of the villagers. He prayed that come daylight, they would not learn that another man of the cloth had sacrificed others for riches. He shook his head. No need to voice his concerns without evidence. "I shall continue to be on the watch for him. Is there something amiss that I may help with?"

Phillipa's eyes widened before she set her attention on the pen's fencing. "No, I...I found it curious. 'Tis all."

Nathan followed the path where Phillipa had been focused mere seconds before. Torchlight wavered near the shoreline. He tugged on the reins, turning Madrigal's head.

"Sir Nathan," she said. Her hand came perilously close to Madrigal's bridle.

"Stay back, my lady." Nathan's gut clenched. Any other person would have been knocked to the ground by Madrigal's massive hooves. Instead, the steed bent his neck so that she could reach that sweet spot behind his ears and give him a good scratch. Nathan took a shuddering breath to steady his own nerves. "You have a golden touch with the animals." He scrubbed at the whiskers roughening his jaw. "What is it that you seek from me?"

Her eyes widened as she fluttered her lashes. "Oh, I, um...thought you should look over there." She pointed in the opposite direction. "A few of the lost sheep might be found in the meadow to the east."

Nathan chewed on his lip. "Are you certain? I have already been over that land. Mayhap we should let Matthew handle the search on that side of the village and keep."

"If you must," she said. "At last count we were down to only a couple of the ewes missing."

He wheeled Madrigal to the west. "If I don't find anything of interest, I promise to return and speak with your servant."

"Look," Phillipa exclaimed. "There's Meg now." She jumped up and down in her youthful enthusiasm and waved. "Over here."

Meg had a cloak wrapped around her body as if to ward off winter instead of the summer breeze. Her lush lips slashed a thin line over her pale face. "I see that almost all are found."

"The hinges on the gate are old, rusted," Nathan snapped out his report. Why did she have to disobey his order? "Did you find what you sought along the shoreline?"

She flinched. Just a slight jerk of her cheek. It was enough to let him know that she was up to something that she did not want to share.

"No. I saw nothing unusual. Only a fishing boat or two in the water."

"Border reivers take to the water just as easily as the field, Lady Margaret. By going alone you put yourself in unnecessary danger."

Her shoulders drew back, unwittingly exposing the curves hidden under bodice and cloak. "As you informed me, 'twas not the work of reivers but of faulty metal."

Nathan wished he could enjoy the view from where he sat above her in the saddle. His fingers tightened around the reins. "But we did not know this at the time. Did we?"

"Meg," Phillipa said. "We are worried because Brother John is missing, too." They turned as a group of villagers carrying torches drew nearer. The flock of wayward sheep trotted in front of them.

"This be the lot of them," Matthew shouted. And all gave a collective sigh.

Phillipa swung the gate shut. "Meg, we must bring out a cask of your best ale to celebrate."

Nathan silently thanked the young girl for redirecting their discussion. The night's task was successful but as far as he was concerned, it was not over.

* * * *

Meg paced her chamber after she sent Anna on to her own room. The smugglers had indeed returned and stole the remains of the casks filled with ale and mead.

She had had enough. Where had Brother John been since vespers? It did not matter the hour. She must speak to the monk. Together they would figure out a way to help Nathan finish his report and send him away. Otherwise she would never have the time or the peace to complete another shipment. The next time she met with the smugglers, she would come armed and ready to negotiate a stronger agreement.

Her feet stalled. Could she involve the Graham's protection without losing anymore?

She whipped on her cloak for the second time that night. There was a rapping at the door.

"Did you forget something, Anna?" She swung it open and gasped.

"Lady Meg," Nathan crossed his ankles and leaned his forearm against the frame. "I would speak with you in private."

"The hour is late," she snapped.

Her skin flushed under his scrutiny. "And that is why you are leaving your chambers?" He rubbed his whisker-shadowed jaw. "I would offer my escort for safe passage."

"Through my own keep?"

"I shall conduct an investigation come the morrow. Until I do, I feel it is my duty to protect all who are here in Fletchers Landing."

Meg huffed and untied the cloak. She flung it on the chair near the door and motioned for the infernal man to enter the sitting room. Her back to him, she closed the doors to her bedchamber and pocketed the key. "You may speak your peace and then leave."

Her brows rose as he selected the chair near the hearth. His proud chin lifted. "Sit. 'Tis certain you are as weary of this day as I."

Her teeth clicked together as she attempted to keep from biting off his head. "I prefer to stand. Any discussion at this ridiculous hour will be short."

"As you wish, my lady," he said. "At least draw nearer so that I don't have to shout." His head tipped to rest against the chair. He closed his eyes, giving her relief from his penetrating gaze. Lines creased his brow. A heavy weariness seemed to settle over his broad shoulders.

Silence stretched between them as he waited for her to do as he bid. A battle of the wills had been drawn. If she were to ever find her bed she would have to concede to his wishes. Just this once. She stepped closer and stumbled as he opened one eye.

"I shan't eat you," he said.

Somehow, that did little to soothe her. Hands clutched together to keep them from showing her nervousness, she took a deep breath. "What do you wish to discuss that cannot wait until morning?"

Nathan leaned forward, propping his elbows on his knees. The leather chausses stretched across his thighs, drawing her attention. "How much do you know about your friar? Can you trust him?"

"Brother John has been with our family ever since our father returned from one of his many trips. Surely, you don't think he cannot be trusted. He is a man of the church."

"And he is human, capable of emotions that many of us do not wish to examine in the light of day."

"I can assure you that there is nothing to fear about that old gentle soul."

"And the blacksmith? Why did he not come when the call for help came?"

"I suggest you ask him that on the morrow when you do your investigation. Mayhap, you will discover that it was simply a case of worn hinges and lack of care. Nothing more."

"I look for no reason to lay blame at their feet. I wish only to offer my protection to you. Your family." He pressed up from the chair and tucked a curl behind her ear.

Her eyelids fluttered. She caught his hand, pressing his warmth to her cheek.

He cradled her face. "Meg, I must depart your chamber before I offend your virtue."

A sigh broke through as she turned and placed a kiss into his palms. "Go," she whispered. "Before we regret our decisions."

The door closed behind him.

Meg stood alone in the center of the room and felt the emptiness grow deeper than any cavern she had ever known.

Chapter 10

After rising early, Nathan waited in the great room and watched the coming and going of the servants. It appeared the household had returned to their daily routine despite last eve's romp through the pastures. He'd had several hours of restful sleep since his arrival. For some that would seem lacking. But for him, the last months had seen more waking hours, wandering the castle hallways and bailey yards. Reliving the torture. This morn, his strength had renewed. 'Twas as if he had clawed his way out of an enchanted faerie hole, finally escaping their spiteful torture.

"Ah, Brother John," he called out.

The old monk slowed his pace across the room. He glanced to the corners as if to look for a means of escape.

Nathan's smile broadened. He had his first victim of the morning in his sights. Brother John blanched under his scrutiny before presenting him with a nod. A halo of gray curls bobbed around his head.

"Good morrow, Sir Nathan. You are up early."

"'Tis a busy day planned."

He nodded. "There are always tasks to be done at Fletchers Landing."

"I imagine some will be moving slower, what with having to chase after a flock of sheep." Nathan let his gaze fall over the man. "I don't recall seeing you there to lend that helping hand the men in cloth are always harping on. Were you unwell?"

"What? You harbor ill feelings for the men who serve God?"

"Not I! I only carry great distrust of them. But that is because I have yet to meet one who truly cares for more than bettering their position."

"I fear you will find many who are not of the church who share those same aspirations. How then do you get along?"

Nathan spread his hands wide. "The past has taught me to treat all with great care and watchfulness."

Brother John nodded and matched his steps with Nathan's. "Mayhap you will one day meet one worthy of your trust."

Nathan sought peace and bit his tongue. They took the path leading to the bailey yard. Nathan had yet to find the best place to start Baldric's lessons. His exercise would serve twofold. One, to discover Brother John's reason for his absence and two, to gain the location for the next steps to regaining the strength of his soul.

"Indeed," Brother John said, "One must always watch over their flock. Even those who are contrary and do not act with wisdom." He shook his head. "There are times that I do fear for us all."

"Is that what you were doing? Watching over someone other than the sheep? I was informed that the keep is safe."

"'Tis certes that you have noticed the lack of chaperones properly suited to watch over the children. The Lady Phillipa was safe amidst the villagers. They would not harm her for they know that she keeps the animals healthy. I set myself between Lord Baldric's and Lady Anna's doors."

"But what of Lady Meg's?"

"She would not nor could not hide in her bedchamber. What would the people say of her? That she is a coward? Too weak to lead?" He scratched the graying whiskers on his chin. "That is my role, though I will admit mayhap that I am getting older, feebler than when I first arrived with their father, Sir Godwin, all those years ago." He cut his attention to wander over the fields. "My time grows shorter, Sir Nathan. It warms my heart to know that you are here."

Nathan narrowed his gaze. Somehow that old man had turned him around. "I do not intend on staying for any length of time. Once I have completed my mission for our king, I shall take my leave."

"Yes? Mayhap, until that time comes, we are all in need of watchful care." He sighed and plucked a yellow bloom from the gorse bush that lined the edges of the path. His foot slid over fallen thorns.

Nathan caught Brother John's elbow. "Steady."

"Gramercy." He righted the cross hanging from a leather cord around his neck. "I would never hear the end of Anna's scolding if I should fall again."

Nathan furrowed his brows. "This has happened before?"

"A common thing when age creeps up on a soul."

They came to a rise in the meadow. Not far from the keep, but close enough to see if a stranger should cross the gates. There was shade and a breeze when it came time to rest. And Baldric would have privacy to learn the steps of swordplay without others watching.

"This will do," Nathan said with satisfaction. Now all he had to do was keep his head once they began their training. Sweat popped out on his forehead. He sat down on a nearby boulder. His hands trembled against his thighs. He curled his fingers under to hide them.

Brother John found a seat and groaned as he settled himself on the other stone. "You're stronger than you realize, young knight. There will come a time when the dark memories no longer have the ability to haunt you."

Nathan grunted. "What would you know of it, monk?"

"Think you that I have always resided on these shores? Nestling in a little cottage waiting to die of old age has never been my plan."

The brother drew his sword and rested it on his knees. The steel glistened in the sun. His gnarled hands slide over the hilt, guiding Nathan's eye. "This was gifted to me. By another man of the cloth. He too was a knight." His fingers slid over a wing etched into the metal. "As am I."

Nathan sat straighter. The itch between his shoulders had returned as he looked closer at the design. Swans in flight, linked their heads and wings. He had seen a similar weapon. They were carried by the men who came before him. The ones who first formed the Knights of the Swan. "What mischief are you about?" Nathan asked.

Brother John dug under his tunic and pulled out a small leather pouch that hung from his neck. "Open your hand."

Taking a deep breath, Nathan unclenched his fists and did as he was bid. A coin like the one the messenger delivered at Clearmorrow Castle and like every other time that the Knights of the Swan were called into duty fell into his palm.

He lifted his head to meet Brother John's watery gaze. "You were the one who called me here?"

A chuckle shook the old knight's body until it loosened a cough. "I only made a suggestion. Though I must confess, I had hopes that it would be heard. The border between England and Scotland is of concern. And I'm too old to chase after border reivers and those who plot against England."

"Henry will expect me to join him in Calais." The journal the king sent became a weight in the pocket sewn inside Nathan's tunic. Did the monk know of it? "This is the only reason you sent for me? To contain the reivers?"

"They are but a nuisance. Lady Margaret keeps them content for now." He shrugged. "But for how long? Who can see into the next day? Or guess when they will change the arrangement and come a roving?"

* * * *

Meg shoved the strands of hair that had come loose from the twisted braid and resettled her cap. Hope swelled, lifting her steps. Her apiary was growing. Basket-shaped hives were lined up neatly in a row. The new swarm of bees had begun to settle in their skep. They buzzed and waggled their dance before landing on the oak slates. Bee after bee crawled through the opening and began to fill the honeycomb. Soon, she would gather the golden sticky liquid for making the mead. The endless process never ceased to amaze her. Mayhap the extra honey would help her fill the smugglers' next order of mead.

Scowling, she yanked off her beekeeping gloves, slapping them against her palm. Thanks to reivers, the wares she had stored were stolen. That Duncan Graham had better have a good explanation for breaking the agreement when next she met with him.

The next load of honey mead and ale needed to be relocated to the caverns. Who could she trust to move it and stand watch until nightfall? For their safety, the villagers were kept unaware of the goings-on in the cavern below the keep tower.

The friar was becoming too feeble. She dared not include Baldric or her sisters. They were unsuited to defend themselves and did not have the strength to fight off the reivers or the smugglers. It was becoming too dangerous for everyone. But what choice did she have?

She replaced the bellows near the hearth. Embers glowed red, reminding her of the lights she had witnessed floating over the firth. The blacksmith, Wayland, was the strongest of the remaining men in the village. What did she know of him? He had newly arrived from Carlisle with his niece. Whether he was swinging his hammer against the metal or speaking with the other villagers there was a sense of danger in him. Could he be trusted to keep silent?

Her teeth scraped over her bottom lip. The sweet taste of apple blossoms coated her tongue, brought back images of Sir Nathan's copper-colored mane as he wiped the sticky substance from her mouth.

She certainly could not ask the king's knight to watch over the shipment.

Their survival during the next winter was in jeopardy. There were no other choices left. She would have to speak with Anna and Phillipa.

Meg looked over the beeswax that would be used to create additional candles. "Thomas, fetch Matthew and have him help you carry this vat of beeswax to the chandlery. Ladies Anna and Phillipa will direct you where to place it once you are there."

"Aye, my lady." The page tipped his head and loped off down the hill toward the gardens.

Meg went in search of her sisters. They were bound to be waiting, impatient to be done with the morning chores and head off to their own pursuits. She cringed. Animal husbandry and alchemy. How would she ever find a husband for either one?

Her sour mood increased with each drudgery-filled step. A frown dug into her forehead. "What are they up to?"

Brother John and Sir Nathan strolled, their heads together, talking of things that had better not include her. Best to nip it before some misguided fool decided something that would be for her own good.

"Greetings—" Her breath caught when her father's old friend stumbled. Her hand dropped to her side. Relief swept over her as Nathan righted him and they continued on.

She held back and followed them to the armory. Baldric stood at the entrance, leaning against the wall. His newly rescued puppy sat beside him, tethered to a shrub with a leather lead. The dog watched his every move and pranced on three legs when Baldric jumped up and pulled out a key.

Meg counted the keys on the ring attached to her belt. Her pulse raced as all three males entered the building. Did they honestly think she would allow her brother to wield a sword?

"Halt! Don't you dare take one step farther." When they ignored her command, Meg lifted her skirts and hurried to enter before they slammed the door on her.

She slipped into the room. Weapons lined the wall. Their usefulness only as good as the warrior who used them. A small blessing that they had been hidden from sight on DePierce's one and only visit. He would have confiscated them and left them completely defenseless. As it was, they had a handful of able-bodied men and women to defend an attack. And their enemies knew this. 'Twas another reason for Meg to despise the man.

"What do you think you're doing?"

Nathan's brows arched. The corner of his mouth twitched. She shivered as his gaze slid over her. "I should think 'tis easy to see that we are about to train."

Her chest squeezed against the bodice, begging for air. She slammed the door shut, blocking their escape. "By whose permission?"

"Meg, don't you recall? We told you last eve. After vespers."

Brother John eased his way past the shields and swords. "I think it is a wise decision. You should be congratulated for thinking to utilize our young guest. Imagine it. Lord Baldric, trained by a king's knight. It will make the villagers sit up and take notice." He patted her shoulder in his fatherly way. "A very wise move, Lady Margaret."

All three males shared an innocent glance as they waited for her to give her leave. She knew when she was being manipulated. Did she not? Yet they did have a point. She hated that they might be right.

"A word, Sir Nathan." She spun on her heel and left for him to follow. Outside, she tapped her foot to keep her irritation from growing. She twitched her skirt out of the way of the dog's teeth. A shadow formed and stretched over her shoulder. "He is just a boy."

Nathan sighed. "He is. But he is ready to become a man."

She turned and tilted her head to search his face. "He is young. Untried."

"Sheltered. Protected. Cossetted," he added.

Meg folded her arms across her chest. "He was only five years of age when we lost our parents."

"And now he is ten years. Past the age a boy is sent to foster with another family."

"I know, but—"

"Boys younger than he are already learning to wield a weapon. You cannot continue to treat him as if he was still wearing nappies."

Forbidden tears stung her eyes. "You've seen him. His...leg. What if he is injured or worse?"

Shards of green jade glittered in return. "What is worse than losing your own respect?"

"We've lost so much already."

"And if you take this away he will lose even more. Meg," he soothed. His arms came around her shoulders. Warmth seeped through the flannel sleeves. "I will teach him to defend himself." He brushed his lips across the hairline by her temple. "Let me show him and you that he is stronger than either one of you believe."

Meg nodded, giving into his pleas.

"I vow to protect him," he said as he released her.

She ached to feel his arms holding her for more than a fleeting moment. "See that you do."

Baldric and Brother John walked out of the armory and kept their faces suspiciously turned from her wrath. "See that you return that dog to the stables before you begin your lessons."

"I thought to bring him with me," Baldric said as he knelt to untie the lead. "Whitefoot needs fresh air if he is to grow stronger."

"You think he can keep up with you," she snapped. "But I wager he'll hold you back." As soon as she said it and read his crestfallen expression, she wished she'd never said the hurtful words.

"'Tis certain your sister has yet to see his many wonderful qualities," Sir Nathan broke in to make peace. "And she does have a good point. You'll want your full attention on our swords. Run along, lad, and return your pup to his bed while I gather our weapons."

Meg chewed on her lip and watched her little brother limp away. Simple as that. Nathan's orders were followed. "I meant him no harm."

Brother John dipped his head. "I shall see to the lad and offer a prayer for you, my lady.

Chapter 11

Nathan wiped his mouth with the back of his hand. What had he agreed to? No matter what that monk had planned, he was not going to prolong his stay. He would set a few matters on the right path. See that the locks were repaired. Discover what secrets the blacksmith held. Find the tunnel that the king was convinced held vast treasure. Make certain that his mind was strong again. And then be on his way.

His plans did not include getting involved with the family members of Fletchers Landing. And yet, here he was.

He and Baldric stood in the pasture. They squared off, their practice swords ready. He took in a deep breath and prepared to teach the young lad a few steps in swordplay.

His blade rapped against Baldric's wooden sword. "Keep your head up. Your thoughts clear."

Fear widened Baldric's eyes. He stepped back, letting his guard drop. His foot dragged across the ground. As the boy had predicted, the weaker leg gave out.

"Keep your feet wide and grounded."

Baldric widened his stance. He repositioned his arms and took a deep breath.

"Be aware of your surroundings," Nathan said. He patted his chest. "Trust your instincts. Notice what a threat is. And what is not."

"Like knowing if a wild boar is charging," Baldric said with a nod.

"Correct. Or is it a sow, protecting her piglet. Both are dangerous."

The lad grinned. "Better to notice them before they're on top of you."

Nathan snapped his attention to the trees. "Do not let a beautiful young woman distract you."

"Who?" Baldric made a face and searched the field. "Do you mean my sister Meg?" His sword arm wavered. "Shite! She must have found Whitefoot in my bedchamber."

"Keep your mind on the situation." Nathan let his shoulders relax. Meg sat on the boulder, her chin resting in her palm. Baldric's puppy lay next to her feet. She had removed her cap and her long mane had come unbound. It flowed over shoulders, a silken waterfall.

His hands were no longer shaking. The sword's hilt fit comfortably in his fist. There was strength in his grasp. His mind was indeed free of the panic that had sat upon him for months. He made a wide arching swing of his blade.

Baldric parried and drew him back to the practice field. Their blades caught.

Nathan blinked and returned his attention to his student. "Keep your stance strong. For now, you'll have a shorter reach and will want to stay in close and swing faster. If your opponent has a longer reach he won't be able to swing in as easily. "

"Like the stairways in the tower?" Baldric bared his teeth and came at him, his wooden training blade jabbing and parrying.

Nathan's breaths came from deep within his chest. It roared in his ears. He clawed away from the crimson stain spreading into his view. There was no turning back. He had to find the control that allowed him to fight without losing a part of himself.

He brought his sword around and braced against another blow.

Baldric was beginning to tire. The flow of the thrusts diminished. His feet began to lose their position.

Nathan caught him as he fell. Their swords tumbled to the ground. Baldric's chest heaved as he gasped for another breath.

"Well done, my lord," Nathan said.

"Next time, I'll be ready for the reivers."

Nathan bent to pick up the sword and return it. He paused, searching for the warning without disparaging the boy's skill. "We have much to work on." He held up his hand. "And we will come again on the morrow. But you are not to take part in a battle alone until I say that you are ready."

Baldric's flushed cheeks wore a darker hue. "And if they come before?"

"Then I'll be in that battle beside you." Nathan ruffled his dark curls and looked over the top of his head at Meg. He could not seem to shake loose of the need to protect and be near her. To let her sweet scent of honey flow over him, pour into every breath. Was that admiration gleaming from her regard?

"Mayhap I should go," Baldric said.

Nathan caught him before he had an opportunity to escape his sister's wrath. He threw his arm over Baldric's shoulder. "Come. Let us speak with your sister. She'll want to ensure that you are in one piece."

* * * *

Meg pressed lips together and jumped up from her perch. She'd been caught staring at Nathan. Again. She wanted to groan, but thought better of it. The man had a way about him that made her forget herself and all of her responsibilities. Whether he was chasing down a lost ewe, swinging a sword, or walking across a pasture, he moved with a graceful stride. But this time, he had a bit of a swagger to his steps. The sun brought glints of gold and auburn in his hair. Flecks of copper glistened on his jaw. He grinned as if he had won the battle of life.

Her little brother tried to match his strides until Nathan noticed and swung him up to ride on his broad shoulders.

"Huzzah!" Baldric cried. He poked the sky with his wooden sword. His cherub's face, complete with damp dark curls clinging to his sweaty brow, was wreathed in utter joy. How long had it been since she had witnessed such emotion? If not for Nathan, he would still not know the wonder of accomplishment.

Her heart warmed. Her insides felt hot and sticky, like one of the pastries Cook baked only for holidays.

"My lady." Nathan bent a knee to let Baldric slide off his arm. He caught her hand to press a kiss upon her fingers. She gasped as his lips left a scorched trail over her flesh and left her speechless. Wide-eyed, she felt her legs begin to melt.

"Meg. Did you see me? 'Twas like battling a dragon." Baldric yanked her back to reality with a tug on her sleeve. Worry seeped into his voice as he knelt beside the bouncing puppy. "Why are you here? Is there trouble?"

She glanced down. "Trouble?" she stuttered. *Only where my heart may be concerned.*

"You never come out here," he said. Suspicion laced through his statement.

She presented the lead, shoving it into his hand. "One of the chambermaids discovered your little friend hiding under your bed. He made a puddle on the floor and ate part of a rug."

"I'm sorry, Meg. He needs me." He glanced up over his hunched shoulder. Whitefoot licked his neck and chin until Baldric fell over and rolled in the grass. He looked up at her and fluttered his lashes. "You did order me to return him to his bed."

Nathan rested his fists on his hips. "You are an obstinate boy but I believe your sister has had more practice."

Meg rubbed her temple and refused to acknowledge Nathan's presence. "Baldric, you and Whitefoot will follow my rules or face the consequences. I'll not allow you to create more work for everyone else."

"Yes, Meg." Baldric sat up, cuddling his new friend.

Good. Finally someone was actually listening to her. "You will have to keep that dog with you at all times. The only way he will be allowed in the keep and your bedchamber is if he is properly trained."

"Phillipa and I have started training him. He's quite smart. Brother John believes Whitefoot will be a good ratter."

"I'll not have vermin in our living quarters," she continued. "The moment a flea of any sort appears in the rushes, he will be returned to the stables."

"Not to worry. Anna has a tonic that we have already begun to use."

"Have all of you spoken about this without me?"

"You've been quite busy, Meg." He shrugged. "We thought it best not to bother you. 'Tis why I'm surprised to find you here."

"I...I..." she sputtered, "I fear my family has united to form a conspiracy against me."

Mortification licked up her neck. Verily, she could not admit that she stole the time away from her concerns to watch the play of Nathan's muscles and sinew. The dance of flesh and strength had nearly taken her breath away. Even now, she wanted to lick the saltiness from his skin.

Nathan saved her from embarrassment and helped her to avoid an answer. "Now that the puppy is settled I believe it is a couple of famished men who stand before you." He leaned over the boulder. "Mayhap dear Meg brought us sustenance."

"I fear not," she admitted. If only she had thought that far ahead. Somehow, he had done it again and caused all reason and thought to disappear. "'Tis not quite time for vespers."

His mouth kicked up. His full lips sweetened his mischievous expression. "Ah, alas no basket." He clasped Meg's hand to his chest. "Then we must away to the kitchens and convince poor Cook to feed our starving souls."

"I shall spread the word." Sword in hand, Baldric squealed and set off for the keep. Whitefoot galloped and weaved beside him.

Meg could not hold the laughter of his lunacy in any longer. She turned her hand so that her palm rested over Nathan's heart. Her chin lifted. If only this once. *Please Lord. Just this one time. 'Tis all I'm seeking.*

The cadence of Nathan's heartbeat increased under her palm. It joined with hers until she could not separate them.

"Ah, Meg," he groaned as his mouth came down on hers. He tasted of pears and ale. Honey mead and sunshine. Light and laughter. He tasted of hope and passion and she could not let him go. His lips found her neck, then they nibbled behind her ear.

Meg wrapped her arms around his shoulders. She stepped closer, pressing until his need became apparent. Emboldened, she found his firm buttocks. Wave after wave of desire crashed into her bones and sinew until she thought her legs would give out.

Why had she waited all these years to feel again? What a coward she had been. But now, there were no betrothals. No promises of marriage. She was free, like a bird that takes wing on the wind, she would soar and this man would help her fly. If only for the time he remained at Fletchers Landing.

"Fire!" someone screamed in the distance. "Fire!"

Chapter 12

Nathan tore his mouth from Meg's. The terror in her eyes gave him pause.

"No," she cried. "No. What have I done?" She scrubbed the remnants of their kiss from her lips.

Together, they ran, hand in hand toward the village. He pulled her along as their strangled breaths threatened to break them apart. "Stay with me," he called.

Smoke billowed from one of the outbuildings. Flames licked the thick black clouds.

Wide-eyed, Meg pointed to the roof. "Dear God. It's next to the chandlery. What of the children? I must find Baldric and the girls."

Nathan grabbed her arms. "Brother John will have reached them before us. He will see to their safety. We must keep our heads. Do you have a plan if a fire should ever leap its hearth?"

"Yes, the villagers know what to do. But we don't have the number of men that we used to."

"Call all the able-bodied servants to you. Have them gather every bucket they can find. Wet the blankets and bath sheets. Bring them to the outbuildings."

He stopped running, and gathered her to his chest. "And Meg, I beg you, be safe." He kissed the crown of her head before releasing her.

She cupped his jaw. "You as well."

Meg gathered her skirts and raced toward the tower. "To me," she screamed. "To me!"

He spun on heel and ran toward the burning building.

* * * *

Smoke lingered in the air, thick and strong; it filled the nostrils and sat upon the tongue. It stuck to everyone's clothing and hair. Everyone would be reliving that nightmare for some time to come.

Nathan's arms and back ached from spreading as much water as he could over the thatched roofs and sides of the buildings. His hair smelled of burnt feathers. All who stood before him were covered in soot.

Meg poured the bucket of seawater over the last glowing ember and sunk down on a low wall. Her face and dark hair were coated in a dove-gray powder. Stains stretched over her skirt and across her bodice. And yet, he could not help but think what a beauty she was to behold. A warrior for her people. She'd fought to save her village and she'd won. The villagers stopped her, speaking a word of gratitude. His heart swelled with admiration. He ached to taste her lips again, to kiss her until they were both breathless with desire.

But there was sadness in her eyes that went far beyond the burning of a few buildings. Why did she blame herself for the fire? If he went to her, would she turn him away even as she did while they battled the blaze together? She had closed herself off and refused to look at him. Made comments to others, but did not speak to him.

He searched the last few hours when they worked side by side with servants and villagers alike. There was no class difference when one was saving your existence from the fires. Through it all, he had not lost himself in the blood-red memories of panic and fear. Relief fluttered over him like a downy cloak.

Nathan looked down at his hands. New burns were added to the scars. Did they appall her?

A cough racked Meg's body. Her cheeks carried trails of tears.

He forced his feet to move forward. Courage against the fire was nothing compared to standing up against whatever weapons she might bring against him. The worst would be her refusal for his assistance.

"Lady Margaret," he said, holding out his hand to help her rise. "Meg, you are in need of clean air." He choked on the smoke working its way around the buildings. "As am I."

Her fingers, warm and alive, wrapped around his. Too weary to speak, they walked the seawall.

"Sir Nathan," the alehouse keeper called out.

"Harrigan," Nathan croaked. He slapped the portly man's shoulder. "We did it."

"Aye, there was a time or two I feared the wind would take it. Indeed, God did shine upon us."

Meg turned her gaze upon them. Her eyes were like two holes burned into a blanket. "Reports of injured?" she croaked.

"One or two that came too close to the flames," Harrigan said. "Lady Anna is seeing to them now." He removed his cap, crunching it between his hands and bowed. "Lady Margaret and Sir Nathan, we give our thanks to your aid."

Meg smiled and curled her fingers around his hand. "And we to you. As you say, it could have gone much worse. My sisters were working in the chandler's building."

Confusion washed over his countenance. His skin flushed as he looked away. "I saw Lady Phillipa escape with my own eyes. But I did not see Lady Anna leave the building. She must have been taking a walk when the fire first started."

Meg gripped the seawall to hold herself up. "I must go to the infirmary. See that my family is safe and not in want." She paused to pull her shoulders back and added strength in her orders. "Sir Nathan, see that someone watches over the smoldering embers. We will discuss this further come morning."

Nathan watched her leave his side. Emptiness filled the space where she had stood. Was it only hours since they kissed? He waited for what seemed like an eternity for Meg to turn back and call to him. And it never came.

"I didn't wish to worry my Lady Margaret, but I've recently heard rumors," Harrigan said.

Nathan pushed away from the despair. "Speak."

"A rider was seen tearing off through the woods right after the call was made."

"Reivers? Have Matthew saddle my horse and gather as many men who are able," Nathan ordered. "We shall track down our visitor and offer our desire to make his acquaintance."

"'Tis unusual for reivers to go a roving in daylight and by his lonesome. They like to travel in a pack. Like wolves." Worry marred his swarthy complexion. "Should we not inquire her ladyship's desire?"

Nathan clapped his hand on Harrigan's back. "You did well in confiding in me. Lady Margaret has enough to carry on her slim shoulders. Prepare to ride before nightfall."

* * * *

"How could you," Meg snapped.

Despite the ache in her back and the pain in her side, she paced the solar. Her sisters stared at her as if she had lost her mind. And perhaps she had. Fear had flayed her, laying her nerves open to the harsh reality that she had caused this. She'd broken her vow. She'd let herself want and desire pleasure. Just this once. Wasn't that what she thought five years ago? The plea had been the same and the outcome had been the same. Destruction for pleasure. She thanked God for the hundredth time that Baldric and Brother John were unharmed and already fast asleep in their beds.

"Meg," Anna said. This time, her soothing tones were more of an annoyance then healing. "I left Phillipa and the chandler for only a short while. The fumes from the melting beeswax and the tapers were stifling. I needed to gain fresh air. So I left. For a short time." She glanced at their youngest sister. "Isn't that right?"

Phillipa raised her eyes. Her pale skin, a mask of distress. Her hands were bound with strips of linen. "She was gone for just a moment or two." Her lids drifted closed. "I was pouring the wax into the molds that you created. Counting the time that I could be done with that task and doing something else. Anything else would have been better than making candles. You know how much I loathe being confined in a room.

"I smelled the smoke before the flames caught in the corner of the building. It moved so fast. I threw my shawl down to smother it but the fire spread like liquid. I tried to save the candles, Meg. I truly did."

"I know, love," Meg crooned. She wrapped her arms around her sister's thin shoulders "I am grateful for all that you did."

"I'm sorry," Anna whispered. "I should have been there."

Meg cringed and resumed the pacing. She should have never kissed Sir Nathan. She ached for the loss. "You are all alive. A few injuries that will require rest, time, and your healing unguents. I give thanks that that is the only price we must pay."

"What of the shipment of candles?" Phillipa whispered. "And the protection payment?"

"It will be impossible to fill," Meg said. She rubbed the ache blooming from her temple.

"Or pay."

"The reivers will hear of our misfortune. They will not strike across the border," Anna said.

Meg slid her gaze over her sister. A chuckle squeezed out of her chest. "And how would you know this?"

"They are people too. They know of pain and loss."

Meg snorted. "Because they are usually the ones to cause it."

She wandered to the casement and looked out over the valley. How much time did they have before they did come a calling? Who would exact payment first? The smugglers? Or Duncan Graham's reivers?

"Thanks to your sister Meg, you know nothing of pain. You should bend your knee and beg for forgiveness." Nathan strode into the solar. He had donned his leather gambeson. The studded gauntlets he wore when she first met him across the stream were wrapped around his forearms. His sword hung on his hip. And a broadsword was strapped to his back. "But I fear if we do nothing, we will know it firsthand."

Meg arched her brow. Brother John brought up the rear flank. Grim-faced Baldric stood to his left. "I thought you were abed. Do you think to take on whoever did this by yourselves?"

"Some of the villagers desire to ride with me," Nathan answered. "Your brother and the monk will stand guard while we are gone."

"And what if they are cunning, outfoxing you all and arrive while you are following their trail that has already gone cold?"

He lifted her chin and smiled. "Then we will rest easy knowing that we have shown our strength and done all that we can."

His lips brushed over hers, holding her enthralled and taking her breath. Under her palm, his heart beat a rapid rhythm through the padded gambeson. She groaned as she fell into the welling need that could not be shed.

Another stolen kiss. Her vow broken again.

Fearing that she had insulted God once more, she tore her mouth from his.

His green eyes darkened. Instead of a gentle green with golden flecks they had shifted to that of shadows and enchanted forests. Should she choose to lose herself in them, she would never return to the woman that she was.

He traced her mouth with his thumb. "We shall talk upon my return."

With that he took his leave. Meg tasted her lips and ached for one more kiss. He was an enchanted potion of which she could not break free.

* * * *

Nathan rode Madrigal through the woods and over the pastures. There were three trails to follow. Two led away from the village; those they lost in the woods. The freshest tracks led to Fletchers Landing and had yet to leave. He would speak with the other villagers and discover who had newly arrived that day. But there were no signs of a large group of reivers.

Relief and confusion warred within. He turned to the two men who chose to ride beside him. "Matthew and Harrigan, what say you?"

"They be gone for now," Matthew said.

Nathan rubbed his chin. "There are no tracks left by groups of riders. Not even a small scouting contingent."

"Do you smell that?" Matthew asked.

Nathan nodded. "Smoke."

"Of course you do," Harrigan said. "We've been fighting a burning building all afternoon."

"Never smelled like that," Matthew added. "This smells of roasting meat." His stomach growled, drawing both men to direct their attention to his middle. He rubbed his stomach. "My innards are telling me that we should investigate."

"We should get back to the village," Harrigan said. "Trouble comes at nightfall."

"It may be a trap. Or just a traveler." Nathan drew his sword from its scabbard. "Best be on alert."

They followed their noses north and came upon a campsite. A traveler sat beside the fire. His supper lay across the fire. He bent over the flames, turning the rabbit skewered on a stick. Nathan moved the branch to size up his opponent. He judged him to be at least a hand taller than himself.

"'Tis a brawny lad. A Graham," Harrigan hissed. "I'd stake my life on it."

"Let's pray you do not need to." They tensed as the man rose from his fire. He stretched his arms out, flexing his back and shoulders.

"I thought they resided farther north in the high hills," Nathan said.

"There are rumors that some wished to ride south to claim the land and anything else they can get their thieving hands on."

"Stay here behind the bushes." Nathan sheathed his sword. "If there are more, they will show themselves soon enough."

He strode out from the trees, showing his hands free of weapons. "You there," he called out.

The tall stranger retrieved his supper and tore off some of the flesh with his teeth. He wiped the grease from his chin with the back of hand. He stared into the surrounding trees as if he could strip the leaves from their limbs. "Aye? Who goes there?"

Nathan took another step closer. "You travel by yourself?"

"'Tis possible." He shrugged. "Not a law against it. Is there?"

His teeth glistened like a wolf Nathan had seen a few years past. He made sure to keep a wide berth of it then and would do so now.

"I come in peace. From Fletchers Landing. You've heard of it?"

"Aye," he bit into the rabbit meat and chewed. "Here and there. Now and then."

"Perchance you heard that there was a fire this day."

He stopped his methodical chewing and swallowed. He bent, his movement stiff, and replaced his supper near the campfire. "Was anyone hurt?" he asked. "The Lady Anna?"

Nathan alerted to the concern in the stranger's voice. He watched his opponent and prepared to pull the sword strapped to his back. "Why do you ask?"

The behemoth shrugged. "'Tis said she has a way with healing. A village would sorely miss someone like that." He scrubbed knuckles over his breeches. "You never said of her health."

"And you've yet to speak your name," Nathan returned.

"Aye, well now, if I do, the ones you have hiding in yon trees are like to come running, blades drawn. And I'd hate to have to harm anyone." He slid his gaze toward Nathan. "At least not when there's nothing to earn from it."

"And if I were to order my men to stand down. To come in peace?"

The dark-haired giant held out his paw. "Then we can all get along. Speak as men, not beasts."

Nathan jerked his chin. A rustle of bushes came in response. "'Tis done." He prayed they understood they were still expected to stand at the ready.

"Name's Duncan Graham." The clansman dusted off a log near a pile of weapons. He looked up and waved him to take a seat. He picked up a small knife, testing its edge with his thumb. "And you must be Sir Nathan Staves."

Nathan eyed the spot across from Duncan Graham. "I am. Suppose you heard that from one of your sources."

Duncan shrugged. "As I said, word comes now and then." He searched Nathan's face. "'Tis your turn." He flashed a wily smile. "A give and take."

So the Scotsman fancied the delicate blossom of Fletchers Landing. Nathan stretched out his legs. "She was well the last time I saw her. A pretty little thing, don't you agree? 'Tis a wonder that she escaped the building unharmed. Her sister, Phillipa, was not as lucky."

"Aye." His eyes narrowed. "How did it start?"

"I've yet to discover the culprit. Someone saw a rider."

"And you thought I might be the bastard to set the chandlery ablaze?" He threw down the knife and it struck the log. Its hilt quivered from impact.

Nathan jumped to his feet. "I never mentioned which building."

"And I said I hear things. But I did not witness it. I would never hurt…" Long tapered fingers wiped his mouth. "Like I told you earlier. If there's no money to be made, I would not be found near it." His chest rose and fell. "Take what I say as truth. Or prepare to arrest me and expect a fight."

There was something about the man that Nathan understood and felt compelled to believe what he said. "I think 'tis best you find your way back to your clan and stay away from Fletchers Landing. It will go better for all if you do."

"Aye?" He rose, towering over Nathan. "Do not think to warn me off of this land. 'Tis a very bad thing if you do."

"And you'll keep your distance from Lady Anna," Nathan added, shoving Duncan Graham back. He tensed for the blow that was sure to follow.

The Scotsman retrieved his blanket from the log and kicked in the fire. "I'll make my way home this night. But you'll want to watch your flanks, Sir Nathan."

"I always do."

He waited, arms folded, his weight balanced on feet ready to leap at any sudden movement Duncan Graham might send in his direction. It was all for naught, as Duncan did as he was ordered and mounted his horse and rode off to the north.

Nathan was ready to do the same and head for home. Darkness was falling and there was no telling who hid in the shadows. He spun on his heel, his sword drawn as Harrigan and Matthew appeared from behind the brush like night wraiths.

"You let him go." Harrigan's reddened face looked like he was about to explode like an overheated apple.

"He's a Graham," Matthew added, explaining to him as he would a child. "He has clansmen who will come a roving."

"He has his warning," Nathan said. Grabbing Madrigal's reins, he mounted his trusted steed. "We've learned all that we can this night. 'Tis time we return to the village."

"Yes," Matthew agreed. "It does little good to chase after a rabbit once it has gone into hiding."

Nathan offered a reassuring smile. "We'll put more men on the wall. I'll take first watch. Then we will assign the others."

"Beg your pardon, Sir Nathan, but we haven't that many to spare."

"Come the morrow, I'll send word. More will arrive to help guard Fletchers Landing."

He wheeled Madrigal around and they set off for home. His thoughts traveled ahead of him. Would Meg be there to greet him? He imagined the reception, arms open wide, pulling her into his embrace, kissing away all thoughts and worries.

Nudging his steed, they galloped toward the keep. The gate, closed against intruders, was a pleasant sight to behold. Madrigal's ears twitched and he did a side hop, nearly costing Nathan his seat.

Nathan whipped his sword from his back harness as a horse and rider came from the shore. They charged through the brush, nearly running over the three horsemen. The horse's dark roan hide was speckled with lather. A crimson stain surrounded its lips.

"Blacksmith, what are you doing out here?" Nathan asked.

The horse fought the bit as Wayland sawed on the reins. "Been running down the reivers who set that fire."

They rode in tight, surrounding the horse and rider.

"Is that so?" Harrigan said. "Never figured you as a tracker."

"By God, Lady Phillipa will have your hide if you continue to do harm to that beast." Matthew warned.

"There were no other tracks." Nathan motioned for Matthew to catch the horse's bridle. He pointed his sword toward the blacksmith. "I think 'tis time we talk."

"What are you accusing me of?" Wayland yelled then slumped over the saddle.

Harrigan held up the weighted bag. "I thought it'd be quieter this way."

"It would have been better to find out what he knows before you knocked him on his noggin," Matthew said.

They escorted their prisoner to the village. The people stared as they did the first day Nathan rode through the gates. Only this time, they pointed to Wayland, whose feet and hands were bound to his saddle.

"What are we to do with him, Sir Nathan?" Harrigan asked under his breath. "There's no dungeon to hold him until we get the truth from him."

Nathan turned. The man looked about to fall over in exhaustion. Matthew did not look much better. "See that he's tied up good and tight in the smokehouse. It won't hurt for him to wait."

All he wanted to do was see Meg, hold her in his arms. He had found healing here at Fletchers Landing and he wanted to share his news with the one lady who was always in his thoughts. He let Madrigal have his head and galloped up the hill to the main tower keep.

* * * *

Dismounting, he handed the reins to the groomsman and raced up the stairs. His footsteps echoed in the great hall.

Raised voices came from the solar. Was that weeping? Meg? Afraid that someone had been mortally injured, he ran into the room.

The children huddled around Meg, consoling her as she wept into her hands. They froze in what they were doing and glared at him over her head. Their stares warned they would rip him apart if they had the opportunity.

Brother John lifted his head, then bent his neck. "Might as well join us, Sir Nathan." He folded his arms behind his back and returned to his prayerful wandering about the room.

Meg's pale face, mottled and puffy from tears, crumbled at the sight of him. "Yes, do come in, my lord." She rose from the great chair. Her fingers curled against her palms. White lines formed around her mouth.

Nathan arched a brow. What had happened to the fine reception that had played out in his mind? What did she mean by calling him her lord? The warning itch crawled its way between his shoulders.

"You!" she said, pointing at him. "When did you do it? Before or after you were stealing kisses. And..." she twirled her finger, "worming your way into our lives." She worked her way past Anna and Phillipa's efforts to stay her wrath. "What did you tell our king? That the Lady Margaret was too weak to manage the property? Did you see the lands and rub your hands together and say, 'Ah, a tasty morsel to steal out from under the people of Fletchers Landing'?" Her chest rose and fell, stretching the bodice to the point that he worried it would rip apart.

"You're speaking in riddles."

"How could you," Meg growled like a feral cat protecting her property. She shoved a crumpled parchment into his hands. "I pray that you choke on it." A sob ripped through her body, doubling her over.

Nathan reached for Meg to offer comfort. Phillipa blocked his way, shoving him away. "Do not dare touch her."

"Come," Anna soothed, pulling Meg away. "You will take ill if you do not rest."

Their brother strode up to him. His blue eyes were filled with the pain of betrayal.

"Baldric, what—"

A single tear slid down the boy's cheek. "I thought you and I were friends." He ran out of the solar. The door slammed behind him.

"Let them go, son. Speak with them come the morn, when heads are clearer and hearts are lighter."

Nathan stared at the missive that bore the king's seal. The other set of tracks they had found must have been made by the king's messenger. Was he still here? Waiting for a response. But to what? His stomach knotted. Had the king found someone suitable to marry the Lady Margaret of Fletchers Landing? Bile rose. The room began to bleed into red-filled panic. He turned to the friar. "Brother John," he said. "What's the meaning of this?"

The deep worry marring the old man's brow made Nathan's organs twist in pain. He knew Brother John had contacted those connected to the old knights but to what extent? The monk waved him to the antechamber. "You will want to read this in private. Then we will talk."

Nathan forced his hands to steady, then slowly unrolled the king's decree.

Chapter 13

Instead of the imagined welcome, Nathan trudged to his bedchamber. Crestfallen, he stood in the hallway, staring at Meg's door, willing her to open it and let him in.

He, the newly appointed Lord of Fletchers Landing, had every right if he chose to wield it; to demand entrance. But what good would that bring if she could not bring herself to look upon him?

What had his king done to him? Henry may have given him a title and lands, but that act tore the heart out of him.

A heavy sigh pressed his feet deeper into the soles of his boots. He retraced his steps to his bedchamber. Once again, he was alone. After stripping off his clothes and splashing his face with the water from the washstand, he fell into the empty bed.

Visions of the fire licking up the wall slipped into his dreams. Screams from the children tore open his heart. Sweat dripped off his forehead. It hissed as it hit the fire, sizzling like meat on a spit. He fought his way into the rooms, one after the other, searching for something. For someone. His sword was no match for fighting the flames.

"Nathan," Meg cried out. "Please! I need you."

He awoke, shivering with fear. He yanked on his chausses and returned to Meg's chamber door.

"Let me in," he whispered as he scratched on the door. "Meg? Please I beg you. I ask only to ensure that you are safe."

Greeted by the silence in her response, he increased his knocking. Worry shifted to anger. "Meg?"

The door swung open to an empty room.

* * * *

Meg walked the cavern on legs that felt more wooden than human. How could she have been so foolish to think that she might trust him? Earlier that day she almost shared the fears that weighed her down.

She gripped her hair. Whom could she trust? No one.

Duncan ducked his head to gain entrance to the chamber. "I suspected you might be needing to speak with me. Just not so soon. Heard you had a wee bit of trouble in your village."

"The chandlery is burned to the ground and all that was stored within it."

He drew up a chair, spinning it so that he straddled the back. "Spoke with your knight."

"Tis not my knight. Ho, no, the man is now our lord. The king has not only torn my land away from me. He has also set my hand in Sir Nathan's for marriage."

"Ah then all is not lost. You'll still live on the lands you've been born to."

She shoved her braid over her shoulder. "All that I've done to keep us safe and now this. Mayhap he is the one who set the sheep loose. Started the fire." She scowled at the behemoth. "Or was it your reivers?"

"No, lass, do not accept that lie. 'Tis another you should look to instead of me or your man."

"Why do you say that?"

"Dinna your man tell you? They have the blacksmith barricaded in the smokehouse."

Meg ground her teeth. "It starts already. He's already keeping information regarding my people from me?" She picked up a ball of beeswax and returned to her pacing. "Why did they lock him up?"

"I'd say that be something you want to give your man a chance to tell you." He shook his head. "Did you give Sir Nathan a chance to speak at all?"

"I…" Heat infused her cheeks. "Perchance I was a bit upset."

"I'd wager you were a bit more than that. Mayhap it would be fair to say you were enraged."

The warm wax rolled in her palm. How did Duncan gain his information? The man knew too much of the goings-on in her keep and village.

"There are worse people to be wed to." He rubbed his chin. "Although, if you wish it, I can see that he is taken away to the hills in the north." He rubbed his paws together. "Bound to be worthy of a hefty ransom."

"And bring more of the king's men down around our ears?" She shook her head. Tempting as it was, she could not bear the thought of Nathan injured and alone. "I beg you, do no harm to him."

"As you wish," Duncan said. "If you should have a change of heart, me and my lads will put the lad in a gunny sack and carry him away."

"No. I'll find a way to convince him that he will not want to linger. That the holding will manage without him as it has in the past. He has already so much as said that he planned on leaving for France as soon as he sends his report to the king."

"Then why did you send for me? I was to be heading to my bed instead of riding out at night."

Meg took a deep breath, repeating the message she had rehearsed earlier. "The fire has impacted the shipment of candles."

"And why does this matter to me? Our women make our own."

She had seen his clanswomen's craftsmanship the last time she went to Carlisle to sell her own wares. Fletchers Landing's candles were the finest. None were comparable. 'Twas why she could charge the smugglers the price that she did. "The loss impacts the timing of payment."

He clucked his tongue. "'Tis a pity."

"Duncan Graham, we paid you well. We'll pay you again in time."

"And you'll receive your protection when we collect our money." He splayed his empty hands. "In time."

"I'm beginning to suspect that you are up to mischief. This fire isn't the first difficulty that has visited our village. Mayhap we're not getting the protection that you promise."

"Spit it out! What are you saying, lass?"

"We had a shipment of ale stolen. I've allowed you knowledge of when these deliveries are to take place so that no one takes advantage of us."

"Now why would we go and do that?" His Scottish brogue thickened as his temper rose.

"You're a Graham. That's reason enough to question where you were. Was it you or one of your men who stole our goods and set the fire?"

"I happen to enjoy your coin too much to steal from you." He stood to tower over her. His nostrils flared his outrage. "And I happen to care for…" His lungs inflated with his deep breath. "Take my word as truth that I've had no hand in your problems. But I vow I'll uncover who's setting up my clan and me to take the fall. I won't be facing a hangman's noose for something I never took pleasure in doing."

"Forgive me. It had to be asked."

He scratched the back of his neck. "Do you think it might be that knight of yours?"

"Of course not. He doesn't know of our agreement. Nor of the arrangement with our merchants."

"That's a pretty way of saying smugglers, is it not? I warned you not to trust them." He folded arms across his chest.

"Yes, you and Anna are a constant buzz in my ear about the dangers. But it has to be done."

"Your sister's a bright woman." His blue eyes shifted as quickly as the direction of his suspicion. "But the fire might be another thing. The knight might want to gain your attention. To prove that Fletchers Landing needs a lord instead of a lady to lead them."

Meg winced and shook her head. "We were together when the cry rang out." The memory of Nathan's mouth pressed to hers, moving together in want, brought a flush to her core.

His brows arched. "So that's the way of it? Well then, we must take him off our list." He sighed. "Since I'm to clear my good name before it is besmirched with lies I'll give you some time until all this is settled." He held up his hand. "Silence. You haven't heard my terms."

"You've already demanded plenty." Wary, she asked, "What additional terms are you offering?"

"I'll present my request when the time is right." He sat down on the chair. "Tonight, I'll stay and watch over what's left of the shipment. Think of it as protecting what's mine."

His wolf's grin should have been enough to make her run to the keep. Instead, she held out her hand. It was an answer to who should take first watch. "Agreed."

"You have my word and now I have yours." Duncan's fingers tightened around her hand. "I'll be certain to let you know what I desire when the time comes."

* * * *

Meg slipped through the door. A form moved from the chair beside the hearth. She gasped, clutching her chest. "Who's there?"

Candlelight created shadows across the intruder's face. A boot heel struck the floor. The chair creaked as its inhabitant stood. "Where have you been, Lady Margaret?"

"You startled me!" she cried. "What are you doing in my bedchamber? Who gave you permission to enter?"

"It was unlocked." He turned to light another taper. "And you did not answer my question."

"You cannot be here," Meg hissed.

"We are betrothed."

Nothing was ever that simple. She took off her cloak, gathering her thoughts. How could she tell him? He serves only his king. He would never understand. Thanks to the troubles of late, Fletchers Landing was nearer to poverty than ever before.

"I could not sleep. The events of the day were too much." She peered under the cover of her lashes. His firm mouth pressed into a thin line as he continued to scowl at the ends of his boots.

"Nor could I," he said. "There is much I would have liked to discuss with you." He shifted his attention to her. His gaze roamed over her body, then drifted to her face. "But you were not here."

Meg steeled her trembling legs as he advanced forward. The gentle stroke of his finger swept down her cheek. "Were you...with someone?"

"No," she whispered. Afraid to look at him lest he see her lie, she closed her eyes. Shaking her head, she pressed into his palm. "I like to walk along the gardens. To gather my thoughts."

"I see," Nathan said. "If we are to be married, we must learn to trust each other. Don't you agree?"

Meg licked her lips. Her throat became as parched as a dry creek bed. "Yes," she croaked.

"Look at me," he pleaded. "I must know if there is another who has your heart."

This was the opportunity for her to claim a lover. Someone who might send him away. She opened her mouth, but could not form the words. "There is no one."

Nathan let loose a ragged breath. He cradled the back of her neck, pressing his forehead to hers. "Then there is still hope."

A tear burned a trail down her cheek. His back was straight and strong under her splayed hands. The warmth of his body, his scent of leather and mint, called to her. A siren's voice that she dared not listen to. "I fear there is very little hope for us."

His muscles twitched against her fingers. "You cannot mean it." He stilled. "'Tis because you believe I am broken. Because of the night terrors?"

"No," she soothed, her heart breaking at the pain that she caused. "I do not fear your dreams. I know that you are a knight and have seen and endured many things. I think no less of you."

"Then 'tis the king's edict." He played with the tendrils by her ear, distracting her from her mission. "I know 'tis unexpected. For both of us. Mayhap the king in his wisdom has created a union that will thrive." He leaned in. Her core tightened as he ran his tongue over the shell of her ear. "There is something between us. Don't you agree? A desire to discover one another. In each other's arms."

If only it could be so easy. "Only a fool lets passion lead them," Meg said.

"On this, we greatly disagree." He grinned at her; an air of mischief in his tormenting lips. "I shall make it my mission to prove you wrong."

"You must listen to me." She had to put a stop to the growing temptation. "Every day, I feared Sir Vincent would return and claim what was his. And deep in my soul, I knew that one day I would be called upon again to wed."

"You've been wed before?" Nathan drew back.

"No," she said, ducking her head. "I have dared to love but once. At least, at the time I thought it love. But I learned the truth of it. By then it was too late."

He lifted her chin. "Tell me."

Her heart ached as she forced her story out. "When I was but ten and seven years of age, I learned that I was betrothed to a young man of influence. My parents believed Geoffrey was the answer to Fletchers Landing's financial difficulties."

"They sold you to the highest bidder?" Nathan remained steady under her palms.

"I am but a lord's daughter, 'tis expected. Most of our wealth had gone to Father's travels and study of ancient history. 'Twas to be a wedding that fall. Instead it was a month of damp and cold. Sickness had run through the Northern towns and villages. I begged Mother and Father to allow me to travel to Newcastle.

"Geoffrey and I had never met and were impatient to get to know one another. We had shared letters of love." She shook her head in disbelief. "As I look back on it, I have come to realize that it was I alone who wrote of love. He wrote of his passion for his horses and the land that he would gain through our marriage. He wished to know all about Fletchers Landing."

The snap of a log in the hearth broke through the silence. Nathan pressed his lips to her forehead, then they traveled to her temple. She pushed at the tentacles of desire weaving through her veins.

"He had been a handsome man, but a recent illness had taken his weight and paled his skin. He swore that his health had returned. And as soon as the ink was dry, he pressed his need into my hands. I was flattered when he spoke of our wedding night. He begged for a taste of what our future held."

She took a shuddering breath. "Although he'd looked unwell, I allowed him to kiss me. I wanted to taste desire. My curiosity led me to disaster."

"Meg," Nathan's voice broke. "Tell me he did not force you."

Her smile wobbled. "He did not. But his mouth had been demanding. He coughed and his hands shook as he demanded more. I thought it was desire that made him tremble."

"'Twas the sickness."

She nodded. "I tore away from him. He called me a bitch, unworthy of his name. He struck me. I cursed him for the bastard that he had become before my eyes. But the curse turned against me."

"He raised his hand against you?" The fury radiating through Nathan was palpable. "I shall run him through."

"'Tis no need." She stroked the base of his spine. If only there could be another chance at love. "Word soon came that the illness had returned and was spreading through Newcastle. Days later, I contracted the coughing sickness and my parents soon followed. However, my precious mother and father never returned home. And I was left to raise my brother and sisters."

"The fault does not lay with you."

"It should have been me who died of the sickness. Not our father or mother. Their deaths were because I put my desire and passion first. I vowed that I would never do that again. The price is too great!

"Don't you see? Trouble has already followed this broken vow. First the sheep escape their enclosure. Then the fire." Her eyes widened. The stolen shipments. She covered her mouth with her fingers. She had broken her vow and brought the troubles on them all.

"Our kiss," Nathan whispered. "That is why you blamed yourself? You pulled away from me. It is not the king's edict for marriage." He forked his fingers through his hair. "You are letting fear steal from you. From us."

Hurt, Meg snapped. "And you are stealing from Baldric. This was to be his holding."

"Not anymore. You knew that. Had Sir Vincent any other living blood relatives it could have passed to him. In truth, you should thank the stars and fate and whomever you pray to, that it was I who killed his only nephew. Hugh was worse than that bastard Vincent."

Meg blinked away the pain. "Worse?"

"God bless Christ on the cross and his bloody wounds, we will wed. And we will make this arrangement work."

He looked every bit of the angry warrior and Meg saw what those who dared to stand against him saw. A man who would not be broken or swayed from his quest. She had to make him understand.

"But I explained to you why I cannot. We cannot consummate the marriage bed." She hugged her stomach, willing the ache to pass. "It would bring more trouble. Mayhap even death the next time."

"Let me remind you that it is Henry's decree that Fletchers Landing is now mine and we are to become man and wife."

"Because that is what the king wants?" Meg narrowed her gaze. "I see. You desire to please your king so that you may return to his side."

"You wish me to wed you and then leave?"

"Is that not what you have desired since your arrival?" She poured a mug of ale and swallowed it in one gulp. If only her hands would quit shaking. Whether he stayed or left, someone's heart was bound to be broken when he discovered the rest of her secrets.

Nathan helped himself to the ale and drank deeply from the mug. His tendons stretched from shoulder to jaw, as he swallowed its contents. When he was finished, he returned the mug with deliberate care next to hers.

Meg gasped as he swept her off her feet. "What do you think you are about?"

"Not all men are cut of the same cloth," he said, as he carried her to her bed. Her heart thundered against her chest. Excitement set her pulse racing. "Set me on my feet," she whispered. The sound of her voice carried little conviction as desire warred with fear. Was that really what she wanted? She did not know anymore. Life spun like a top. "I'm not a babe to be carried about."

"Indeed. 'Tis a fact I have noticed since the moment we met across the stream."

The skin over his cheeks and around his mouth was stretched taut. His heart vibrated through his tunic, galloping against her shoulder. Her hip skimmed his flat stomach. To her surprise, he ignored her order and carried her to the bed. He paused long enough for her to wonder if he'd reconsidered. Then he nudged aside the heavy drapes and removed all doubt.

He let her slide down his chest, stopping only to place her on the mattress before releasing her.

Meg dug her fingers into the coverlet and wiggled to stand. "I cannot... we cannot do this."

"Be still for a moment." He gently pressed her shoulders so that she remained seated.

Her eyes burned. "If you force me, I will fight you," she warned. "Of this, I vow."

"Meg." He tipped her chin, forcing her to meet his gaze. "I desire you. I admit it freely." There was an air of pride as he spoke. "But set your heart at ease. I have never forced a woman to slake my needs."

She fought the urge to nip and taste his flesh. Her fingers clenched and unclenched. Her core tightened.

He stared at her mouth, rubbing the pad of his thumb over her lips. "When we do come together it will be on your terms."

"Confident, are you?"

"I think you want me, too." His head dipped to the side. "You're just too stubborn to admit it."

Meg squashed the thrill that threatened to float up from her belly. She watched, wide-eyed as he knelt and lifted her foot, placing it on his knee.

"I keep thinking of when we first met. Beside the stream. I believe you started lusting over me the moment we first met."

He removed her shoes and let them drop to the floor. The soles echoed in the wave of silence hanging between them. "You, my sweet, were staring at my feet."

Meg gasped. "I never—"

He ducked his head so that she could no longer read his expression. The curls of his auburn hair tickled his neck as he chuckled. "Not a very skilled liar, are you?"

"How dare you," she withdrew, tugging to free herself from his hands.

"I've been told many times that I dare too much." He nudged her skirt out of his way. Warm breath skimmed over her leg. His hands encircled her ankle, prodding the aching joints. Then he worked up her calf until he arrived at the top of her stockings. He played with their edge. "Ah, I do believe I recognize these. Hello, my lovelies."

"Nathan." Instead of chastisement, his name sounded like a plea of passion to her ears. Her core clenched and unclenched. Her nipples pebbled. Meg closed her eyes and bit her lip to suppress the groan.

Slipping a finger under the fabric, he rolled them down her leg, baring her feet. Her toes curled at the pleasure. A sigh filtered through her lips as he rubbed his hand over the aching bones where her shoes often pinched. She searched for his head to pull him closer. For what, she did not know. Would it be after this night that she no longer came to him a virgin?

"Please," she whispered in defeat. Raking her fingers through his mane of curls, she drew him to her bed.

"Not tonight, my lady," he murmured. Lifting both legs, he tipped her back until she rested on the bed, her head upon a pillow. "When we come together you will no longer question your desire."

"Sleep," he said, placing a kiss upon her forehead. His lips scorched a path to her mouth. "Perchance you will dream of me and see us in the future. We will speak of our new arrangement come the morn."

Meg stared at his retreating back. The door clicked shut. Desire flooded her limbs. Pressing her thighs until she ached with need, she stroked the many places that he left untouched. Frustration lit like a wax taper. Her only satisfaction found that night was the knowledge he too would ache with unresolved need.

Chapter 14

Nathan's cock would not allow him to sleep. The fire haunted his dreams when he closed his eyes. And when he lay awake all he could see was Meg. Her glossy dark hair splayed upon the coverlet, eyes pleading for passion's release. Thighs opened for him to plunder, teasing him to take action.

Once again, his cock rose to attention at the thought.

If a glimpse of her fair calves turned him into a rutting hart, what would it do to him when he saw the whole of her? Every inch of flesh would require stroking and tasting. It startled him to think what kind of control she could have over him. If he allowed her, she would be devastating.

He rose from his bed and prowled the keep halls and found his way to the portraits of Meg's ancestors. They looked down their commanding noses. That should most certes clear the lewd thoughts from his mind.

Those who came before him knew of their heritage. They had fought to protect the Fletchers Landing's people and maintain prosperity. Some succeeded where others failed.

Nathan felt like the imposter that he was. His family had died so long ago, that he never felt the need to unearth the roots of his heritage. His place had always been in service to the king. The Knights of the Swan were his brothers. He had no need for more than a solid set of armor, a strong horse, and a few coins to help him entertain the women in his bed.

And now, through marriage and Henry's favor, he had inherited another family. What would those who came after him have to say about Sir Nathan, Lord of Fletchers Landing? Would he be up to the task that he'd been given?

He raked his fingers through his hair. Time and time again, he had scoffed at his friends as they were saddled with land and buildings in need of repair. And now, with one stroke of the pen, King Henry had handed over these holdings. Why grace him with this gift now?

"Good morrow. I see you rise early." Brother John joined him in the hall and stood at his elbow. "Have you adjusted to your good fortune?"

Is that what it was? Judging by the looks that he'd received the night before, he should feel blessed that they hadn't tried to poison him. "I fear the family is none too pleased."

The good brother's deep sigh echoed against the cavernous walls. "Aye, but it is as the king wills." His crystal blue eyes followed Nathan. "What do you intend for them? The unknown is but a heavy weight around one's neck when there is fear. But when there is hope, one can accept change with a little more ease."

"I had no foreknowledge that this would come to pass. I was tasked to glean information from a journal. Not to accept both land and Lady Meg's hand in marriage."

"You will need to accept it all or displease our king." Brother John turned and began his slow amble out of the keep. "No one knows for certes what a king will take into his head." He folded his hands behind his back as they walked through the gallery.

"There is always a price when someone meddles in affairs," Nathan said.

"I take it that you disapprove of my interference in the fate of Fletchers Landing."

Nathan stopped to squeeze the old man's shoulder. "I'm still doing my best to understand all of your motives. Where does Lady Meg go at night?"

"Speak to her. She keeps her secrets for good reason. But she needs you even though she does not realize it."

Nathan cut his attention to the shore. That was the direction in which he had seen the lights every night since his arrival. "I spoke with her last eve. She is displeased with the notion of marriage. Nor is she pleased with my taking of the holdings."

A glint of anger sparked over the monk's visage. "I am well aware of your visit to her bedchamber."

A rush of heat found its way to his ears. "We spoke. That's all that took place."

"See that it doesn't until you are wed. And in the meantime, woo her. Convince her that marriage to you is a blessing. Not a curse."

How long would that take? Nathan did not relish the idea of a prolonged betrothal. He wanted it finalized as soon as possible.

"Two days hence, you will officiate at our wedding," Nathan announced. "That should give adequate time to prepare for the celebration."

"So soon? Do you not wish to discuss this with your betrothed?"

"She may not want a celebration, but I think it best that we proceed with or without her approval. I will speak with Meg and the children and make it clear of my plans. I waited for her to rise, but have not seen her leave her rooms. She avoids me. But I will be lord of this domain. I wish to see the ledgers."

Worry marred the monk's brow. He looked up at the tower and pointed to the high windows. "The master chamber was where her father conducted Fletcher Landing's affairs. I will take you there."

* * * *

Nathan marveled at the resplendent chamber. Glass windowpanes reflected a rainbow of colors on the walls. Books, lined up like soldiers, filled the shelves.

He ignored the guilt as he walked on a thick rug. These were now his private chambers, his library. He was Lord of Fletchers Landing. No longer an intruder. So why did his skin prickle? He pushed open the shutters and inhaled.

A navigator's glass rested on a stand near a double-wide window. Its shining copper tube glistened in the sun. Nathan swung it about, searching the land leading to the firth. Beyond its shores lay the sea. A handful of fishing boats bobbed in the waters. Merchants should be coming here, looking for fine wares to sell. Instead the harbor was deserted. What dangers kept them away?

A worktable sat in the middle of the room, angled to catch a wide view of the village and fields. After replacing the smaller, feminine chair with the solid heavy one standing in the corner of the master chamber, he sat behind the overlarge table and surveyed the stacks of leather-bound ledgers Brother John had pulled for him.

Nathan scrubbed his hands together. Thankful he had been given the opportunity to be schooled in mathematics, he settled in to learn of his new home. His breath rushed from his body.

Home?

He could not recall the last time home was a reality. A place you could trust that no matter what events befell you in your travels, you would be received with open arms.

The hours spent reading through the numbers scribbled across the parchment had begun to make his eyes water. He rubbed his cheek when it jumped. Thanks to the strain, a tic had formed. The words swam and danced behind his lids.

He would rather battle a horde of Frenchmen or chew off his leg than read another page of jagged shaky handwriting. He closed the tome. Picking up another, he flipped it open and sighed with relief. This hand was more meticulous in the numbers and letters.

Hunched over the pages, he read until daylight turned to night. Drawing the candle nearer, he reread the entry. The calculations did not balance.

A scratching came from the other side of the door.

"Come," he ordered, marking his place with his finger.

The handmaid entered with a food-laden tray. She was a pretty thing with rosy cheeks, her flaxen hair pulled back and tucked under a cap. "'Tis long past your first meal, my lord."

The deep curtsy brought her cleavage under his notice. She lowered her lashes, creating delicate shadows over her cheekbones. "I thought you might be hungry by now. You, being our new lord and master, should be seen to. Given the best treatment and care."

There was a time when he would have been enticed to have a tumble with her. Instead, his little head slept. Glowering, he laid his pen down on the table. "And who might you be?"

Bidden by his question, her smile widened. "Millicent, my lord."

Nathan folded his hands over his chest and leaned in his chair. "You accept me as your lord so readily? What of the Lady Margaret?"

"That she dragon locks herself away from the rest of us, playing with her hives and bees. Not natural, is it?" She caught her lip with her teeth. "I probably shouldn't have spoken so clearly. My uncle is always telling me I speak my truth too loudly."

Nathan rose, towering over her diminutive figure. "How long have you worked in this keep? You need to be taught discretion."

He jumped as she plopped down and knelt beside his knees. Her fingers dug into his thigh with a claw-like grip. "Mercy, my lord. I meant no harm," she wailed.

"Shite, Millicent, stand up." He extracted her nails from his person. His attempts to put the desk between them proved difficult. The wench was as slippery and determined as an eel.

"What are you doing, Sir Nathan?"

"Meg," he started.

"Unhand her at once." Meg's nostrils flared. She pushed past him and lifted the serving wench from the floor by the elbow.

"If you take notice, I was not touching the wench. In truth, she was climbing up my leg like an alley cat."

Meg turned her dark glare on Nathan and swished her skirt around him as if he had the plague. "Return to the kitchens. Wait for me there."

Nathan watched the comely wench turn her waterfall off and on with expert ease. Her mouth pursed in a bow.

"Yes, my lady." Eyes cast down, she stepped toward the door to make her escape.

"Inform Cook that our evening meal will be taken one hour later," Meg said.

The serving maid was not so talented to hide the glare cast behind Meg's back. The treacherous woman smoothed her hands down her apron and over her hips. She licked her lips, offering up her foul treats for his use. A blond spider spinning her web.

As soon as the door clicked shut, Meg's frown deepened. She stood before him, a warrior; a sight to behold. Her scowl was fierce enough to force a Viking to flee back to his ship. "You will not bed every wench in Fletchers Landing."

"My lady," he said. "You are the only woman I wish to bed." He drew her to the chair beside the stacks of ledgers.

She nudged one of the heavy tomes. "What are you doing in here? This is my parents' private chamber."

Nathan hooked a hip on the table and braced his other leg on the floor. He bit his lip to keep from noticing that her gaze kept slipping toward his groin. Good. Let her be as off-balance as the damn accounting.

"As Lord of Fletchers Landing, I am to go over the accounts. Am I not? Who keeps this mess?" he asked, pointing to the hated pile of numbers.

"I do," she said. Her arms crossed below her chest, lifting her bosom higher.

"Then, my dear betrothed, we will be spending every waking hour, straightening them out."

"Mayhap too many battles have scattered pieces of your brain matter. There is nothing wrong with my numbers."

He scrubbed his fingers through his hair. She'd struck too close to the center of his fear. But he had never given up field position before and he was not about to start.

"Send word that we will take our meals here. We will not stop until you and I have gone over everything."

"Meals?" Her mouth made a pretty little circle. One he wished would someday be used on him in many exciting ways. He tore free from the fantasy.

"As many as it takes."

He stopped her as she turned to flee. "Meg, you may also want to inform Cook that we are to be wed in two days. I expect a small celebration."

"Two days? Do you not wish for your friends to bear witness?"

"Your brother and sisters will suffice." He lifted his hand to stall her complaints. "A messenger has been sent."

"Two days is impossible." She swayed on her feet, threatening to topple over at the least provocation. "There's no time," she muttered under her breath. Her skin blanched the color of cream.

Nathan rushed to her side and caught her waist. He returned her to the chair, pressing her head down. "Good thing my pride is not so easily bruised. I hate that the mere thought of me as your groom makes you take ill."

"Don't be a fool," her voice floated up from between her knees. "'Tis no reason to rush. You have the holding and title, your lordship. If we must marry, I would at least like to know who I'm wedding." She swatted blindly in his direction. "Do let me up."

"Do not fall over in a heap," he warned.

When she turned her head to cast a withering glare, he did as she bade him. He chose to remain perched on the table should she threaten to faint again. "I explained to you why we cannot wed. Why do you persist?"

He cleared his throat. "Brother John is aware that I came to your rooms. He agrees that we should not delay the event any longer than we must."

"We did nothing sinful."

He shrugged. "It's all in perception. You believed that I would touch that wench. Why?"

Meg rose from her chair. The color had returned to her fair face. "She was on her knees by your..." Her hand waved in the direction of his cock.

"And that wench needs to be cast out of the keep. If she is willing to present herself to me, she must be watched." He twirled his pen. "Keep her away from Baldric."

"My brother is an innocent."

"Then let us keep him that way. There is trouble about her. I can feel it."

"She has newly arrived. Why would she hold a grudge against us?"

"Whose family does she reside with?"

"Wayland."

"The blacksmith?" They looked at the meal Millicent brought to the chamber.

Meg grabbed the contents on the tray, and hurled it out the window. She dusted her hands, then poured water over them from the pitcher.

"I shall speak with Cook myself."

Nathan nodded. A wave of pride swept through him, piercing his heart. She could one day be his lady, his wife. By all that was holy, his lover.

"Meg," he called out. "Remember, return to me posthaste. We have work to do."

"But 'tis nearly evening. Vespers will be called. Brother John will expect me to attend service."

"Not tonight. This night, we shall share together."

* * * *

Meg stared at the door to the master chamber. It, a trap, waited to snatch her from the life she had known for the last five years. Had Nathan truly gone over Father's numbers? To say they were in disarray would be an understatement. She should have thought to provide a separate set of ledgers. Then no one would have been the wiser. But she did not. And now Nathan poured over those pages, tallying up profits and losses.

Would he be furious when he discovered the truth about Fletchers Landing's financial state? She had warned him off when she gave him her reasons why their marriage could not be one of passion in the marriage bed. Even then, the holding had begun to show signs of financial ruin.

Her hand shook as she pressed down on the lever. The hinges complained as the door swung open. The blacksmith had been charged to repair many of the locks and hinges. But since he was still kept prisoner in the smokehouse, there was little promise that the repairs would happen until Wayland cleared his name. She would have to speak to Nathan. See that it was done soon.

Taking a deep breath, she steeled her resolve and strode into her parents' chambers.

Candlelight swathed Nathan's auburn hair with threads of gold. His broad shoulders were hunched over those damn books.

Memories of her father swirled into the room. Sir Godwin, too, had poured over numbers, trying to find the magical spell that would multiply their coin. Unfortunately, he had more skill in spending and losing wealth than he did in creating it.

She had thought to keep her secrets to herself. But mayhap it was time to share with the man who would inherit more than buildings in need of repair. He stood to lose a substantial amount of wealth. Baldric was in need of fostering. Her sisters would soon be in want of marriage and dowries.

Nathan looked up and laid his quill pen near the pot of ink. A ghost of a smile swept up his lips. "'Tis good to see you," he said. His voice, soft like a feather, stroked over her skin. "I began to wonder whether or not you intended to ignore my wishes." He rose to come around the table and join her.

Meg inhaled, pulling in his scent of mint and leather. She would forever think of him whenever she entered the stables. Even after he had left them all.

He covered her hand with his. "Tell me, dear Meg, how Fletchers Landing's accounting of goods and expenses do not add up. And yet, by some miracle the tables are laden with food and drink."

Now is the time. She should explain their troubles. That if she did not take the measures that she did, it would be impossible for them to eat through the winter.

"We are frugal in our measures. And we grow most of our food. The fields produce what we need. Phillipa's skill with the beasts keeps them bred. Anna keeps us healthy." She gulped. How much more should she say?

"And you make your meads and ales," Nathan helped her. "Selling and bartering with nearby villages."

"Yes." Relief attempted to shake her off her feet. "We do what we can."

He prowled around his worktable, scraping his fingernail over the spines of the books. "And yet, it still does not balance. Why do you keep the numbers from your sales off the books?"

Meg closed her eyes and prayed Father would not hear her lie from his grave. "I fear I have no head for figures and very little time to work my way through them." She fluttered her lashes. "Mayhap now that you are lord, you will take over the task."

The book he'd been examining fell to the floor making them both jump. Taken aback by the expression on his face nearly made her burst with laughter. But then the desire whether to chase him away or keep him as lord warred within.

She followed the dimming light outside the window. Shadows stretched. Soon her presence would be required in the caverns.

"I will hire someone to look after the ledgers when I have returned to my duties," Nathan offered.

The thought of him leaving pinched her heart. "Already you plan your departure?"

Nathan made a circular path around the room until he once again stood before her. "I must always be prepared. 'Tis the nature of my role."

"I spoke with Cook. He complained that he has not seen Millicent since she brought you a tray." She hugged her arms, aching for them to no longer be empty. Swallowing her foolish sorrow, she added, "There is talk that she is not happy here and wished to return to her home near Carlisle."

He leaned against the table, his hip near hers, but kept his distance. "Do you believe the rumors?"

She shook her head and plucked at her skirt. "The girl is quick of wit. Mayhap she realizes she acted a fool and is too embarrassed to show her face."

"The wench travels alone? 'Tis not safe." Worry brought a furrowed to his brow. "And her uncle?"

Jealousy reared its head. It almost left her speechless. What was Nathan asking? She waited, hoping he would repeat himself and clarify.

"Wayland, the blacksmith?"

She latched on to the information. Of course. It must be the sleepless nights that made her thoughts wander. "Still waits for you to speak with him. Do you intend to keep him in the smokehouse forever? He should not be punished if he is innocent of treachery."

Nathan pushed off his perch and went to the navigator's glass. He peered into it, focusing on the outbuildings. "I mean for him to be ready to spin his tale when next I see him."

Following him, she looked out the window with him. "What do you see when you stare into that thing?"

He turned his head. His mouth near hers. All that was required of them was to lean into each other. Her tongue flicked out, searching, tasting her lips. The now-familiar ache had awakened and called to be fed.

Nathan must have heard it too. He drew her to him, wrapping her in his embrace. He called out her name as their lips met. "Meg," he groaned against her mouth.

Chapter 15

Nathan came up for air. He did not know if he had the control to keep from bedding Meg that night. What madness possessed him to think they could be sequestered in the same room while still keeping his hands from roving over her succulent body? Why did he agree to wed in two days? The vows should have already been completed. Then they would have found their way to their bed, consummating their marriage.

Meg squeezed his arms, pushing him away. She locked her elbows. "We can't. We mustn't."

"We can. We should." He leaned down, nipping at her kiss-stung mouth.

"Not yet." She pulled away.

Nathan sighed and swept his hair out of his eyes. He knew he should move slowly with her, assuage her fear. He had even promised to wait for her. But every time they were with each other, they were tempted to kiss. He wanted more. And she was afraid.

"Meg, we must discuss our upcoming nuptial. There is more to a marriage than saying the vows." Wrapping his arms around her, he pressed her back into his chest. "I want more than that. With you."

She bowed her head, refusing to look at him. "I'm well aware of what goes on between a man and his wife." Her voice held a mix of annoyance and fear.

He turned her to face him and tightened his embrace when she threatened to pull away again. She shifted between his legs, her skirts brushing his cock. He could feel her apex pressing into his need. His body leaped to attention. He swallowed, aching to reach down and touch her bud of pleasure. "Are you now? 'Tis good to know. Though I cannot but wonder how you came about this knowledge."

Intrigued, Nathan watched the color rise up her neck.

"Through Brother John. Same as Anna and Phillipa."

He fisted his hands. "Baldric?" His eyes burned. The dreaded burgundy color of wine began to seep into his vision.

"Not yet." Her soothing voice worked through the red tide. "I believe the monk will instruct him in the fall when he is old enough to understand the way of things."

"I'll kill him. With my own hands, I'll strangle him." He flinched when she touched his cheek, smoothing the tic by his eye.

"Nathan, 'twas only the rutting of beasts of the field. Though my mother might not have approved, how else would we comprehend the violence of breeding?" Her eyes brightened with humor. A soft chuckle lifted her shoulders, brushing her breasts against his shirt.

Nathan sucked in a harsh breath and released it. The rage washed out with it. There were enough repairs required at Fletchers Landing. The thought of the women being damaged by the monk's lust had nearly caused him to take another life. He shook his head and thanked God that he would not have the blood of one of God's own on his hands.

"Brother John, a monk, talked to you regarding the pleasures in bed? He's a damn monk. What could he possibly know of it?"

A soft chuckle lifted her shoulders. "I'm told he did have a life before he took the vow to serve God. He chose to teach us through nature's way and let us witness what takes place between the animals."

Nathan pressed his forehead to hers. The warmth that surrounded her, seeping through their clothes, reminding him of what little space was keeping them apart. How was he to undo that monk's damage? "My sweet Lady Meg. There is a great deal more that goes on between a man and a woman."

Her fine brow arched with skill. "If you recall, I had taste of it with Geoffrey. It left bitterness on my tongue and life."

"I am no Geoffrey. Of that, I vow as truth. When we come together, it will not be rutting like your previous fiancé."

"Then you will keep your word? You will not take me to your bed?"

He released Meg, offering proof that he would not force her. "I gave my word." He caught her wrist, staying her for a moment longer. "But I did not promise to not give you reason to come to me when you are ready. Nor will I give you reason to fear me when the time for our lovemaking comes."

He brushed his lips over her knuckles. "Because you will come to me. Of that, I am certain."

* * * *

Although Meg desired to stay within Nathan's embrace, she withdrew her hand and restored the space between them. If they were to remain as close as they were, enclosed in the room, improperly chaperoned, another night would not pass by without her losing her virginity.

She was afraid. Would their mating be like the stallion and mare? Would he mount from behind? She had seen the nipping and biting, heard the mares squeal. Seen the blood.

Geoffrey had caused pain when she refused to please him. Nathan had yet to show that side of him. He was a knight. A soldier familiar with battle, violence, and bloodshed. And yet, he was a gentle man with the animals and her brother. The loss of her mother's advice left an ache in her heart. What if she and Nathan found a love as deep as her parents? There was still a chance for it to bloom into something wonderful and breathtaking.

She fiddled with the navigator's glass, turning toward the firth. The moon glistened on the rippling water. The dark night sky sparkled with faerie lights.

They had studied the ledgers together, side by side. The hours had slipped by unnoticed. Her pulse quickened. Time for the delivery of the last shipment had come. Thankfully, that Scotsman, Duncan Graham, would be there to oversee and ensure that proper payment was received. And she must be there to be certain that all the money owed to her was handed over.

Lights winked near the shore. She had to find a reason to leave Nathan to his muddled ledgers and numbers.

"Be warned, Sir Nathan, this will be a loveless marriage," Meg warned. "Nonetheless, I thank you for your vow of patience. 'Tis late and I must take my leave now before everyone has found their beds." She flicked her attention outside the window. The lights were moving in an odd dance. Something was going wrong. "I suggest you find your bedchamber. I bid you good eve."

She swept up her skirts and did her best not to run down the stairs.

* * * *

Nathan started to take off after her and stopped. She might not have thrown his pledge in his face, but she came damn near to doing so. He threw down his quill and paced to the window. He spun the spyglass with the flick of his finger. The shiny metal caught his reflection. Around and around, the harried face of a warrior came back to stare at him. Did he truly look the madman? The days and nights had folded upon each other until it was no longer clear the length of his stay. He no longer desired to hasten back to his king's side. The lady of the keep was more enticing than any quest the king might send him on. This was his home now and he would find a way to claim her heart. If only she would trust him.

He spun the tube again. His image shifted and wavered with each turn and click of the glass. It was much like the journal pages: flip them faster and the hidden map appeared. His pulse racing, he dug into his tunic and pulled out the journal. As the pages were flipped faster and faster, the drawn lines of the shoreline connected.

He looked through the lens. The moonlight and shadows matched the map. He popped up to stare out the window and then at the map. A medallion formed along the shore. By all that was holy, he had discovered the place to start his search for the king's treasure.

A movement caught his eye. Lights flickered across the firth. They bounced and swerved along the rocky edge. He grabbed the telescope and leaned in. Someone ran down the path that led to the water below. "Meg?"

What or who did she run to? The bite of jealousy clamped onto his heart. She had lied to him. She ran to her lover. Swearing a possessive oath, he doused the candle and set off down the circular stairs toward his bedchamber. "By all that is holy, there will be a price for this behavior."

Sweeping up his broadsword and the short blade, he ran to the stairs. The short blade slid into the sheath at his hip. His boot heels clattered down the steps leading into the deserted great hall. The hour had long passed vespers and the evening meal. Everyone had taken to their beds.

"Everyone but our Lady Margaret Grace," he growled as he slammed through the double doors. They crashed against the stone, and bounced back, nearly closing on him.

What if trouble had drawn her from her bed, his conscience countered. Mayhap she needs your help.

Nathan drew in a deep breath to bank the fiery rage. It would do them no good if he lost himself in the dark thoughts again. He would return to the lessons he learned as a Knight of the Swan. He would listen and learn. "And then execute," he muttered.

He followed the path he had seen Meg take moments ago. The moonlight aided in navigating the steep incline. More than once, his heel slid over a pebble, forcing him to slow his pace. He grabbed a branch lining the rocks to keep from falling to his death. His heart pounded in his ears. What forced that woman to navigate a treacherous path in the middle of the night? Surely a lover would not demand she take her life in her hands. "I'll kill the bastard and apologize to Meg later."

Nathan stopped. The lights had stalled in their movement and clustered together in the safety of the boulders. He slipped into a crevice, pressing his back flat against the rock.

The world shook as Meg ran to a man dressed in his padded jak of plaite and gripped his arms. The padded vest not only enhanced his form but also would allow him ease in movement. A leather sporran hung from his belt. The unsheathed claymore gripped in his fist was large enough to cut down a small tree. His shaggy mountain pony, tethered to a bush, lifted its head. The beast turned in Nathan's direction and nickered.

Meg and her lover swung around. The Scotsman. Betrayal from both liars tore Nathan's control from its mooring. He should have heeded Matthew and Harrigan's advice and run him through. Too bad, Meg will have to witness the Scotsman's death this eve.

Before he stepped out to confront the two deceivers, a group of marauders attacked from the other side. They yelled as they swung their mace and hammers.

The hiss of unsheathed swords announced the battle had begun. His stomach twisted. Meg stood in the middle. Outnumbered, she and the giant Scotsman braced their backs together. Their attackers circled their prey.

Nathan counted only three. Not too many to handle. He'd deal with them first. And then he would take care of Meg's lover.

Woefully unprotected in his simple jerkin of wool, he gripped his sword and charged into the melee.

Chapter 16

"Watch yourself, lass," Duncan said. "I don't suppose you have a weapon in that wee shoe of yours."

"I have my dining knife."

Meg unsheathed the little blade and positioned it so that it pointed outward from her chest.

Duncan grunted. "Well, I suppose something is better than nothing."

They turned in a circle, slowly following the path of the smugglers. Their feet scuffed the ground as they came closer.

"What do you propose to do?"

"I plan on keeping us alive. Thanks to your untimely arrival that's about as far as I made it in laying out a plan."

"We should have let them take it all."

"And allow the bastards to steal from you and me? I protect what's mine."

Blood had already stained the side of his head. "You're already wounded. It's not worth the price of a life."

Duncan grunted. "Aye, I don't intend to give mine or yours to them. Talking to the fools dinna make a difference. Guess we'll have to take lives instead. Are you strong enough for this end of the game?"

Meg gulped. Her legs had turned to water. Her bladder threatened to relieve itself. "Yes?"

Duncan grunted again. "That's encouraging. I don't suppose your man knows of your clandestine meeting with these fetid thieves."

"No. I—"

Meg stiffened, terrified as the men came at them. She turned her head. "I'm sorry, Duncan."

"Tried to warn ye. Stubborn lot of women in your family."

A battle cry exploded from the boulders. Relief washed over her. And then if it could be possible, she became more frightened that she had been seconds earlier.

Sir Nathan swung his sword. The blades rang as they crashed together. He attacked again and ran a man through. Blood exploded from his sliced neck and shoulders as Nathan worked his way to her. Another fell like a sack of grain. Duncan leaped to one side, narrowly escaping the sharp blade arcing in his direction.

"You'll pay for this," Nathan growled.

Meg squealed as he grabbed her wrist.

Before he could make good on his vow, three more marauders ran to the aid of their men. Nathan turned, creating a wall with his body. The smugglers' men regained their strength, forcing them to step back. Nathan wedged his shoulders between Meg and Duncan.

"'Tis good to see ye, Sir Nathan." Duncan said. "I'd hoped ye wouldna miss the festivities."

"How many more," Nathan snapped.

"Ye took down two. By my reckoning, we have four more to rid from this earth."

Meg marveled that Duncan sounded like he was enjoying the danger they were in. "Why so many? There are usually only two smug...men." Who were they? How did they know about the arrangement?

"Aye, well, lass, at last count there were five all waiting for me to hand over the goods free of payment. I took umbrage at their demands and let them know they could carry their arses back to the hell they came from. That's when one of them tapped me on the skull with their cudgel."

"Enough talk," Nathan snapped. "Your woman's safety is paramount."

The anger simmering in Nathan vibrated through their bodies and foretold that the night was far from over. If they survived. He pulled her behind a boulder and forced her to kneel behind it. Duncan followed, leaping down beside them.

Duncan chuckled as he checked his weapons. He pulled out a small blade from his boot. "She's not my wench, my lad. A bitter mouthful is that one. I wouldna take on the lady dragon for all the whiskey in Scotland."

"She sure as hell looked snuggled in your arms a moment ago."

Meg peered through the crevice. "If you two are finished besmirching my name, I'd like to know what we mean to do."

"He and I are going to finish this," Nathan said as he glanced over his shoulder. White lines had formed around his mouth. "And you—" he jabbed his finger in her direction, "will stay here."

"Oh, but I—"

"You'll do as you are ordered. And when we are done, you will confess everything to me."

"Excuse me, lass and laddie, but it appears our guests wish to play a wee bit more."

"Fools," Nathan muttered.

"Aye." Duncan grinned at him. He pointed to the blood-matted spot on his head. "I don't mind a scuffle or two." He fisted both weapons and jumped to his feet. "Care to play?"

"Try to stop me." Without a glance in Meg's direction, Nathan joined him on the other side.

Offering a prayer of protection, she listened as their grunts and curses wove their way toward the shore. Meg crawled away from her hiding spot and rose.

Three bodies littered the ground. That left three more. She still did not like the odds. Her blade would even the score. Following the sounds of battle, she ran down to the shore. Shadows danced and wavered. Blades struck and struck again.

Only two of the thieves were left standing. Their fight carried them into the water. Duncan's footing slipped and he went down on one knee. His arm rose to deflect the blow. He cursed as the mace caught his wrist and ripped the sword from his fist.

Meg pressed her knuckles to her mouth to keep from crying out. Sea spray mixed with her tears. She searched the beach. Where was the other man lurking?

Nathan impaled his opponent, and pushed him off with his boot heel. He spun to aid Duncan. He fought the muck, his legs churning to reach his next victim.

A sword in one hand, he swept the other weapon from the sheath strapped to his back and attacked with both weapons. The man went down with a strangled gurgle. The water sprayed as Duncan rolled out of the way.

Another charged Nathan from behind. He swung his war hammer.

"Nathan!" she screamed.

He stumbled, falling onto his back. The man crashed through the waves, his weapon aimed at Nathan's head.

The image of Nathan's blood mixing with the sea was too much. Lifting her skirts she ran toward them. She had to do something to save him. The weight of her dress slowed her progress. His head went under the water and did not resurface.

"No. No. No!" she screamed again. "Nathan!"

He shot out of the water's hold. His mane and clothes streamed with bracken from the firth's seabed. Roaring, his empty sword hand lashed out and missed.

A few more steps. Her fist tightened around her knife as she struggled to reach them.

His opponent bent over him and grinned. "Ah, the great Nathan Staves finally dies at my hand. Say hello to the DePierce men on your way to hell."

"Do it yourself." The blade from Nathan's back harness slammed into the man's chest. Blood bubbled as he fell and floated into the firth's mouth.

Nathan stumbled toward Duncan and lifted him by the shoulders. Meg slipped under Duncan's other arm, and together they carried him to shore.

Bending over, he pushed his palms against his thigh to catch his breath. "He'll need Anna's help. I'll send Brother John as soon as I reach the keep," he said, his voice harsh with emotion. Refusing to look at her, he turned without another word and left.

Meg's legs trembled, threatening to collapse under her weight. "How am I going to repair this?"

* * * *

After Nathan roused Brother John and Matthew from their beds and sent them to clean up the mess in the cove, he slammed through the double doors. The household may be dark, but he found his way to his bedchamber. He stripped off the wet and bloodstained clothes and threw them in a pile. Rage tore at him like wild boars, attacking, bringing blood and pain. Any wound he had ever received dimmed at the realization that Meg did not love him. He drew in a ragged breath filled with a thousand blades. She loved another. He yanked on his hair. How could this be?

He sank into the chair beside the hearth. Someone had seen to replacing the one he broke earlier in a mindless nightmare rage.

His hands dropped to the arms. Was this why she could not accept him? Did she fear him?

He shot up and began prowling his chamber. He'd certainly showed her the beast within. The night's events unfolded in his mind with each step. What could he have done differently? Nothing. He had fought and claimed lives for his home. Damn it. His home. His king's gift was becoming a stone around his neck. And now he found himself betrothed to a woman who apparently did not trust him with the truth and was plotting behind his back all along. For what? A few barrels of ale. A handful of coins.

He threw himself into the chair and reached for the flagon. Pouring a generous helping, he justified his outrage. He'd killed men in the past. But this time held a passion that he'd never known before. He feared for Meg's life. Beyond all reason, he feared for the woman who wanted another and he would do it again.

Drinking deeply, he let the ale swish over his tongue then slide down his throat. Time and time again, he completed the ritual until the events slowly receded. All that was left was the raw pain of taking another life. The knowledge that there was no other way did little to cool the burn.

It was like every other battle. The regret and the resignation.

Nathan sat up a little straighter. He did what he had to, to save those who were threatened. And by God, he would do it again. It was who he was, but would she ever see him in that light?

Would Meg ever look on him as she did the Scotsman? The worm of envy inched through his thoughts. He had to discover what drew her. Why did she leave the master's chamber only to run to Duncan Graham?

Nathan threw the mug into the fireplace. The flames licked at the alcohol. It made him want to weep. But that ability had been removed when he was a child. The king did not cherish tears. Therefore no one was allowed to show that weakness.

He tried to rise from his chair, but his body refused. The bruises were beginning to form. He probably should have sought Anna out for an unguent to dab on the cuts he had received. At the time, knowing Duncan and Meg were ensconced in the keep was comfort enough. That thought made his stomach twist. She was his betrothed. By God, he would not allow their dalliance to go on any further.

Lurching forward, he grabbed the door's latch and lifted the lock.

The door swung open. Meg stood before him. Wide-eyed and beautiful. His warrior maiden.

"By all that is holy," he choked out. "Why are you here? Are you a vision or sent here to torment me?"

* * * *

Meg stood outside Nathan's door. How she came to be there she did not know. Ever since the battle, for one could never call it a skirmish; it took lives. She could think of nothing else but finding comfort in Nathan's arms. Whenever she closed her eyes, all she saw was Nathan, his life about to be extinguished by the swing of an arm. And she relived the terror that he would no longer be in her life.

A shuddering breath that shook her to the bottom of her soul reminded her that she came for a reason. To only check on their new lord. That was all. Wasn't it?

He stood, barring the doorway, as if she were the enemy. His chest, sprinkled with copper coils, blocked her view into the bedchamber. She dropped her gaze and rejoiced in the lean hips and bared flat stomach. The mad desire to lick his stomach nearly brought her to her knees. And that would never do.

"I ask you," he voice rough with emotion, "why are you here?"

Meg gathered the courage that threatened to break away like a wild mare and contained it. Did they not call her the dragon lady behind their hands? Tonight, she would wear that badge proudly. Beside it was the only remaining thread that kept her from running to her bed and weeping into her pillow. She swallowed the fear and pushed him aside. "Giving my report, my lord." She swept off her night robe. Her chemise, the armor protecting the only item in which she had to barter. "Anna is seeing to the Scotsman. He is bound to the bed as you ordered." She paused to gauge Nathan's mood. "His wounds are not mortal."

"So your lover lives." He poured himself another hefty serving of ale.

"I will tell you once more, he is not my lover. Do not insult me again by making that assumption." Meg gritted her teeth and walked into the lion's den. Thoughts of the scene made her question leaving Anna and Duncan alone, but she felt it imperative to right her relationship with her betrothed. God help her. "Apparently my sister is most pleased with this news."

Nathan grunted. "I know what I saw."

"You understand nothing of what it was." It pushed her patience. Could the man at least save that for his men and a battlefield? Where was the knight that serving maids whispered about with feverish hope to turn his head? All she saw was an angry arrogant ass. "Damn it. Nathan. What more do you want from me?"

"My lady," he whispered. He stroked the gossamer material that barely contained her breasts. "I want nothing more than honesty."

She gasped when he flicked a finger over her nipples. Yes, she had come to him, baring all, but the want was more than she anticipated. Denying the fear clamping down on her soul, she placed her hand over his heart and pushed her way deeper into his chamber. To her surprise, he allowed her entrance without argument.

He caught her hand, trapping it under his. "You will explain. Now."

Gentle kisses rained down her lips. His tongue probed, seeking permission to enter. And she gave all that she had, opening, allowing; removing all barriers. If only this would continue on into the night, she would not have to reveal the secrets she had been guarding. She just wanted to feel loved and cherished. Was that too much to request? The thought of him turning away from her, ripped at her with furious claws.

"Can we not speak of this in the morn?"

He drew back, questioning what she offered. "We were to be wed in the morn. I have found you in a questionable position with another man, and I have thus killed others, and you wish to not speak of things?"

Sighing deeply, he set her aside. "My lady, when we do come together, we shall indeed find pleasure in our bed. But not this eve."

"You are refusing me?"

"I am saying until you are truthful, we cannot consummate this marriage." He reared back his shoulders. "The woman I take to wife will be my partner in all things. Until you understand and accept this, it cannot be."

"But the king," she sputtered.

"Will take exception, but I will bring our case to him. He will understand eventually." He ducked his head. "I spoke with Brother John earlier. We are agreed. We will postpone the nuptials."

He turned her, cradling her elbow, as he directed her to the door. Meg blinked. Her skin flushed at his refusal. "Please, you must let me explain."

Nathan lifted her hand and pressed a kiss to her knuckles. "My lady, I will gladly listen to what you have to say on the morrow. But if you press further, I will take you to bed without another word. Is this truly what you want?"

Meg turned and touched his firm jaw. She reached on tiptoe to press her lips to his. "Yes."

In less than a breath, he swept her up, barred the door, and placed her ever so gently on his great bed.

"My God, the thought of still having you possesses me." He stroked her face with one finger then trailed down the column of her neck, over her collarbone. He toyed with the ribbons that held her chemise together. The string fell away, exposing her breasts. "You are more beautiful that I imagined."

The cool night air slid over her bared flesh. Meg did not know whether to reach for him or cover herself. No man had ever seen her as such. Naked and needing...something. Instead, she let him look upon her. His forest green eyes brightened. If only he would touch her.

She squirmed, searching for what her body hungered for. She lifted her breasts. They felt heavy and wanting, waiting for his mouth to suckle. Her nipples pebbled.

Rewarded with his sharp intake of breath, she circled her breasts, cupping them, bringing them closer to his lips.

He watched her, a hawk following its next tasty meal but kept his hands clenched to his sides. "Is this truly what you want?"

Meg ran her hands down her chemise. The room had become too warm. The soft linen too hot to wear. "Yes. I recall your vow: That you would wait for me to come to you when I am ready. And here I am."

Grazing his thumb over her breasts, Nathan groaned and knelt beside her. Bracing one arm, he leaned over drawing her wrists over her head. The heat from his knee warmed her thighs. His breath caressed her skin as he hovered over her nipples. He stroked her belly with the flat of his hand, then skimmed across her mons. "Because you fear being put aside?"

His tongue flicked over her sensitive flesh, circling her nipples.

"No. Please," she whispered. Her hips writhing, she lifted her hips for him to slip his hand under her chemise. And yet he did not. What was he waiting for?

Nathan released her wrists and sat back on his haunches. A bemused look shadowed his face as he watched her. His chausses bulged at the apex of his thighs, proving his desire. "Then tell me why. Explain to me. Show me what you want from me."

"I don't...I mean I want to..." Meg bit her lip. He slid his hand over hers and pressed it to her mons.

"Your virginity is still intact?"

"You know this to be true." Meg scrambled to stand, fighting the unease that she had committed another blunder. "Mayhap I was too hasty." She gathered the edges of the chemise to her neck and attempted to leave the bed.

"Forgive me." His body blocked her path of escape. "I ask only because of the Scotsman, my lady."

"He is but a paid protector. He keeps the reivers from roving over our land." Meg winced and squeezed her eyes shut. Now she had done it. He would be furious and take it out on everyone involved.

Nathan tipped her chin. Instead of fury, she was greeted with a smile.

"Then we will begin here." His full lips claimed hers with a gentle kiss. He probed the rim of her mouth and Meg responded, tasting the ale on his tongue. She matched his dance of circles and swirls, testing the passion that simmered out of reach.

The length of his muscled body pressed into hers. The ridge of his engorged flesh pumped next to her belly. Separated by too many layers of clothing, he lifted the hem of her chemise.

She tensed, prepared to hear the rending of the soft material. Instead, his hands slid up the back of her thighs, cupping her buttocks, slipping a finger between her cheeks. He nudged her legs apart, giving him access to her slit.

Obeying, she held on to his shoulders as he devoured her mouth, her face.

Her legs quivered as he continued to explore her body. His fingers splayed over the small of her back. The chemise rose higher. Exposing her mons for his perusal.

Fingers trailed up her rib cage, encircling her breasts. He broke from their kiss to suckle and lave her nipples, and then carried the chemise over her head. It fluttered to the floor.

"Ah, Meg, you're as sweet as that honey that you covet." He opened her legs a little more and slid a finger between her folds.

Gasping, she could no longer keep her body still. She had to touch him. Feel his slick skin under her palms. She slid them down his shoulders, retracing the path he took on his back. Her fingers hooked his chausses. These had to come off.

She fumbled with the string holding them up. His anxious flesh poked at her hand, making her tremble even more.

Nathan stopped her efforts. His nostrils flared, reminding her of the stallion as he readied to mount his mare. "Patience. We've only just begun." He nipped her lips. "I shall explode if you touch me know."

Irritated, she ignored his command and continued to tug on his chausses. "'Tis unfair. I wish to see you. Touch you." Emboldened by his panting breath, she licked his nipples. "Taste you." Fascinated, she watched his nipples pebble.

"As you wish, my lady." Picking her up, he cradled her, her bottom exposed for him to explore. His fingers and hands left a fiery trail. Meg thought she might lose her mind by the time he laid her back upon the mattress.

She lay naked before Nathan. Waiting. Please God. To strip himself bare. She squeezed her thighs together. The muscles clenched and unclenched, sending jolts of pleasure to her core.

Nathan watched her as he untied the string and let the chausses drop to the floor. Freed from confinement, his cock tapped against the planes of his flat belly. He cupped his engorged flesh as if to tame it.

She gasped. So large. Too large. How was that going to enter her narrow slit? There must be pain. 'Twas why the horses coming together was so violent. Unable to bear the thought, she shut her eyes and turned away. Maybe she could convince him she had fallen asleep.

The heat between her legs began to cool. There was still time to change her mind. The mattress bent with is weight.

"Meg," Nathan said. "Look at me." His eyes still gleamed with passion, but they held a gentle expression that promised to do her no harm.

Meg rolled over. He lay on his side, facing her. His appendage in question still pulsed between them. He stroked her hip, tracing the crease between her thigh and abdomen. Her nipples contracted as he stared at her mouth. She licked her dry lips. They felt swollen to her tongue.

"Let me pleasure you," he whispered his voice laced with passion.

He traveled to her mons. She sucked in a breath. It had become more sensitive than before. He lifted her hand and placed it under his. "Your body already prepares for me."

She eyed him warily. "But you are so big. You will tear me asunder."

He rocked over, pressing her hand into the button of flesh while palming his burgeoning root. "I vow, when we do come together, you will be able to take me. 'Tis why I cannot let you touch me. Not yet."

She stared into his eyes. Did she trust him to care for her, to give? Not just take? A slow, lazy smile lifted the corners of his mouth as he slid down on his belly. He encircled her ankles and spread her legs. Waves of pleasure rippled up her thighs as he traveled toward her opening. Catching the back of her knees, he lifted them until her legs were bent. Tasting and feasting the whole way, his touch created shivers through her body. Meg clutched the bedsheet. Her toes curled as she clawed to maintain control. She did not want to let go. She wanted this feeling of pleasure to last for hours, if not days.

Her muscles clenched. He tongued wherever his whiskers scraped across her skin. Meg rolled her head. She gripped his broad shoulders, tugging at him, to bring him closer. There had to be a way to be closer. Skin against skin. Their sweaty bodies slid together.

Meg gasped as his mouth moved over the swollen lips of her core. He sucked on the nub of flesh, flicking it with his tongue. She dug her heels into the mattress, her hips lifting and lowering, aching for release. When he slipped his finger into the entrance between her legs, a keening moan slipped past her parted lips.

She needed more. Sweat glistened over his shoulders as he maintained his position despite her efforts to unseat him. His mouth closed over her as his fingers swirled inside. His thumb massaged her sensitive pearl. Her inside, clenched. Muscles she never knew existed bunched and released as she bucked against him.

Meg arched her back and cried out as wave after wave crashed over her. It pulled her in and out like the tide until she thought her soul was torn from her throbbing body. And then it slowly receded, leaving them panting, their bellies pressed together.

Nathan lay between her bent legs. He braced his arms, holding his weight off of her, as he leaned in to kiss her. He tasted of sex, of lovemaking.

"That was lovely," she said. "I never knew." She glanced down. His cock looked just as large. Dew clung to the tip. "But what of you?"

He bent his head to suckle her breast. First one and then the other. He looked up, that boyish grin on his face. One of mischief and the need for repentance. "This is where I take your virginity."

"There is more?"

"Indeed." His hand stole between them and found her apex. Fire reignited, sending trails of pleasure through her limbs.

She groaned at his touch and spread her legs. "Oh, yes, my lord."

Nathan shifted position and raised her arms over her head. Her breasts were left exposed, giving him access any time he pleased. She arched her back to graze her nipples against his chest, to have his silken hair tickle her sensitive flesh. The head of his cock pulsed against her entrance. Her hips lifted of their own volition giving him permission to take her.

He pressed deeper. Her opening widened, taking him in. "Meg," he whispered. Sweat glistened on his forehead. His arms trembled as he moved his hips.

Releasing her wrists, he spread her legs, lifting them over his shoulders. Meg grabbed his buttocks. Kneading the hard planes of his cheeks. Liquid slid between her legs, allowing him to rock in and out. Deeper and deeper.

He slipped his hand between them again and found the place that sent lightning through her core. She held on to him, her nails digging into his back, as her body quaked. Never could she have imagined that giving her virginity to her future husband would bring so much pleasure.

His body tensed as he raised his hips and lowered to the base of his root.

Meg's breath caught in her throat as she cried out. Stinging pain wrung the liquid desire from her core. She clamped her legs around his waist.

Nathan paused over her. He held his body firmly in place. "Forgive me. I didn't intend to hurt you."

"No," she said, stopping him from pulling away.

She cupped his jaw. His full lips showed signs of lovemaking. The reddish tints in his hair reflected the candlelight. "I'm fine. I just need a moment to catch my breath."

His hips rocked against her, returning to the rhythm that they found together. In no time at all she matched his pace. Faster and faster, they panted and cried out as they were carried over into a swirl of need that neither wanted to end.

Meg settled into his arms, her bottom nestled against him, and sighed. He kissed the back of her neck, nuzzling her ear. She flipped onto her back, her legs entangled with his, and smoothed his curling mane from his shoulders.

Letting her gaze burrow into those fathomless eyes that had seen and done so much, she feared that she might fall deeply in love with this man. What was she to do when he left and never returned from the battlefield?

She started to rise from the bed. How would she ever endure it if she were to lose him too?

"Stay," he said. Drawn to the warmth of his body, she wiggled next to him.

"But the others. Someone will know."

"I'll carry you back to your bedchamber before anyone is the wiser." He kissed the tip of her nose and snuggled closer. "Get some sleep," Nathan ordered. "'Tis our wedding day."

Hours later, as the morning birdsong began to filter through the windows, Meg rolled over in her bed. Still naked, she searched the room for Nathan. He'd done as promised and had delivered her to her bedchamber. She searched for her clothing and muttered a curse. Her chemise was not in her room.

Meg turned as a servant scratched on the door. She leaped into bed and drew the bedsheets up to her chin.

"My lady," the girl said. "My lord suggested you might want to sleep later than usual." She set a tray laden with bowls of steaming oats and whey and berries. "Though, I imagine you'll want to make haste." She glanced over her shoulder as she shook out the dress from the day before. "This being your wedding day and all."

Meg cringed. "Have you news where my sister, Lady Anna, might be? I wish she might attend me."

"Oh, yes, my lady. She's caring for the injured Graham a lay'n the bed. Brother John had him taken to the chamber next to the kitchen. Cook is near beside himself. Says he won't be feeding no thiev'n Scotsman. The man is a large one, ain't he?" Her eyes widened in appreciation of their guest and giggled. "In all sorts of ways, I'd wager."

"Brother John…"

"Summoned to our new lord's side. They be walking the village and outer buildings." She offered a hungry grin. "Another large one for certain. Is he not? You are sure to be blessed with children in no time at all," she predicted.

Meg did her best not to roll her eyes. "Please deliver a message to my sister that I will be there shortly." What were they thinking, leaving her gentle sister to tend to Duncan Graham? It was like leading a little lamb to a highland wolf.

Meg did not languish in the tub but made haste with her toilette and hurried down the hall to the chamber by the kitchen. Once she freed Anna from their guest, she would search out her future husband. Their union was a mistake. A moment of foolishness. She still intended for their marriage to be a passionless one. It was the only way she could protect her heart.

Voices drifted from the small chamber they used to house the vegetables during the winter months. The hair on Meg's neck prickled as she recognized Duncan's low rumble, followed by her sister's soft soothing voice.

"Be still. What have they done to you? Why are you bound to the posts?"

"All better for ye safety," Duncan teased.

"I'll have a word with my sister. You saved her life."

"Not the way your lord and new brother see it. I'm a threat." His chuckle belied his declaration. "Come here, lass. Sit awhile and let me take comfort in your presence."

"You know how it is, Duncan. Soon, though. I vow it."

"You'll come with me, Anna."

"I can't. You know this. Stay in Fletchers Landing. We can sort this out."

"No matter what ye think. They won't agree."

Meg picked up the candle's stand and let it drop on the side table near the door. She cleared her throat, making certain that she did not enter with them in a compromising position. It was hard enough not to rail at them for their stupidity. What nonsense was that Scotsman spewing, attempting to woo her sister? They had only met a few hours ago when he was brought in wounded from the skirmish against the smugglers. He required Anna's healing skill. Not her heart.

"Lady Anna," she called out. "Ah, there you are." Unwilling to wait for a reply, she straightened her skirts and squared her shoulders before charging into the room.

"Meg." Her sister leaped away from her position where she sat on the cot. Anna had neatly bound his head, covering part of a bruise that spread from his cheekbone and into his hairline. One arm was cradled in a sling.

The other one was attached to the bedpost by a stout rope. His large feet stuck out from under the thin blanket. A twinge of guilt pinched. He should have been given a better room in which to heal. The man had been injured while protecting her from the smugglers.

Then she spied the indentation where Anna had sat too close to her patient. Mayhap Nathan's decision to hold him here should be applauded.

"What brings you?" Anna asked. After smoothing her mussed hair, she ran her palms down her skirt, and tipped her chin in an air of defiance. Meg's worry increased as her pliable sister shifted into a woman intent on protecting her man.

"I came to check on our prisoner."

"Patient," Anna snapped.

Meg nodded, and took another route to pry Anna from this room. "I am to be wed this day, am I not?" She did her best to pout. "I expect to have my brother and sisters nearby, to bear witness to the nuptials."

"His lordship still intends to wed you after you admitted your arrangements with the thieving bastards?" Duncan eyed her from his bed. "'Tis a forgiving man that you marry."

Meg glanced out the chamber door. Did someone listen to their conversation the same way she had moments ago?

"Ah," he said, nodding from his bed. "Then ye wish for the plans to continue as your king commands.

"'Tis good your sister is an obedient servant to the king," Duncan said to Anna. His fingertips trailed up her arm.

Anna and he shared a look, sending alarms through Meg's body. Her hands curled, flexing into fists.

"Take your hand off my sister, Duncan Graham."

Anna gasped. "'Tis no need for unkindness. Duncan must heal before he leaves us." She untangled her arm from his grasp and stepped out of reach. But not before she smoothed his bangs from his face.

"Forgive me, Duncan Graham." Meg's stomach clenched as she dipped a curtsy in his direction. "'Tis certain I misspoke. A man, such as you, would never take advantage of a maiden in the safety of her home." She caught his gaze and held it.

"Och," he exclaimed. "It never entered my thoughts." He shook his good arm, making the bed tremble like it was made of kindling. "Least not while I'm trussed up like a boar for slaughter." He chuckled at their discomfort. "Come now, my ladies, I was only jesting."

"Lady Anna, your presence is wanted in the kitchen." Meg added before she could offer an objection. "Please see to Baldric."

"I'll attend to him at once." Anna turned, her cheeks flushed, she began gathering her salves. Her voice rose. "As soon as I—"

"At once," Meg snapped. She had to put a stop to the way Duncan followed Anna's every movement with hungry eyes.

"Lass," Duncan called from his bed. He swung his bare legs out from the coverlet and searched for the floor with his foot. "Cease your rushing about. I'm well enough to see to myself. Release me now, and I shall be on my way."

Anna pursed her lips and lifted her patient's leg, returning it to his bed. "We have no right to keep him bound to the bed."

Meg had seen her sister minister to other's needs many times before. Many times Anna had directed that her patient needed their clothes removed. Whether from chill or damp, fever or wound. But there was something about this patient that made her aware of his nakedness under the coverlet. She must speak with Brother John.

She caught her lip between her teeth. That too would change once she was wed to Nathan. The king had given away more than just their family holding; he had given away her rights. Who would seek her out for advice? Would Cook inquire her desires for the meal or look only to please his lord? Her parents dealt with each other in a partnership. Was it possible to build a similar relationship with Nathan? There was much she must discuss with Nathan before they wed. And if they could not come to an agreement, she would have to leave. Mayhap even flee to the land in the north.

"Meg," Anna said. "If you insist on lending a hand, at least pay attention. When do you intend to confront Sir Nathan regarding my patient?"

Quashing a shiver, she turned her focus away from the unknown and tied back the drapes surrounding the bed. She threw open the shutters. A sea breeze cooled her skin. A sigh slipped past her lips. "Sir Nathan is Lord of Fletchers Landing. 'Tis his command. Not mine that keeps you here."

The basket filled with flagons of oils and unguents hit the floor with a heavy thump. "Duncan helped saved your life. I cannot help him if you insist on treating him as a prisoner." She returned to his side, lifting the flagon of ale to his lips.

"In Sir Nathan's eyes, that is what he is," Meg said. Ignoring the flash of anger crackling in the room, she added, "Anna. I must speak with you and expect you in my bedchamber anon."

Duncan lifted a sardonic brow. "Where is the lady dragon's fire?" He stretched the leather thongs tied to his wrists. "You've ordered me manacled to the bedpost, lass. I shan't be attempting anything nefarious while you're away." He flicked his fingers. "'Tis an auspicious day. Go now, run to your man, Lady Meg. Your beautiful sister and I will find a way to keep ourselves amused until the time comes."

Meg gritted her teeth. "We have an agreement."

"Aye, but you've broken it more than once. From now on, 'tis the Lord of Fletchers Landing that I mean to deal with."

"You took money for protection," Meg hissed under her breath as she bent to straighten the bedclothes.

"And I mean to keep that bargain. But not from this bed. Find a way to change it." He pierced her with a glare. "Those men have comrades who will come looking for them. Their assault is not over."

Meg's hands stilled.

"My lads will take notice of my absence soon enough. They'll seek me out. You know this to be the truth."

"We'll send a messenger.

"'Tis not that simple, as ye well know, my lady."

"Certes, when they learn of your injury and that we are caring for your wounds they will maintain peace until you give word otherwise."

"And if they don't? If they fear for me, they will come and do more damage than any night of roving." His auburn main of hair caught the sun as he shook his head. "Smaller misunderstandings have caused great pain in times past. We have not only placed your village in danger. We have placed the members of my clan in its path, as well." She felt him searching for the weakest link in her armor. "Would you have their blood on your hands, my lady?"

Chapter 17

Nathan paced through the village and surrounding outbuildings. It was high time he acted like the new Lord of Fletchers Landing. He glanced at the monk striding beside him. Did the man know that Meg spent the night in his bedchamber? Nathan's groin tightened. His heart beat a rapid rhythm in anticipation of seeing her, having her in his bed. He attempted to shake off the distraction. Was that all it took to turn his mind away from his responsibilities?

They walked past the chandlery. Little remained of the building. The scent of wood smoke lingered despite the villagers' efforts to rebuild the structure. Puddles of melted wax stained the stone path.

"Matthew, we'll start with this one." He directed the steward to the charred rafters. "I want the roof material changed from thatch to shale."

The woman clinging to his thoughts appeared at his elbow. He would forever link the taste of honey to that of her lips. None could be compared. He offered her a gentle smile, his gaze lingering on her mouth. How much time would have to pass before they wed and shared their bed? Memories of her soft moans sent his blood coursing through his veins.

He tucked her hand through his arm. "Good morn, my lady. I trust that you slept well."

His arm tightened as Meg stumbled and broke eye contact. She yawned, barely covering her mouth. "'Twas an uneventful night."

Nathan swept his gaze over her face. Her lie brought a pretty flush to her cheeks and brought back fresh memories of their night of passion. Her curves fit perfectly next to his. "Mine was beyond exciting. Thrilling even. I still wear bruises from our adventure at the cove."

A soft rose color spread up her neck. "Not all of us knew of that incident," she said under her breath.

"'Tis a small village, my lady," Matthew reminded her from where he trailed behind them. "The aftermath of the battle was a rare sight for some. The old ones retold long tales deep into the morn."

"You could have brought reinforcements," Nathan muttered to the monk and steward.

Brother John cleared his throat. "Aye, it was noisome at all hours." He glowered at Nathan. "Mayhap I should move to the chapel after today's festivities."

"The wedding can wait," Meg said in a rush under her breath. "I must speak with you. In private."

Nathan arched a brow. In private? Had she searched him out for a reason? Perhaps to smile and warm him as she had a few hours earlier? Her sighs of pleasure had remained with him throughout the morning.

Her fingers trembled against his arm. Mayhap she still feared that foolish curse of hers. He always appreciated a challenge and he had only just begun to show her the pleasures to be found in their bed. Without another thought of the two men in attendance, he brushed his lips over her temple. "Once we are through here, I shall escort you to the master's chambers. We will speak of many things then."

Brother John cleared his throat. "The Lord of Fletchers Landing wishes for the moving of the outbuildings. He wishes them rebuilt with stronger, safer materials. Starting immediately."

Meg gasped and regarded Nathan from head to toe. He itched under her frowning scrutiny and had come to the conclusion they would have their meeting in private sooner than they thought. "Meg, 'tis not that difficult to comprehend."

She withdrew her hand and stepped away from him. Her nostrils flared, reminding him of a wild mare. Anger snapped from her dark brown eyes. "I understand more than you realize. You forget that I have been in charge since the death of my parents." She whipped her skirt away from him as if she feared vermin would leap from his tunic and take residence on her body. Meg cut her glare to Matthew and Brother John. "I disagree with our new lord. It'll cost extra. Extra that we don't have at the moment."

"Worth it if we don't lose everything in a fire." He redirected his thoughts and surveyed the rest of the small buildings. "They should be moved out and away from the tower keep. Again, the roofs made of shale will help slow a fire if one does start again."

She pivoted on her heels. "Whose treasure do you intend to use?"

"Mine." He watched the color from her cheeks drain. Did she think that he came to her as a pauper? Nathan grunted. Her disdain came from more than their night of passion. If she wanted a battle on the village streets instead of in private, so be it. He would not be the one to start it. He took a deep breath. "I've had some of my spoils of war set aside."

"You intend for this before winter falls?"

"Not enough time. The materials for the structures will need to be sent for."

"We haven't the manpower," she argued. Her steps quickened.

"Not to worry, my sweet. I've sent a messenger to Lockwood Castle to the south. Sir Darrick is lord of that land. He'll send a few of his men to help rebuild and strengthen Fletchers Landing."

"Why would he do that?"

"He owes me." He slowed Meg's pace by curling his fingers around her hand.

"But we have no need of more men. We have managed well without soldiers underfoot."

"I disagree." Nathan tucked her close to his side. "Your disregard is insulting," he said under his breath. "You wished to speak with me, and so we shall. Look around you, my Meg. Do you wish for everyone to worry that they are no longer safe with either of us at the helm?"

The villagers milled around, offering signs that they were busy about their tasks. Nathan knew otherwise. He had already noticed their nervous conversations. They moved about but produced nothing with their labor.

He dipped his head in salute. "How goes it master ale keeper?"

"'Tis a fine day, my lord," Harrigan touched his cap as he struggled to load a keg onto a cart. Worry tugged at the older man's mouth.

"A moment." Nathan left Meg to help with the unwieldy barrel. He would have shared a cup of ale if not for the woman standing alone, looking as lost as he often felt.

"Move over, my man." He nudged the bearded one over. "Let me show you how our king's knight is able."

"My lord," Harrigan groveled. "I cannot let you dirty yourself."

"What, and take away the opportunity to display the strength my betrothed is receiving in the marital bargain this afternoon?"

"No, my lord." Harrigan swept off his cap, crushing it in his meaty fist. "Many thanks, Sir Nathan. I thought to handle it all by myself. 'Tis a wonder King Henry has let you leave his side."

Nathan offered Meg a sly wink as he returned and tucked her hand in the crook of his elbow. His heart warmed when a suppressed chuckle filtered through her fingers.

"You're right. I have been foolish." Meg's rib cage expanded and compressed with each shuddered breath as she released the tension.

He flexed his arm, offering a gentle nudge. Hope began to build.

They walked past the unusually quiet smokehouse. Nathan's brow furrowed. "Brother John, what news have you regarding our guests?"

"They were a godless bunch," he said. "Those that clung to their last breath refused prayer for their soul. A few of them mentioned your name, Sir Nathan. Expected you'd soon join them where they were headed." The monk crossed himself. "I left the lone survivor with the smithy Wayland. They appeared familiar with one another."

Nathan's shoulders began to crawl, alerting him to danger. He tried the door and the rusted iron locks flaked away in his hand. His mood began to sour. "By whose anvil and hammer were these created?" A fearful silence followed on the heels of his question.

"The blacksmith," Matthew uttered.

"The only place to stow our prisoner and we put him in here? Shite." Nathan cursed his misfortune for the king's gift of rot and fools.

"Stay where you are, Meg," he ordered. "Matthew, stay by your lady and protect her. If you fail I will cut you down myself."

Brother John drew his sword as they pushed open the door. It swung on rusted hinges, announcing their arrival. A torch wavered as the breeze caught it. The scent of fish lying on the drying racks filled his nose. Legs of smoked mutton hung from the rafters. Vessels of preserved goods lined the shelves. But the improvised cell that should have held the blacksmith was empty.

Nathan knelt and tested the corroded locks. They, too, were brittle to the touch. "More of his handiwork?" He rose, dusting his hands free of rust.

"Aye," Brother John growled. "I curse him for his deeds."

Nathan gripped the man's cassock as they left. "Tell me what he's worked on since he arrived."

Brother John began to list the items. Nathan's stomach began to twist by the time they reached Meg and Matthew. He would have someone's hide for this blatant negligence.

"Matthew, are you not steward of the keep?" he snarled. The steward's tunic wrinkled under his fist. The man's face turned a mottled purple as Nathan tightened his grip.

"Cease this madness," Meg cried. She pried at his fingers, breaking him from his rage. "You're killing him."

Nathan shifted his glare, placing it on all of them. "I would it be him, and not you or your family."

"My lord," Matthew choked out under the stranglehold, "we learned that Wayland and the wench Millicent came from the direction of Carlisle. Mayhap the others did too."

"Or they work with Duncan Graham and his clan," Nathan said. "'Tis time I discovered why our large friend was waiting at the cove."

He released the steward. The time for punishment had passed. Their need for answers grew with each moment they delayed. "I want every lock and hinge checked."

Matthew nodded as he rubbed the raw spot on his neck. "Aye," he said, then trotted off to do Nathan's bidding.

"Meg, you and Brother John wait for me in the master's library. I will meet you there once I've had a word with Duncan Graham."

"I implore you to listen, my lord," she cried.

"The time for pretty speeches is over, my lady," Nathan said. He pushed open the double doors. They swung on silent hinges. At least one door was in good repair. Thank God, since the door's size and weight would kill should it happen to fall on an unsuspecting victim.

Meg planted her feet to block his path. Her slim hands pressed into his chest. "I must explain. In private."

Nathan nodded and took her by the hand. "Brother John, I assume you'll need to attend us." The monk swept his tunic up in his fists and followed on their heels as they climbed the winding stairs.

The heavy doors stood before them. No longer locked, the room behind the doors proved to be a welcoming haven that Nathan had not anticipated. He bit back the smile. No use in allowing Meg to know his pleasure. Judging by her mood, she was intent on forgetting the pleasure they shared the night before.

He shoved through the doors. Meg still pinned close to his side. "You have your privacy. Speak as you wish, but do so with truth or not at all."

* * * *

"Truth?" Meg's chest rose and fell rapidly. One of the first items she intended to address when life had returned to some kind of peaceful normalcy was to slow the speed in which he strode. A lady cannot maneuver the steps as easily when laden down with skirts. "Why are you pursuing the need for men? I do not require them."

"You...we," Nathan corrected, "do not have enough able-bodied men to watch our walls. And 'tis apparent we do not have protection for our keep or our village. The people know this. Why are you so damn stubborn and refuse to accept this fact?"

"Our protection is handled." Meg cut her gaze to Brother John. "What say you, monk? Have you nothing to add to ease your lord's soul?"

The brother's grayed curls quivered. "No, child. 'Tis not for me to share."

Meg rolled her eyes. "When have you never had an opinion?"

Nathan puffed his chest. "I will not tolerate secrets. Whatever pertains to Fletchers Landing will be told. Or punishment will be met."

Where had the gentle man from the previous night gone? Did he retreat when the sun rose overhead? Would she know him only in the dark hours? His eyes scoured her until she felt raw from the distrust in his gaze.

Meg took a deep breath and prayed God would find a way to soften her news. "I paid Duncan Graham for protection. To keep the reivers from roving over our land. It has been a peaceable agreement. Until now."

The crease in Nathan's brows deepened. "I've seen the ledgers. How did you do this?"

Meg looked to Brother John. Would he support her? Or release her to the winds and let Nathan's ire send her to punishment. She received her answer when the damn monk found the navigator's lens more interesting than their discussion.

The old man sighed and spun the glass as he turned. A rainbow of lights bounced across the wall. "Your arrangement with the Clan Graham is flawed. 'Tis why I sent for your assistance, Sir Nathan. Our Lady Meg is trusting of so few, but when she does relent, it is to a fault."

Her breath caught. Betrayed by her father's trusted confidant.

Nathan turned, his glare seeking hers, searching. "How much trusting has been done?"

She cleared her too-dry throat and poured a healthy helping of ale. The cool liquid quenched her thirst and then left her just as nervous as before she took a drink. Her hand shook as she set the pitcher down. Would their marriage begin on distrust and hatred? She could not allow it. She had bared herself body and soul. They had shared the night. He knew of the places that made her toes curl when he licked and sucked.

And she knew what made him lose control.

She slammed the empty horn cup on the table. "You know for yourself that there has been nothing shared between the Scotsman and me."

"And yet you trust him. Over me?"

"He has proven himself worthy of my trust. What of you?"

Meg felt the blood drain from her face. The room spun as panic built. Would he take offense and beat her? As lord, he had that right.

"Leave us," he ordered the monk.

"I think, mayhap..."

"You will do as I say," Nathan warned.

Meg trembled, awaiting the eruption that would surely come. A part of her soul broke off to argue with her conscience. Would he call off the wedding? Defy the king? 'Twas what she wanted. Was it not?

Brother John did not argue as she anticipated, but nodded and did as he was bid. The door thumped shut. Meg stepped back as Nathan approached her, cutting the distance between them. She ached for the time when she found safety in his arms. Was it so easily fractured?

"Meg." His voice soft as lamb's wool wrapped around her, sealing her fate.

Nathan cupped her chin, forcing her to look into his eyes. She nearly lost herself in their mossy warmth. This is where she wanted to stay, but she feared it was created by the faeries. A trap; easily found and rarely escaped.

"You mentioned the need to speak in private. What is it you wish of me?"

Heaven help me. If only she could tell him how her body still hungered for him. Instead she was forced to explain her agreement with Duncan and the smugglers. Her throat tightened. What if he turned her family from the land? It was all that they knew.

"Help me trust what you say," Nathan said. "Tell me your secrets, my lady."

"And what secrets do you keep from me? Either we do this together, or we are already lost."

"I vow to share this keep. This land," he murmured.

She arched her neck as he nibbled a trail down her neck. A sigh whispered through her lips. Her legs threatened to wrap around his middle on their own volition. Meg tore away from his hold, putting distance between her breasts and his masterful lips. The floor called to her. It begged for her to lie on her back and spread her legs. She wanted him to return, to sink deep and ride with her to the brink of madness and joy. Panting from the mere thought of what could be, she drew in a breath and prepared to tell him all. Her nipples brushed against her bodice. They pebbled, aching for more. At what price? She stepped out of reach. The loss of contact with his lips flayed her skin and broke open her heart. If only he would listen.

"We keep the peace by paying for protection. That which we make, we sell," Meg said in a rush. Nathan's scrutiny bore into her, demanding all. "And that which we cannot sell in Carlisle, we sell to the smugglers." She glanced through her lashes, clenching her jaw until her teeth ached. What would he say?

Nathan walked to her father's spyglass. It swung back and forth as he searched for something. Meg waited. The silence stretched.

When his outrage and blinding blow never came she dared cut the distance between them. She placed her hand on his sleeve. The muscles tensed and bunched under her palm. "And what have you to reveal before we are wed? What is it that you want from me?"

* * * *

What could he say to her? *I thought I was losing my mind, my soul. Then I found you. And then the pieces began to return. Only now they no longer resemble who I was. But who I am. Only I don't know who that is anymore.*

Nathan played with the tube. It was easier to touch the cool metal. He knew if he allowed himself to reach out for her, he would take her on the table. Too many things were unresolved. He never wanted to see her looking at him with fear. Never again. Coward that he was right then, he would ride away before he let that happen. So, instead of seeing the distrust in her eyes, he forced his attention on the navigator's glass.

It fascinated him to know that he could look through a set of lens and be brought so close. Mayhap he would send it to Henry. A gift to remind his liege that he was needed on the battlefield. He searched the bailey and then the tilting yard below. The movement brought the terrain in sight. It was clear that the path to the private cove was the beginning of the map. Did he dare reveal the primary reason his king sent him?

Ah, but there were the smugglers. And the Scotsman. How was he to move forward with any plans if Duncan Graham hovered over him? He could not find fault in Meg's plans. They were set in favor of the village. The only one who paid was Meg. And what a dear price she had forfeited. There were weary lines about her mouth and eyes. 'Twas his duty to see them removed.

If only she would give him more. She had told him of the guilt she bore. She revealed the heartache. One in which he believed she should never have accepted. To come to him, offering up her trust, had nearly brought him to his knees and he never wanted to break that fragile trust that had only just begun.

Judging from the skirmish, there were few smugglers remaining. They had mentioned his name. Linking it to the bastards Vincent and Hugh DePierce. Mercenaries without someone to pay their bills were an angry and hungry lot.

Nathan's stomach cramped. His heart slammed into his chest. They would stop at nothing to gain what they determined was theirs. He gripped the wooden table, fingers digging into its surface. The leather journal Henry sent to him rested near his hand. A breeze must have caught a corner of the parchment, lifting it enough to draw his attention.

What could he offer, but his own truth?

Nathan dropped his hands to his sides. He flexed his fingers. The only saving grace he could latch on to was realizing he had not slipped into a mindless walking nightmare. He almost wished that it was. Then he could awaken and find himself nestled against his new wife. Unable to look upon the contempt he feared he might see, he turned his back to her. He braced his hands over the window casing and peered into the bailey.

"I desire a woman to love me for who I am. Not because it pleases the king. Or seals an agreement that keeps her safe from poverty. I desire a woman to challenge me, and respect me, and trust me. I desire a friend in whom I can confide. One who I can share my bed and body with and know that when I have grown old, we will still come together and hold each other. I desire my woman, no, my wife, to want me as badly as I want her. I desire to create a family that I can oversee, protect and nurture. I desire my wife to love me."

He shrugged his shoulders. The aches and pains from all the battles he had ever fought never left him feeling as raw as in that moment. "To love me. For. Me. A broken knight. One who still has dreams and aspirations."

Silence filled the room. Had she left him as he bared his soul? Gathering his courage in case he faced an empty chamber, he turned to face Meg. "I thought I had found all that I desired and so much more in you."

"Imagine my surprise when I discovered you standing across the stream. My beautiful warrior. Our king sent me to search out a treasure." He shook his head, running his hands through his hair. "I never intended or knew that he would hand over Fletchers Landing or force us to wed." He turned, lifting his head, he searched for her understanding. "I swear it."

Fearing what he might see, he shut his eyes. His flinched at the first touch of her hand. Meg stroked his back. His muscles contracted and then turned to liquid as he reveled in her gentle caress. "I might have failed in finding the king's treasure. But instead I found something greater. I found you, my healing Margaret Grace."

"'Tis a bit frightening. Isn't it?" she whispered.

Nathan turned, catching her hand to kiss the crest of her fingers. He blinked, surprised by the tears scorching his lids. "I never meant to harm you or your family."

"Tell me of the treasure," she whispered. "How may I help?" She traced his cheek. Her fingers danced over his jaw, down his neck. "I must confess.

I've scoured those caverns. Followed the paths into the caves. There is no treasure to offer our king."

Nathan cupped her chin, drawing her deeper into his embrace. Their lips grazed, sending a tension to his loins. "Years ago, while in my youth, I vowed to never give in until my dying breath. I will stand and fight. And this I vow again, to King Henry and to you."

Meg swiped at the tears streaming down her cheek. "I do not ask that of you. My wish is that you live to a ripe old age. If you wish to be a treasure seeker, than we shall do it as one."

Nathan's spirit lightened. Years had passed since he felt this light. Knowing that someone cared whether he returned from battle or not brought a grin that he could not contain.

"Then let us away to our patient. Mayhap Duncan Graham has an idea of the hill or valley our prisoners have run to."

Meg dug her heels in as she held him back. "He is a good man. He saved our lives. You shared a battle. I ask that you take this into consideration."

Jealousy, wrought in a dragon's form, reared its head. He curled his fists wanting to strike out at anyone who stood in his way. "I spoke with him once. The man lied."

"Patience. For me." Her slender fingers wrapped around his upper arm, drawing his attention. He sighed. He was lost. The woman had but to wiggle a finger and he would come running. He dared not reveal the power she held over him. "I'll speak with the head of the Clan Graham when we are through here."

Meg's gasp surprised him. Her beautiful obsidian brown eyes widened and drew him into her spell. "Head of the clan?" she squeaked.

Nathan could no longer ignore the lure of her mouth and leaned in. "Aye," he said. "I'll speak with him anon."

Her fingers dug into his hair, tugging, kneading until he wanted her to consume him. What could he say? He was lost into her charms and he did not want to turn back.

"They'll come for him," Meg warned, her lips moving against his, driving him to distraction.

"If they do, we'll be ready. Either the man will call them off or there will be a battle."

Meg pulled away, leaving a yawning empty cavern that he never wanted to know again. "A battle. We are a village. Not an army of soldiers. Families. Women and children already striving to survive while their men are away."

"There will be peace."

"How can you know this?"

Desperate to ease her heart, he swept up her hand and caught a fingertip with his tongue. "I will make it happen. This I vow."

She sighed despite the concern etched on her brow. "How? You will be too busy searching for the king's nonexistent treasure."

"I have to do this."

"And you have to protect your people. They depend on you. On us."

Nathan growled and shoved his hands behind his back to keep from slamming a fist into the wall. All he wanted was the sharing of secrets. Easy things like admitting to pleasuring oneself when no one was about. Not the refusal of taxes. Or the information gathering of the people to the north of the debatable lands.

"Meg," Baldric called. He stood in the doorway. A questioning glance swept over them. "Is there truly treasure hidden in the caverns?" He bit his lip, an accusatory glare swept over the chamber and stopped on Nathan. "Mayhap you won't have to wed the bastard after all."

Chapter 18

"Baldric, never say such a terrible thing."

"'Tis true isn't it? I heard them talking in the village. He's Nathan Staves of nowhere. He's not good enough for you. To be our lord." He limped forward. His little sword drawn from its sheath.

Meg rushed to her brother and knelt before him. His little body trembled against her chest. "Baldric, my love. Where did you get this fine sword?"

"From the blacksmith. He," Baldric said, pointing in Nathan's direction, "ordered it from Wayland before they locked him up."

"Put it away." She pried his fingers from the hilt. It clattered against the floor. "'Tis not as simple as that. We must do as our king edicts."

He lifted his head. Angry tears slid down his cheeks. They dripped from his chin and stained the leather jerkin. It joined the myriad of stains from days before. He had determined he must wear the garment ever since he had his first lesson of swordplay with Sir Nathan. When he had thought of the knight as a friend. "I won't let him harm you, Meg," he cried.

Her heart broke. "Nathan would never harm me. He is attentive. Gentle. Do you not recall how he championed Whitefoot for you?"

"I heard you arguing." Baldric sniffed, wiping the tears with his sleeve. Lips still turned down, he glared at Nathan. "I saw him grab you. Rough like. You were fighting him."

She glanced over her shoulder. Nathan stood still, his hand hung limp at his sides. His skin had paled visibly next to his auburn curls.

Worry.

Sadness.

Compassion.

These emotions flitted over his countenance. Nathan cared what she thought of him. She knew in that moment that what she said was not a lie. Nathan did care for her. He would never purposely harm her or her family. Would they ever fall deeply in love? How did one truly know? She had to give them a chance and hope that it would happen. Meg offered an understanding smile over her brother's head. Nathan rewarded her with an arched brow. The corner of his mouth wavered and tugged upward.

She gripped Baldric's shoulders. They had become stronger, wider than she recalled. It was time she treated him like the growing boy that he was becoming. He attempted to turn away, forcing her to bring him to face her. She winced. "Baldric, how did you come by that bruise?"

He moved under her hands. "I don't recall. I must have tripped. You know how clumsy I am."

Meg closed her eyes. The image of his limp had already embedded itself behind her lids. Perhaps it was best not to make a fuss over it. "You're growing. It happens to the best of us."

"'Tis why I can protect you now, Meg." He gripped her hands. "You don't have to marry him or anyone else."

"Baldric, you must listen. Sir Nathan and I are to be wed. On this day." She brushed his damp forehead with her lips. "I ask that you be strong and welcome him as your lord. He will be part of our family."

"Mother and Father…?" Worry marred his fair complexion.

"Would have approved." She nodded, and locking her gaze to Nathan's, they shared a moment. He took a step toward them, before pausing to scrape his fingers into his hair.

Meg grinned. Hope began to bloom. She had confidence that that her family would grow to care for him. Just as she had.

She looked at Nathan, her betrothed. A shiver of anticipation ran through her body. "'Tis time for you to wash, Baldric. You'll want to present yourself in a good light as I want you, Phillipa, and Anna to bear witness to our marriage." She stood, tugging Baldric with her and nudged him toward the door. "Sir Nathan and I are to see one of Anna's patients."

"The big burly one? He's much larger than you, isn't he, Sir Nathan? Imagine that sword fight would be a great one I would hate to miss seeing." Not waiting on a response, he grabbed her hand. "May I linger a little while longer, Meg?"

Nathan chuckled. "He enjoys the lens. Let him stay, Meg," he said. "What harm could it do?"

She bit her lip. Baldric's foot dragged a little heavier than usual. She would ask Anna to check with him and perhaps give him one of her boiled bark unguents that returned one's health. She prayed he was not coming down with a sickness. Dread gnawed at her. Had she dared Fate yet again by seeking her own bit of happiness?

Baldric narrowed his liquid blue eyes over Nathan. "Many thanks, Meg. 'Tis true that I like to look out the window and imagine what the world is like beyond Fletchers Landing." He held out his hand. "I ask for your forgiveness, my lord. I should have never repeated what our people were whispering."

Nathan bowed his head and gave a nod. "Mayhap we shall be able to continue our lessons of swordplay come the new day."

"Mayhap," Baldric muttered. He spun on his heel and left them with only his back to see.

Appalled, Meg shook her head in wonder. She must look into his training. "You will return and apologize again. This very moment."

"Let it be," Nathan said. He held out his arm. "He'll come around eventually."

Meg let him lead her down to the sickrooms that Anna had set up in the tower.

* * * *

"'Tis not true," Nathan said quietly. "I'm not a bastard."

Meg nodded and kept her focus on lifting her skirts to clear the stairs. "It does not matter."

"It does," he argued. "Though both of my parents died from sickness, my bloodline is strong. I was young, but old enough to foster into Sir Damien's castle. He would have preferred that I stayed in the kitchens. But I demanded to show my strength. Much like Baldric has." The memory made him smile. "I knew that disease took my family from me, but I wanted to find a way to protect those I cared for. And the only way that I had was by using my brawn." He winked in an attempt to make her smile. "And my quick wit."

She slipped her hand into his. "You misunderstand. It does not matter to me. I will speak with my family. Show yourself to be a good man. Then they will accept you as you are."

Nathan shook off the sadness that threatened to tear him down. When had he become the ogre in Baldric's eyes? The boy had mentioned overheard whispers in the village. And witnessed an argument with Meg.

He glanced down at Meg. Her ebony hair shined like luxurious silk. His betrothed. Did she fear him too? How were they to come together in their union if they could not get beyond this impasse?

"Do you intend to join in questioning the Scotsman? Would you not wish to prepare for our nuptials?"

"You've met him before. You know the man that he is."

Nathan sighed, and paused on the step below her. "I met him over a fire, and he answered my questions with lies."

"And you met him again. His back pressed against ours as we fought."

"His sword arm is strong. I'll give you that."

"And now we keep him a prisoner."

"Because you have not been forthcoming with information. Now I must demand answers why he was there in the first place."

"I told you. We had an agreement for protection. There were difficulties with the smugglers. Someone was stealing our supplies and the orders ready for delivery. He went to the cove to ensure that there were no more problems."

"He did a pathetic job of it, wouldn't you agree? S'pose he is taking two bites of the Shepherd's pie?"

Turning, he led her into the solar. Two of their servants had scrubbed the room, leaving behind an herbal fragrance in their efforts. Fresh flowers adorned every available surface in preparation for the ceremony.

"Leave us," he grunted at the women cleaning out the hearth.

"'Tis no need to be rude," Meg muttered. Hands planted on her hips, she dug in her heels and returned to the source of their disagreement. "Duncan Graham helped to save our lives."

Nothing would please Nathan more than to rid his land of that man. But he could not do so without ensuring that he had not released a wolf into the henhouse.

"Where was he during the fire? Is he working with the blacksmith? Or the smugglers? DePierce's mercenaries? Or is he a clansman who searches for additional ways to pad his purse?"

Her eyes widened as she absorbed his suspicions. "He would not do that. I'm sure of it."

"You have a good and caring heart, Meg love. And mayhap, you are right to trust him. But I have yet to determine his motive for not returning to his clan when you informed him there was no longer immediate coin to be found for his services."

Her rosy cheeks paled. She compressed her lips as if to seal off a confession. What did she hide? Was there more than protection money that kept the Scotsman from finding his way home? "Ah, Meg," he groaned. "Alright, I vow to keep our conversation peaceful."

His gaze followed her lips as they widened into a smile. "And if he gives good solid answers you will release him?" she asked."

"Will it please you if I agree to your request?"

He could not fight the temptation any longer and slipped his fingers under her long tresses. She tilted her cheek toward his hand. Like a kitten seeking a long stroke over its pelt. Her sigh stroked his skin.

"I should find my sisters and seek their help with the preparations," she said, but made no effort to move from his embrace. His heart skipped. They had shared a moment that he thought only available to his friends, Darrick and Ranulf. A woman to hold through the wee hours of the morn and never tire from his touch. A wife to mother his children. Family.

"'Tis been a while since I've spoken with your sisters. Do they, too, despise the sight of me?"

"No." She pressed a consoling hand on his arm. "Don't be foolish. They are busy with their tasks that come from the heart."

"Passions like your beehives?"

"And my honey meads." She wrinkled her nose. "But they are not near as compelling as their passions. Phillipa would never leave the barns and fields if I allowed it. And Anna cares for her gardens as if her plants were children, but never more than when she is caring for those in need. Family usually acquires the last position of importance. We do it for the people of Fletchers Landing."

"It sounds like a lonely existence." He recognized the lost soul in her description and wished to improve it. He slid his thumb over her lower lip. "Soon, we'll have each other to keep us company."

She smiled that soft smile that he enjoyed seeing when coaxed out of hiding. "Does that mean you'll help me gather the honey from the hives?"

Nathan suppressed a shudder. He had never considered bees as an enticing element to lovemaking. But if it kept her smiling, he would do his best without complaining. Until one stung him. Then he'd have to find another way to make her sigh.

"Go." He turned her toward the main keep. "Find your family. We'll make this event one to remember."

She rose on her toes and kissed his cheek. "We must search out Brother John to officiate."

Nathan nodded. He did not want to lose what gains he had made. Unwilling to let her go, he drew her closer so that he might taste her. Nightfall could not come soon enough. "The ceremony will be quick and efficient. No unnecessary words," he murmured over her neck. "I would that we forgo the wedding."

He perused the location he planned to lick next. Perhaps the delicate shell.

Meg jerked the fine hairs at the base of his neck. He winced as she increased her pressure, dragging him away. What game was she playing? He nipped her earlobe and she rewarded him with a kick to his shins. "Ow!" he yelped.

Her teeth bared, anger shimmered from her glare. "You wish to cancel our wedding? How dare you...you jackanapes donkey," she sputtered. "I gave you my virginity!"

"My lady, I don't..."

Confused by her outrage, he let her drill her finger into his chest until he feared she might puncture a lung. Or, God forbid, if she aimed for lower points of attack. He scrambled for safe ground as she followed him around the solar.

"King's knight or not, I'll see you suffer. You... horse's arse."

Despite his fear of damage to his nether regions, he swallowed to keep from chuckling at her curses. Her black tresses flared out as she shook her fist at him. "You'll find yourself stuffing in a gunnysack and used as a fute-ball on the loamy marshes of Scotland."

My God, the woman is a passionate sight to behold.

Her breasts threatened to escape the confines of her bodice as she took a shuddering deep breath. His gaze stuck on the vision. Her breasts. He wanted to lose himself in their lush mounds. His little head nodded, pressing for release from his chausses.

What did she say? Nathan tore his attention away from his lusty thoughts. "Fute-ball? What do you know of fute-ball?" Jealousy made him want to claim her as his wife. Again. "How much time have you been spending with our guest?" He spat that last word out like it was spoiled fish. Closing the space between them, he made certain she could not damage his already aroused body parts.

"What does it matter?" she yelled.

Sorrow pinched his soul when she flinched as he wiped his mouth with the back of his hand. His chest ached. Her words were like a mace to his heart. "What does it matter," he croaked. He shook his head and rubbed his breast bone. Mayhap his heart was already dying from the blow.

"I already gave you what you demanded."

"Demanded? My dear sweet Meg. If memory serves, you came to my bedchamber."

"Excuse me," Phillipa called from the doorway. They both jumped and separated like two naughty children caught in the act.

She eyed them, first Nathan and then Meg. "Have you seen Baldric?"

"We left him in the master chamber." Meg's brow furrowed. "He had his orders and should have found you by now."

"He probably lost track of time," Phillipa said.

"Or is sulking," Nathan added.

"Mayhap he went in search of you in the barns and your paths passed in opposite directions."

Phillipa tucked a stray curl behind her ear. A clump of dirt stuck to the toe of her boot and she scraped it over the rushes covering the floor. "'Tis odd though. He hasn't let his pup out since he went to speak with you and Sir Nathan. Poor Whitefoot has been whining and barking, scratching at the gate. Both of them had been in a sour mood all morn ever since they returned from the village. 'Tis certain they would have caused one of the mares to foal early. That's why I sent him to you. To get it off his chest and give me peace."

Dread began to creep its way between Nathan's shoulders. "Phillipa, did he mention the reason he needed to seek us out."

"He didn't confess his foolish mistake?"

Meg wrapped her arm around Phillipa's back. "What was it he was supposed to share with us?"

Her sister growled, as she began pacing the solar like a bear. "Foolish, pigheaded boy. Serves him right that I tell you instead." She picked up a pitcher and let it roll between her hands. "He was worried about the commissioned sword. He went to see the blacksmith. When he learned that he was a prisoner he was beside himself with worry." She set the pottery on the side table. "You know how emotional he gets, Meg. You have to do something about it."

Meg rolled her eyes at her sister. "Later. Baldric," she urged. "Why was he so upset?"

Phillipa glanced at Nathan then turned her back to whisper.

"He did what?" Meg yelped. She gripped her throat, her voice cracking. Phillipa nodded and hung her head. Her shoulders slumped.

"Share it," Nathan said. "What did he do?" He handed Meg the cup he had filled with mead. She knocked it back in one long gulp.

"He's the one who released the blacksmith," she croaked.

"'Tis not entirely his fault," Phillipa chimed in. "The wench Millicent convinced Baldric that the only way he could have his sword was to unlock the smokehouse cell. One of them struck him." She tapped the corner of her eye. "'Didn't you notice his bruise? 'Twas one of the reasons I sent him to you to deal with."

"He said he tripped." Meg said. She squeezed her eyes tight. "And I believed him."

Nathan laid his palms on her shoulders and caressed them. "We all did. Wallowing in guilt can wait. We need to find him and set his mind at ease."

Meg kept her hand in his and rose. Their fingers locked, woven together in unity.

"Phillipa, why didn't you send him to Anna? Lord knows she has greater healing skills than me."

She sighed dramatically. Nathan had this uneasy feeling that this was only the beginning of family issues among brother and sisters. "He was upsetting the beasts. I was tired unto death of his weeping and since Anna was too busy rubbing the brawny Scotsman's muscles and cooing over him, I figured you were the next best person. May I return to the barns now?"

"No," Meg snapped. "You will stay and help us locate your little brother. Go to the master chamber and look for him there."

She and Nathan locked gazes. "We must go to Anna. Now."

* * * *

"I will throttle her if she has done what I fear," Meg ground out through gritted teeth. Why had she ever agreed to let Anna place healing rooms so far from the main keep? Because of disease and contaminants? Her sister knew of her fear of vermin and she had used it against her.

Nathan grabbed her wrists, slowing her down. She glared at his fingers, daring him to maintain his hold. "Care to share with me what that is? Do I need to carry both of my broadswords?"

"Both?" she asked. Visions of him swinging two great weapons, his muscles bulging, had distracted her for only a moment. It was enough. He had succeeded and he knew it enough to offer a mischievous wink.

"I can wield two at one time. I'll demonstrate once we are finally alone."

Meg's skin flushed, warming her ears. What else could he do with his brawn?

She licked her lips and felt pleasure in knowing that his attention was drawn to her mouth. Two could play the game of distraction.

Her heart lurched. He had done it again and turned her, a responsible lady of the keep, into a wanton wench. She had to save her sister from the same fate. "I must stop her before it is too late for her, too."

Nathan's brows arched. He had the nerve to grin back at her.

"If you yell huzzah, and slap Duncan's back when next you see him, I vow I will smack you."

She bit her lip when he covered his groin. "My lady, my role will soon be that of protector of all the women in my household. Duncan Graham will thank his lucky thistle that my name is not yet written in the family's holy records. When that is done and the ink is dry, I'll be forced to call him to the tilting yard. But until that time, let us seek out dear Duncan's sickbed."

Meg prayed no one but the patient remained in his bed. She was beginning to think wantonness must run through their family blood.

Fingers locked together, they slipped through the unnaturally quiet hall leading to the patients' quarters. Nathan whistled under his breath. Bottles and baskets littered the shelves. Dried herbs hung from the rafters. Jars of unguents and liquids lined the cupboard. A pot of something that Meg dared not sniff, simmered over the fire.

"Is your sister an alchemist?"

"She's a student of the art of healing. That is all." She tugged him toward the room where she last saw Duncan and Anna. Her lungs squeezed, strangling the air.

"Shite," Nathan said. He broke free of her hand and marched into the empty room.

Chapter 19

"How could you?" Meg shouted. Whether from anger or fear, or a blend of emotions that she had never known before, she was ready to put all of her sisters into a dungeon. If they had one. Which fortunately, up till now, they hadn't had the need. Now, she was ready to order one built the first chance she had. She would even help lay the first block of stone.

Her wedding day came and went without a ceremony. Instead, it had become a nightmare and she had no idea how to make things right.

"I had to," Anna shouted back.

"Thanks to you, our brother is lost out there."

"Duncan would never harm Baldric. Not for any amount of money."

"You don't know that," Meg growled. "He took good coin with the promise of protection from his own thieving clan. What manner of man does that?"

Nathan stared into the fireplace. The master's chamber had once been a place of peace. Now it had become a war room. Meg wanted to go to him. Coward that she was, she did not have the courage to take the chance and stroke his rigid back.

Brother John refused to leave the window, but stared out into the night. The crash of the firth slamming into the shore reached their ears. A storm brewed in the moonless sky, stirring the sea into a rage.

Phillipa paced like a caged animal. "When may I return to the stables? The animals need to be fed."

Meg spun on her little sister. "You did check the barns. Am I right?"

Phillipa shrugged her shoulders. "I looked. I called out for him. Whitefoot was still there, barking and scratching at the door. Same as when Baldric left him." She sniffed as a tear slid down her cheek. "What if something horrible has happened to him?"

They all turned as someone knocked at the door.

"Enter," Nathan bellowed.

Their steward Matthew tugged on his forelock. "My lord, you told me to come for you if I have news."

"Spit it out."

"Two messengers arrived one after the other. Neither of them saw a young boy on the road." He cut his eyes to the side, and whispered out the corner of his mouth. "Nor in the stream."

Meg gasped and found both of her sisters had launched into her arms. Nathan snatched Matthew's tunic sleeve and tugged him away from the weeping women. Meg was grateful that he made certain to keep within earshot so that she might hear the news too.

Nathan closed his eyes and leaned his palm on the mantle. "Was that all?"

"One came from the south and brought a missive for your eyes only. Other one came by boat. They had tied it to a rock and tossed it onto the beach. I almost missed it. No telling when it arrived." He dug a stone out of his pocket and held it out for Nathan to take and scurried off to return to his position as guard over the keep.

Meg watched as Nathan unrolled the first parchment. He palmed a round disc and tucked it inside his belt. It did not look like any coin of the realm that she had ever seen. What did it mean? She waited; praying that he would tell her what was in it. Did it come from the king? Surely he had not received word that the marriage did not take place. Nathan looked up. "The men I requested to come have been detained." His chest rose and fell. "When they do reach Fletchers Landing there will be more to help scour the land for Baldric."

Meg left her sisters. She stroked his back as she had wanted to do all along. She needed to feel him under her palm. "And the other?"

He untied the string. A torn piece of parchment fluttered to the floor. Meg bent to pick it up. She could not bring herself to read it and held it out for Nathan. "Please." The word came out strangled.

Nathan read the note aloud. "Bring the king's treasure or he dies."

A roaring sound entered the room, filling Meg's ears. The room began to spin as her legs turned to liquid. Nathan caught her before she hit the floor.

Everything receded until all she saw was Nathan's face. He cradled her in his arms and bent over her. "I vow that no one will harm him." He glanced up, including everyone else in the chamber. "I will protect all of you."

"I know you will, love."

All but one member of her family huddled around her. Brother John cleared his throat. Anna held out a cup for her to sip. Phillipa knelt on the floor. All but their little brother was there. Tears burned her lids.

She forced a smile as Nathan kissed her fingers. Threading her fingers into his auburn curls, she pulled him near. She no longer cared who saw her do it, so she let go and kissed him.

When she finally came up for air, she smoothed Nathan's jaw and ran her finger over his lush lips. His gaze poured into her, filling her with his concern, and perhaps, love.

"What are we to do?" she asked. "There is no king's treasure."

Nathan settled her next to him, but did not release his hold. She snuggled deeper into the crook of his arm. "First we will learn who we are dealing with." He turned to Anna. "Make contact with Duncan Graham."

Anna blushed. "I don't know how…"

"'Tis not the time for deception. Find him. Let him know that Baldric has been missing the moment you set Duncan loose. He's a smart man. If he is innocent, he'll come to our aid. If not, then we'll know where to look first."

"He's a good man. You'll see." Anna swept up her skirt. She paused at the door. Her bottom lip caught between her teeth.

Was this the reason she had pressed so hard for Meg to find a husband? "I pray you are correct," Meg said.

Brother John hovered nearby. His gnarled fingers rolled over the cross hanging from the leather thong around his neck. "Perhaps we should continue with the plans of the day. Securing the marital vows in the holy pages."

"No," Meg said. "I cannot agree to that."

"Gives you a way to escape the king's marriage net. Doesn't it?"

"I will hold to our agreement. But I cannot think on our wedding day and not worry about Baldric. He's missing. Out there." She waved toward the window. "Alone. Afraid."

Nathan kissed her forehead. "He's still alive. Trust it. Otherwise, they would not use him as bait."

Meg tensed as someone knocked on the door. Cook carried a tray laden with food. She swallowed a sob. Another servant, almost Baldric's age, carried one filled with pitchers and cups.

"We thought it best to fill your stomachs and maintain your strength, my lady," Cook said.

"Aye," the boy piped up. "I'm sorely sorry for the loss of your brother."

Cook flashed him a glare and motioned for him to leave. "Forgive him, my lady, if you can."

Meg rose to address the man who had cooked their meals since they were babes. He too would be worried for the little lord. Even if he was no longer the Lord of Fletchers Landing. She covered his burn-scarred hands with hers. "We will find him and bring him home. And when we do, I ask that you prepare his favorite dishes."

"I shall be honored, my lady." Cook swallowed and dabbed the corner of his eye with his apron and took his leave.

"Brother John, continue to pray for Baldric's return."

"Aye, child, I will as I search for answers." He picked up a trencher of bread and stew. Steam swirled from the creamy concoction of vegetables and meat as his spoon broke through the flaky crust. He returned to his position by the window.

The door swung open and Anna stormed in. Her head held high, she announced, "A message has been sent."

Meg nodded. What more could she say on this eve? The distance between she and her sister had widened, making them even further apart. She had failed at keeping her family together. They were fracturing in front of her eyes.

Nathan poured a healthy portion of ale into a mug and held it out to her. Then he cut a chunk of cheese from the wheel and slapped it into her other hand. "Eat. The day is nearly over and you've had nary a bite. You need your strength. Come morning, we will tear this land apart looking for your brother."

He drank deeply from his mug. The bands of sinew and muscles working as he peered across the room. His head cocked to one side as he slowly lowered the cup made of horn.

"Meg, did you happen to move the leather journal from the worktable?"

She swallowed, watching him. "The one the king gave you? No. Not since we spoke of it earlier."

"And that was when Baldric could have overheard our argument."

Her heart began to beat faster. It thumped a cadence against her rib cage. "You think he may have gone in search of the treasure?"

He gripped her hands, pulling her to her feet. "I do."

Her smile fell. "But we don't know where to start looking."

"Not true." He told her. "Baldric and I had spoken of the possibilities where it could be hidden. He's a smart lad and pointed out the map that dances across the pages when they are flipped."

He dragged her to the table where the navigator's tube stood pointed toward the shore. "There's a cavern nearby. Isn't there? Brother John, have you touched this? Bumped it in any way?"

"Not I," the old monk said. He bobbed on his toes. "I think you are on the right trail, my son."

"Lady Anna? Phillipa?"

They shook their heads and linked arms with Meg.

"Then it's still pointed in that direction?" Phillipa asked. She craned her neck to see out the window.

"I believe so," Nathan said.

"Then what are we waiting for?" Phillipa raced to the door, only to have her escape stalled by his wide hand pressed over the panel.

"If we go unarmed or without a plan we could lose so much before we even have a start."

Meg drew her sister back to the chair. "Nathan is right. He has experience with this. Trust that he'll know what to do."

"Before dawn, we will meet back in this chamber. Brother John, keep watch from the window. Ladies Phillipa, Anna, and Meg. I ask that you sleep in the same bedchamber. Call out if you hear anything amiss."

Meg ran her hand up his sleeve. "And you, my lord?" Tired lines were already forming by his eyes.

"I will make the preparations for the morrow." He slid his palms along her neck. Long fingers kneaded the building tension in her muscles. She sighed. Her mouth opened, seeking his kisses and he did not disappoint. He found her lips, offering promise and hope in the days to follow.

* * * *

Dawn came on the heels of their rising. Meg, Anna, and Phillipa were dressed and ready to find their brother before the sun could shine through their windows.

Unwilling to wait until someone came for them, Meg pulled open the door and found Nathan lying on the floor. He blocked the threshold, his broadsword drawn by his side. His long legs stretched out.

Her sisters ran into her back and squeaked their surprise.

Baldric's pup was pressed against Nathan's side. Whitefoot lifted his muzzle from Nathan's thigh. A low growl warred with the confused dog's tail thumping. Phillipa lowered to untie the dog's lead and scratched behind his ears.

Nathan's lashes fluttered against his cheek. He raised his head to meet her gaze with bloodshot eyes. "I don't recall giving you permission to leave."

She winced. The pallet he had slept on, constructed of his wadded cloak, made her want to groan. Guilt threatened to make Meg become a bigger fool and inquire the state of his health. He would not appreciate her concern for his night's sleep, whether or not the nightmares had once again inflicted their pain. Or was it duty that brought him to her chamber door?

"My sisters and I have need of the garderobe." Heat rushed up her neck. "If you must know, we intend to seek out the latrine."

"No, Meg, don't you recall the plan we discussed?" Phillipa asked. "Anna is to check the spot where she and Duncan have been meeting."

"I don't know that which you speak of, Phillipa."

"Don't mind her," Anna added with a shove to their little sister's back.

Meg swept her skirt out of reach and nudged her feet past man and dog. He caught the hem and began reeling her in.

"Unhand me, Sir Nathan." Meg freed the material from his grasp.

Shoving his bangs out of his eyes, Nathan struggled to rise on stiffened legs. "You look dressed, my Lady, Meg. Ready to meet the day's challenges, Phillipa and Anna."

He stretched his lower back, hips jutting forward, drawing her hungry eyes toward his groin. She could not turn away when he bent to retrieve his sword. Instead she admired the view of his backside and recalled the strength in his thighs. The way her hands molded around each cheek.

He cocked his head. A shadow formed along the ridge of his jaw, outlining the growth of whisker stubble. "Allow me to escort you."

"It's down the hall. Our parents installed it years ago. They chose to build it near our bedchamber." She rattled on. "For privacy."

"I know where it is, Meg. I bathed in the washtub." He chuckled. "I don't mean to join you."

"Anna and Phillipa…"

"Would like to find the privy, if you please," Anna called out.

"Let them pass," Nathan said. He waved her on. "Make haste. The sun is nearly up and we've yet to speak with Brother John."

Meg grabbed his hand. "Have you word?"

"Not precisely."

"Then what have you done, besides bringing that hound into the keep?"

"Do you recall your sister's concern for Whitefoot?"

"She worries about all the animals." Meg made a face. "I'm surprised that we didn't have to share a bed with it."

178 C.C. Wiley

"He's a strong pup. Much like your brother. 'Twas all I could do to get him up the stairs." Do you want to know the direction in which he wishes to run?"

Nathan nodded at Meg's gasp. His fingers flexed around hers as they shared a look.

"The cove where the smugglers attacked Duncan Graham."

"And the same direction as where that navigator's lens was pointed. What else can you tell me about the place, Meg love?"

"There's a cave. But Nathan, there's nothing there but a tunnel." She bit her lip. Had the smugglers stripped it bare? If not, she would have to explain away the wares that were tucked in every nook and cranny.

Anna and Phillipa joined them and chimed in. "Do you suppose they'll agree to exchange Baldric for the barrels of mead stored there?" Phillipa asked.

"Don't be foolish," Anna said. "Without Duncan's protection they will have already taken it."

Meg stepped out of the way before her sisters could do more harm with the information they revealed. "Unless he planned it all along."

Anna's back stiffened. "I told you he would never do harm to Fletchers Landing."

"And why would he not?"

"He wishes to wed."

"I have not given permission for a union between you and Duncan."

Nathan eyed her with a wintery gaze. She shivered as the cold seeped into her bones. "I had suspected that you stored the shipments somewhere. Had even hoped that there was a vast supply that we could use to leverage ransom for Baldric's return. Is there anything else for them to take?"

Meg shook her head. Welling tears blurred her vision, threatening to overflow. "I fear we are lost."

"Anna, Phillipa, go to Brother John," Nathan ordered her sisters. "Tell him where we believe we'll find your brother. Have him call the steward and gather all the men. Have him wait for my signal. "

Wide-eyed, Meg watched them leave to do his bidding without question. "You intend to go after Baldric alone?"

Nathan adjusted his weapons. "I'll have Whitefoot to aid me."

"And me."

"I will not put another member of your family in danger. You will stay in the master chamber with Brother John."

Chapter 20

Nathan stopped Meg in the stairway. He cupped the back of her head and tipped her chin up. Her lush bottom lip quivered until he could no longer resist the urge. He took her mouth. Demanding that she respond and kiss him in return.

She rewarded him by bunching his tunic in her hands. She gripped his hair, tugging him closer. Their bodies pressed together until he could feel her heart thumping through their clothes.

When he did finally release her and come up for air, he gazed into her sparkling eyes. They swirled with emotions, glittering back daggers of anger. Her nostrils flared. "I am going with you."

"I forbid it."

"You are not my husband yet, my lord." She lifted her skirts and ran down the stairs. "You'll need a dog handler. To keep your sword hands free. I know the tunnels."

Nathan grunted. She had a point. Damn her sweet hide. She would have the temerity to ignore his orders anyway. He might as well give in to her demands. Otherwise, he'd be looking behind his back the whole time.

Pebbles rolled under their boots as they climbed down the sloping hill to the shore below them. "The path is steep," she warned. "We'll need to see where 'tis safe to place our feet."

He shook his head when she reached for a torch. "We must go under the cover of early dawn."

"Then we will go slowly. Protect our steps."

"Follow Whitefoot's lead." He had pulled up his tunic, to muffle his voice. "I'll catch you if you start to fall."

"I fear I already have," she whispered under her breath.

"What's that?" He caught her sleeve, tugging on it to slow her pace. "Meg?" he pressed.

"Hush. The rock formations carry the sound." She coughed into her leather work gloves. "Listen for the shifting of the tide. That's the direction we'll want to take. That will help cover any sound we might make."

They crossed the meadow that led them to the cavern he had seen in the navigator's scope. He swallowed. A bead of sweat tickled his neck. "How far do the tunnels run?"

"Deep under the land." She looked over her shoulder. "I have never been to the bottom of the cave. It was too steep and unstable. Only a fool would venture that far."

"Then let us pray that we are not dealing with fools."

Her quiet chuckle lifted her shoulders and she stumbled. Rocks slid off the path, clattering off the walls of the cove. He caught her, his heels digging into the dirt, and dragged her away from the edge. Pebbles bit into his arse. Fire burned in his lungs as he fought the dizzying sensation that they were still falling. He tightened his arms around Meg and refused to let her go.

Whitefoot ran off into the trees that lined the ledge. A flash of tail signaled that he was near the opening.

"Nathan," Meg gasped and muttered a strangled curse. "Loosen your hold. I can't breathe."

Her voice brought him back and he sank into the feel of her body next to his. Her back pressed into his chest. Her curved bottom nestled in his lap. Hips, pressed into his thighs.

If it weren't for the realization that he'd nearly lost her, he would have enjoyed the moment of having her body cradled next to his. He tucked his head into the base of her neck. She smelled so sweet, alive.

Panting, they pulled in ragged draws of air. The noise they made had bounced off the rocks. It echoed in the cove and was loud enough to draw a hermit from his lair. They sat next to a scrubby bush and waited. No one came to the entrance.

Nathan wiped his mouth. He should have waited for help.

Meg wiggled her fingers into his hand, burrowing until he could no longer feel the quake trying to take over. Her breasts brushed his forearms, distracting him from the danger they were in.

"Are you certain Baldric would have taken this path?" Nathan asked.

Meg shook her head. Threads of silken hair danced over his skin with the movement. He shivered. "Not unless he was forced. His balance is too unsteady."

"Treacherous even for a goat. Or a Scotsman." Blood ran through his veins like lightning and made him almost giddy. "One and the same, really."

"'Tis why we came this way, is it not? Less chance of meeting someone climbing up?"

"Or a goat." Something dug into his backside. He shifted his hips and her crease between her bottom cheeks found his erection. Air hissed between his teeth. "Don't move."

She swung around, eyes wide, she searched the vicinity of his belly. "You're aroused?"

Chagrined, Nathan looked for something to cover his crotch. "How do you think I became the camp prize amongst the wenches?" He wiggled his brows. "I was always willing and ready."

"Braying donkey." She struck him in the chest. Evidently, his effort to tease had the opposite effect. He did his best to put her at ease. At least the color had returned to her face. That was a blessing, wasn't it? She was far from fainting on him.

But when she tugged her bottom lip between her teeth, he wanted to take her right there among the grasses.

He shifted again, digging under his hip. "Shite!" He pulled the king's journal out from under his hip.

"That must have been what I stumbled on," Meg whispered. She knelt to peer over the edge.

"Careful," he said as he reeled her back.

She looked up at him. Brown eyes sparkled with unshed tears. Rocking on her heels slid farther into the brush and covered her mouth with her fingers. "Whitefoot is gone. Do you suppose he's entered the cave?"

"'Tis where his instincts have been leading him all this time. I fear we've made enough noise, someone is bound to come out and check the area." He smoothed the raven strands from her dampened cheeks. "We'll get Baldric."

"Alive." The single word hung between them.

Could he promise the outcome would bring the boy to them unharmed?

"I had hoped that we had come for naught. That a messenger would deliver a missive that he was found safe in his bed," Meg said. She tilted her head. "But you knew, didn't you? You feared he was in terrible trouble."

Nathan's heart slammed into his chest. "The men that we fought are more ruthless than your smugglers."

"But how did you know?"

"I recognized some of their voices. From the dungeons at Balforth Castle." Sweat popped out on his forehead. It trickled down his cheek. Damn, was just the mention of those torturous days and nights enough to break him? He should have waited for help to come. But what if he had waited too long already?

"Look," Meg grabbed his wrist.

Nathan squatted behind the boulder and stared at the hole burrowed into the wall of stone. "You mean to tell me that you were allowed to enter that thing? Your father and the monk should be hung from their genit..." Recalling that he was about to speak ill of someone she loved, he corrected himself. "Thumbs."

He rubbed his forehead with the back of his sleeve. The sun had already begun its ascent. If they didn't enter the cavern soon, they would be too late.

A bearded man strode out and set the lantern down on a fallen log. His leather gambeson covered his chain mail. It clinked as he walked the shore, searching the trees. His stained chausses sagged from his hips. He scratched himself as he yelled, "Who's out there? Is that you, Sir Nathan? Heard you were here. No doubt hiding under your woman's skirts."

Nathan tensed. That voice had clung to him like a sticky web since the first day they crossed paths at Balforth Castle.

Meg trembled beside him. Tight-lipped, she gripped her small dagger in both hands. Her jaw clenched.

He could not let anything happen to her. Gritting his teeth, he shoved her out of the way and stood in front of her. Nathan knew what this one would do with women. There was no way he would let the bastard mercenary take her.

More soldiers emerged from the black hole. The traitor blacksmith, Wayland, was among them. They swarmed like ants pouring from their nests. It was like the one that he saw the day he left Clearmorrow Castle. The day he nearly killed Darrick. Nathan shook his head to clear it of the vision.

A dog raced out after the mercenaries. Whitefoot bared his teeth and launched his body toward the men. The hound gnashed at their faces, ripping and tearing at flesh. He yelped when he was knocked to the ground.

"Whitefoot," Baldric screamed as he limped out. He struggled to free his wrists from the soldier.

"There are so many," Meg cried.

"Stay here," Nathan said. He did not know how, but he intended to end this. All of it. At the dawn of this day. He skidded down the trail. Leaping from one boulder to the next.

A loud whistle tore through the air. Rocks sailed over Nathan's head. He ducked as one shattered, splintering blade-thin shards into the trees. One after another, they rained down, striking the shore, then shooting off toward the men near the cave. He did not know how Darrick and his men had found him but he was never so relieved. Nathan bared his teeth at the mercenary charging toward him. "Come taste my steel."

The Knight of the Swan had returned.

Baldric broke free from his captors. He scooped up the hound and ran past Nathan. White-faced, Meg stood beside him. Her blade drawn, she gritted her teeth, daring anyone foolish enough to get between her and the boy.

Nathan shot a glance over his shoulder. His blade arm wavered. 'Twas not his brothers in arms but the Scotsman, Duncan Graham, astride a shaggy little pony, leading his band of men. Once they hit the shore, they ran toward the fray. Their claymores clanged against steel as they met the cowards attempting to escape. One by one they fell. The lads of the clan succeeded where Nathan had not.

"Sir Nathan." The man who haunted his days and nights now held his blade against Meg's throat. He spit out a stream of blood. "Your woman is feisty," he yelled. "Wager she's a handful when you rut."

He renewed his grip, yanking her head. Meg slapped at his hands, struggling to break free. Air hissed through her lips as his knife cut into her skin.

The red haze began to seep into Nathan's vision. Only this time, he knew that he could control it. Empowered by his rage, he stalked the bearded one. He focused on the marauder's tang of sweat and locked gazes with Meg. *Trust me.*

Duncan had left his men to tend to the prisoners who still breathed. He strode toward them, looking as large and proud as a bear ready to take down his next meal.

Nathan cocked his head toward Baldric. Understanding, Duncan blocked the boy's path and wrapped a beefy arm around his small shoulders.

Ensured that no one else could be harmed, Nathan turned his attention on the bearded one. "Let her go," Nathan growled.

"Give me the king's treasure and I'll be on my way."

"What treasure?"

DePierce's man narrowed his eyes. "D'you think that I've sat on my haunches all this time, waiting for nothing? My lord DePierce got wind of this treasure long before. 'Tis why he coveted this godforsaken land. He's long dead now thanks to you. In my mind, you owe me for wages lost."

"You're a fool," Duncan shouted over their heads. One hand on his hip, the other still gripping his claymore, he barked a laugh. "There hasn't been a treasure kept in this cavern since the Knights Templar stowed it."

Duncan's distraction was working, drawing the soldier's attention. "Where is it?" he croaked. He cut his gaze to the cavern. "Bring it to me."

"Och, laddie, I fear you've wasted your life for nothing, if you believe that bedtime tale." The large Scotsman shook his head. "They sailed away with it years ago."

"You lie." His face blanched, then flushed. His arm tightened. Spinning with indecision, he rocked on his heels. His boots scraped through the stones scattered over the shore. "I won't leave empty handed. It's either the treasure or this wench. Imagine someone will pay for her services."

Nathan saw the red haze. It seeped in, giving him strength to keep from charging the man and impaling him on his sword. He had told Baldric not to lose his balance. To remain calm. An opportunity would present itself.

The bearded one nipped her earlobe and Meg elbowed him in the gut. The padded gambeson deflected the blow, but it was enough. Nathan locked gazes with Meg. He took the opportunity and charged.

Meg let her legs go limp, dragging her captor off balance. Nathan struck. His blade did the damage the king's blacksmith had planned so many years before at the forge. But all that mattered to Nathan was Meg was no longer in danger.

She fell into his arms. She was safe.

He gulped the air, filling his lungs. The visions had not come during the fight for their lives. They'd remained silent. Ironically, it took the threat of death to make him see that he might be free.

Truly free of the nightmare.

He tensed. If that were true, would his king expect his imminent return to the battlefield?

Meg tilted her head. Blood seeped from the wound on her throat. He tore a strip of fabric from his tunic and pressed it to stop the flow.

"My love," she whispered as she brought him down. Her mouth covered his, and for once in his life, he had found a home for his heart.

To Nathan's horror, she sank into his arms, and went limp.

* * * *

Nathan paced the solar. Anna had already had him removed from Meg's bedchamber. He should have demanded the right to stay by Meg's side. She was still his betrothed. They were still to be wed. And he was the damn lord of the keep. God help him, even the head of the household.

Brother John eyed him, then ducked his head, his voice rising as he continued to pray.

Duncan stood in the corner nursing a flagon of something he called his clan's secret elixir. Two men, nearly the size of Duncan, flanked his sides and pretended to drink from a horn cup. These brawny men, who had come to their aid, Nathan had learned, were Duncan's brothers. Robert and Lawrens Graham nervously watched everyone waiting in the room for news of Lady Meg.

Though he had downed most of it, the Graham seemed to become stronger, more aware. He adjusted his sporran, and fidgeted.

Grunting, Nathan abandoned the worn path and joined Duncan. He swiped the flagon from Duncan's fist and took a deep swig. It burned down his throat, warmed his stomach, then seemed to ignite his whole body.

Duncan grinned and thumped his back. "You'll learn to love the taste of the Clan Graham's golden elixir."

Meg snorted from the doorway. "Is this how my betrothed now spends his time?"

Nathan's heart melted. Anna had worked her healing magic and though still pale from their ordeal, Meg stood straight and proud. The linen wrapped around her neck, only seemed to accentuate her raven tresses.

"Go to her, laddie," Duncan urged under his breath.

Nathan handed him the flagon and strode toward the woman who had managed to capture his heart. If only he dared to believe that she felt a fraction of what he did, then theirs would be a strong marriage. A strong bond between a man and a woman. Husband and wife.

Chapter 21

Meg watched Nathan leave the men and stride across the solar. His long legs ate up the distance with little effort. The room seemed to narrow until all she saw was the man she had come to care deeply for. If only she was courageous enough to admit it.

Love.

That single word scared her almost as much as hope.

Hope.

Her heart thumped against her chest, threatening to break every rib. Liquid heat formed in her belly, warming her core. Her knees trembled at the thought that one day this would be her husband. They would find joy in each other's arms.

She stepped toward him. The fear of dreaming of love faded as they drew near each other. She would no longer be alone. She would dare to speak of love.

His intense gaze deepened. The mossy green of his eyes darkened. His lush lips lifted. She knew not only that she could trust Nathan. This was the single man in which she could place her heart and soul and know without a doubt that he would never harm her.

"My Lady Margaret," Brother John said, his voice booming as if he intended it to carry over a congregation. "'Tis good to see that you have recovered. God be praised."

Meg tore her concentration from Nathan's seductive mouth. They needed to settle the monk in a new home. Mayhap one far from the master's chambers. The sooner the better.

"Brother John," her voice still hoarse, she nodded in his direction.

Nathan linked his fingers with hers. He kissed her knuckles. Under the guise of bending his knee deeper, he added a mischievous lick to the side of her thumb.

A languorous smile lit up his face. Her breath hissed between her lips. How had she ever thought this man would be her downfall?

Phillipa and Baldric skidded into the solar, nearly knocking Brother John over. Meg and Nathan chuckled at their excitement. "You've returned," Phillipa cried. She batted her lashes at the hulking Duncan Graham, including him in her praise. "Huzzah!"

Whitefoot danced around them, barking and leaping on his three legs. Phillipa snapped her fingers and he settled at their feet. If only Anna were in attendance their family would be reunited.

Nathan quirked a golden eyebrow. "You've decided to allow a hound in the keep?"

"After his heroics," Meg shrugged, "I fear I'll never have the heart to send the hound to the stables."

Overhearing her proclamation, Baldric wrapped his arms around her waist. "Good news. Phillipa said the blacksmith left behind a few more pups. 'Tis up to us to care for them. Don't you agree? We'll be one large happy family. Pups and all."

"That is up to my lord, Sir Nathan, to decide."

Nathan's eyes twinkled at Meg over her brother's head. "I've always desired a family."

"Takes a wedding to make that happen." The old monk winked and rubbed his hands together. "Shall we be about it come the morrow?"

"No," Meg and Nathan said.

Nathan's smile vanished. The skin over his cheekbones tightened.

Meg's chest constricted, threatening to burst open. How could she have been so wrong?

Nathan grabbed her wrist. "Excuse us."

Without another word, they climbed the staircase until they reached the upper floor. Meg's feet tangled in her skirts and she bit out a curse. Why was he enraged? She was the one being manhandled, tripping over steps. All she wanted was to have Brother John say the words that day. Mayhap, nightfall, at the latest.

By the time Nathan unlocked the doors and dragged her through them, they were both out of breath. She stared at him as he turned and cupped her jaw. He brought his mouth down, covering her, devouring her lips. His tongue probed, tasting, licking. His lips sucked and drew, nipping until they were breathless.

When he broke free, unshed tears sparkled. Was this goodbye?

* * * *

"You don't desire to take me as your...your wife?" she stuttered. She wrapped her arms around her middle.

"You made your desires known." Nathan turned away. To look into the hurt in her eyes was too much for him to bear. He had vowed to never cause her pain. And before the day was even close to being over, he had succeeded in doing so again.

Meg tugged his sleeve. "You will not present your back to me. My lord," she added to her command.

Nathan flared his nostrils. "What do you want from me, my lady?"

"To be heard," she said. "You once told me what you wanted in a lady that you took as wife. But never gave me," she thumped her beautiful chest. "Me. The opportunity to tell you what I want."

His heart ached. Did he really want to listen to his faults? He already knew what they were. He closed his eyes. He was too much of a coward to see her disdain for him. "Then tell me," he said, repeating the very words she had given him.

"I desire..." She started slowly. Her breath caressed his cheek. Would he ever again know the pleasure in her touch when they were through? "I desire a man to love me for who I am. Not because it pleases our king. Or that it protects my family or the people of the village. But for me."

Nathan opened his eyes. She stood before him. His beautiful warrior woman. The lady of his heart. The sun shined all around her, creating a halo. Tears glistened against her flushed cheeks.

She took a step forward, linking her fingers with his. "I want a friend. Someone to challenge me. Support me. Hold me when I am afraid, and when I am done listing my fears, kiss them all away."

Nathan sipped in a breath, afraid that if he moved she would slip away and take his heart with her. Her fingertips danced over his mouth as she continued.

"I want to share my family with my husband. The duties and the joys. I desire children. And I want a husband who wants this as badly as I do. But more so, I want someone who simply wants to share his life with me. Share his secrets and desires. To build a life together. To love me."

She kissed the corner of his mouth. "Just. Me. The dragon lady of Fletchers Landing."

Nathan could no longer resist and pressed her to his body. His hands spanned her narrow waist and he returned her kiss. "I love that lady," he declared. "The one who raises bees, raids their hives, fights for her family, takes chance with rogues and knights. All for the sake of love and devotion."

Her fingers slid through his hair. He shivered as her nails scraped over his scalp. "But most of all, I love you, Lady Margaret of Fletchers Landing."

She pulled back, an unexpected pout lined her lips. "Then why do you resist in wedding me?"

Nathan barked a laugh. Lifting her off her feet, he spun her around until they both were dizzy. "My love. I want to wed you. I fear I'll die of thirst if I do not sip from your body this very eve."

Meg fell into his arms. "Thank God. I don't want to wait any longer."

Nathan swept her into his arms. "Let's find Brother John and the children."

They turned as the door swung open.

The steward bent over, panting in the doorway as if he had run up three flights of stairs.

That warning itch threatened to creep up Nathan's spine. "Matthew, what is it?"

"There's an army of soldiers riding this way. The Scotsman has fled for fear of arrest."

She squeezed Nathan's hand. "Let them go."

Love poured into his soul. "Aye, a wedding gift to us both."

* * * *

Meg's legs trembled, but not out of fear this time. She knew what to expect once the celebrations were completed. Her core tightened in anticipation for the pleasure they would share on their wedding night.

She stood arrayed in her best gown of the softest lamb's wool. The bodice cut deeply, providing a most advantageous view of her breasts for her new husband. The gilded belt, woven of fine linen and studded with pearls, enhanced her waist.

Nathan's brothers in arms, Sir Darrick and Sir Taron, watched over them, their armor reflecting the sunset. And, since Nathan had vowed to share his secrets, he had explained briefly, that they shared more than a bond in knighthood. They were members of the Knights of the Swan. The king's selected few.

She took in a shuddered breath. They still had a great deal to learn of each other. And she prayed they had a lifetime to do so.

She and Nathan would finally be wed. His fingers tightened around hers. She caressed his newly shaved jaw.

Nathan smiled down at her as Brother John intoned the vows. They repeated them. Swearing promises to God and king, but most importantly to each other.

They kissed to seal their agreement. His eyes radiant with adoration, he lifted his head to look over those who witnessed their union. She followed his gaze as he took in all who now became his family. His brothers of the Knights of the Swan grinned at him. Darrick and Taron elbowed each other as if sharing in a secret joke. And her brother and sisters. They too, had become his to care for.

Their steward, Matthew, stood beside Phillipa and Baldric. They were dressed in their finest clothes. Whitefoot, freshly bathed and brushed, wore a ring of flowers around his neck. He sat obediently on the pew bench waiting for Baldric's next command. And Anna...

Meg's heart skipped a beat. Dread seeped into her bones. Had she once again tempted Fate's jealous heart? "Nathan, where's Anna?"

"Let us find out, my lady love." He kissed her forehead and led her to the children.

A piece of parchment stuck out from Whitefoot's festive collar. Baldric held it out to her. "This is for you." He tugged on his lower lip. "She said 'twas a surprise for you on your wedding day."

Meg unfolded the missive.

My dearest sister. Now that you are wed, and have found your love, I must bid you goodbye. I believe you now must understand how love cannot be denied when it is shared with the one you are destined to be with.

Not to worry. I am in Duncan Graham's care and loving protection. And as you know, he is a man worthy of trust. He will not come roving over the hills and shores of Fletchers Landing.

Leave a note in the great oak tree should you ever be in need.

God be with you until we meet again.

All my love,

Lady Anna

Meg crumpled the missive in her hand. She should have heeded her misgiving and kept Anna from tending to Duncan's wounds. "She's left. With Duncan."

Nathan braced her, holding her gently in his arms. "We shall run them to ground if that is what you desire."

She shook her head and cupped his strong jaw. Though she hated to admit it, she knew that one day her sister would leave their home. And

Anna had tried so many times to tell her that she had found someone to love. Meg had been too afraid to listen. Until now. "My lord husband, how can I deny their love, when we have just discovered ours?"

"Nathan, our men are at your service," Taron said as he joined them.

"Mayhap this will allow us an opportunity to penetrate beyond the debatable lands," Darrick added. "King Henry will be pleased to discover what the Scots might be brewing."

"Politics will manage for a little while longer without our aid. We will stand down, for today," Nathan said. "When we meet with our new family, it will be in peace."

Meg stroked his neck, threading her fingers through his hair. "And we will pray for their union as well as ours."

"My lady wife, it is decided." Nathan swept her up in his arms. "On this blessed day, we celebrate for us. And for the peace that mayhap their union will bring to these lands."

He bent down, claiming her mouth. And in their kiss came the sweetness of life. To choose hope and joy over fear. The dream of love had now become their reality.

Nathan raised his head and marched out of the chapel, leaving all but Meg behind. He paused at the panel doors and turned. "May King Henry be blessed! This is the finest gift a lonely broken knight has ever received."

"Huzzah!" shouted one and all.

Meet the Author

C.C. Wiley is a longstanding member of the Romance Writers of America. She lives in Salt Lake City with her high school sweetheart of over 35 years and their four wacky dogs. When given a choice, she prefers a yummy, well-written, historical or contemporary romance that is chock-full of hope, love and a Happy Ever After. She believes there are wonderful courageous characters waiting for someone to tell their story. It's her hope that each adventurous romance she writes will touch the reader and carry them away to another place and time, where hopes and dreams abound. Visit her website at ccwiley.com, find her on Facebook at CCWileyAuthor, and on Twitter @AuthorCCWILEY.

Printed in the United States
by Baker & Taylor Publisher Services